P9-CET-529

DOUBLE JEOPARDY

Double Jeopardy

A NOVEL BY

Jean Echenoz

TRANSLATED FROM THE FRENCH BY

Mark Polizzotti

DAVID R. GODINE · PUBLISHER
Boston

The translator wishes to thank
Jodi Daynard, Jean Echenoz, David Godine,
Julia Hanna, Mario Polizzotti, and François Samuelson
for their help and forbearance.

A portion of this translation
previously appeared in *Yale French Studies*.

The publisher wishes to acknowledge a
translation grant from the French Ministry of Culture.

First published in English in 1993 by
David R. Godine, Publisher, Inc.
Horticultural Hall
300 Massachusetts Avenue
Boston, Massachusetts 02115

Originally published in French in 1986 as L'Equipée malaise
by Les Editions de Minuit

Copyright © 1986 by Les Editions de Minuit
Translation copyright © 1993 by Mark Polizzotti

Library of Congress Cataloging-in-Publication Data
Echenoz, Jean.
[L'equipée malaise. English]
Double jeopardy : a novel = L'equipée malaise */ by Jean Echenoz ;*
translated from the French by Mark Polizzotti.
p. cm.
ISBN *0-87923-916-6*
I. Title.
PQ2665.C5E6813 1993 92-5224
843'.914—dc20 CIP

FIRST EDITION
Printed in the United States of America

I

1

THIRTY YEARS earlier, two men had been in love with Nicole Fischer.

The stranger she'd preferred to both of them, a fighter pilot by trade, had had time neither to marry her nor to bail out of his spinning prototype, which slammed into the Haute-Saône under the noonday sun of May. Blonde and baptized Justine three months later, the fruit of his labors would thus bear her mother's name. The latter, her mourning over, her daughter born, conceived the idea of seeing her former suitors, Jean-François Pons and Charles Pontiac; she would have liked to know how they were getting on without her. But her search proved vain: they had loved her so much that their lives had been shattered the evening when Nicole, in the Café Perfect, had nervously revealed the flyer's existence to them. Pons and Pontiac had distanced themselves, first from each other, then from the outside world. Their names were now missing from the phone books; even the memory of them had faded nearly without trace.

Charles Pontiac disappeared first, going underground, without notifying anyone. He was thought to be dead, and over a two-year period fewer and fewer people spoke of him. As for Jean-François

Pons, he announced his departure only to his sister, a relatively young mother abandoned by a certain Bernard Bergman, who had only just recognized his child, then called out that he should be named Paul J. through the window of a train that was picking up speed. Pons said a brief, solemn farewell, rested a hand on the already formed head of young Paul J., then took a plane to Southeast Asia, about which he knew nothing.

Having no concept of Burma or Siam other than that of a large park, no image other than uninterrupted green, Pons's settling-in required much care and effort, which killed off the past as he had hoped they would. He learned other languages, and so began to see things differently. These transformations soon gobbled up his savings. When all his assets were gone and he had to find a means of livelihood, someone from the consulate spoke to him of a fellow named Blachon who lived in Rangoon. Blachon wore a canvas hat whose brim he chewed while reflecting. There might well be that business in Malaysia to take over, perhaps, following the death of an elderly European planter. Explaining the thing, Blachon drew on his open left palm with his right index, as if to illustrate his point.

Not far from the Malaysian coast, due east, a rubber plantation had suddenly been left to its own devices—its owner, born in Tulle, having just expired in the Ipoh hospital. As his legacy had triggered lawsuits and countless appeals, the law's representatives were obliged to recruit an interim manager; a French-speaking candidate would take a load off their minds. Jean-François Pons, whose recent past as a printer offered every guarantee of reliability, was immediately hired. After Blachon calculated his commission in the palm of his hand, he proposed stretching the payments over a period of eight months.

For eight months and more Pons knocked himself out, rising early in the morning to coordinate the teams of agricultural laborers, going over the accounts in the hottest hour of the siesta, and spending his nights reading between the lines of Bouychou's *Hevea Planter's Manual*. Very soon he was on closest possible terms with the peasants, who saw him, like them, plant grain in all kinds of weather, fertilize the soil, bed out the shoots and graft seedlings, tap the trees at dawn, and carry the sap to the plantation's little factory, located near a pond fringed with untamed kapok. He had perfected his Malay and begun studying Chinese with the foremen. He never abused his status as manager. He partook of the local noodles, the local bedding; he was given credit for two children in a neighboring plantation, whom he willingly supported. He knew how to make himself liked.

Wouldn't a new name be the crowning touch of this new life— a life that had been transformed so completely? The imaginative Pons would, for example, have liked to be called Tuan, an established title of nobility, but the peasants proved reticent. Duke, he thought one evening. Duke, perhaps. Sounding enough like a first name of local vintage, this label was more readily accepted. Duke, Duke Pons, laughed the rustics, who gladly went along with the harmless whim. It soon passed into common usage. In short order Pons became Duke Pons; was known by this title even among the bankers of Kuala Lumpur and the businessmen of Singapore, with whom he dealt more and more frequently, more and more successfully. Indeed, by 1967 the plantation had regained its former prosperity, even surpassed it, producing a gross ton of gum per hectare per year.

Meanwhile, those who stood to inherit it had granted each other neither truce nor compromise, complicating the matter to such an extent that it could be resolved only by the decease of one of the parties. This came to pass long years afterward in favor of a Mrs. Luce Jouvin, the wife of a waterworks engineer. One November second, in Kuantan, Luce and Raymond Jouvin staggered from Flight 337 of the Malaysian Airline System. They were tired, dismayed at being immediately soaked by the northeasterly monsoon. Luce, between air pockets, had consumed too much duty-free liquor. Ever since morning, the winds had enjoyed scooping out the China Sea and brutally dumping it onto this part of the peninsula. The sky no longer bothered to separate into drops, but instead relieved itself in a soggy flood that exploded without respite on the roofs of the taxis amassed in front of the airport, drowning out the drivers' choir.

In the shelter of the jeep, Pons was tense. He immediately identified the Jouvins, but it was they who approached him, after two mirthless cases of mistaken identity. Jouvin had no shoulders, parted his hair on the right flank of his skull, and was always raising his eyebrows over washed-out eyes; like Luce, he wore size 8½ shoes. The rain stopped suddenly. Luce Jouvin felt the heat and started drinking again, perspiring her alcohol almost instantly. Jouvin was too dazed to talk during the ride to the plantation, and Pons was thinking too much about his future. Outside Gembang, rabbits hopped across the road. Luce found this surprising: she would have preferred to see other, less familiar animals; she felt a bit disappointed, and reassured at the same time. She made a vain attempt to express all this before falling asleep in the back seat.

Jouvin, who had specialized in water for too long, quickly understood that it wouldn't be so easy to adapt to rubber—all the more so since Pons was casually making every effort to render the whole affair incomprehensible. One evening, after the noodles (to which the couple had trouble adjusting), Jouvin suggested that Pons might retain his technical duties for an unspecified length of time. For now, Jouvin would familiarize himself with the accounts, orders, and personnel management; he had already been given this job once, as a replacement for the Culligan man. Pons accepted: freed from these administrative chores, he could occupy his spare time with the study of celestial bodies, as the Duke had also acquired a keen interest in ancient observatories. But mostly, his more flexible schedule would allow him to devise a plan for eliminating these stupid Jouvins, who threatened the middle term of his future. He liked his second life (now almost as long as his first) too much to let it go. He would defend it. He had no intention of forfeiting his ducal prerogatives. On the one hand, Jouvin demonstrated a naive confidence in him; on the other, Pons knew he could count on the support of the locals. He would play both sides against the middle. But first he would let a little time go by.

For the Jouvins, the noodles still left something to be desired. Two evenings a week, over a background of gastric protests, Pons tried to teach them the main principles of rubber-growing. But after he had recapped Bouychou's pointers, summarized the theses of the French Rubber Institute, and reiterated several innovations developed by the Michelin plantations, his teachings began to distort. Throwing the wool over Jouvin's eyes with his technical glossary, improvising for Luce on a *gutta-percha* melody, with no apparent logical flaw he soon demonstrated the bitter necessity of stiffening the working conditions. Several anti-labor propositions followed, concerning salaries, working hours, benefits, days off, and penalties. "Perfect," said Jouvin, "if that's your opinion. If you say so, I personally have nothing against it. We'll tell them about it tomorrow."

"*You* should talk to them," Pons observed. "After all, you're the boss. You're the boss, you're in charge. *You* talk to them."

"Perfect," said Jouvin.

Two days later, of course, Duke Pons was sounding off among the bushes about the tenor of the measures announced the previous day by the waterworks engineer. Unnerving the locals with hints at other iniquitous dispositions, he then invoked, in dull tones and short sentences, as if he were talking to himself, the principles of trade unionism. These principles were unfamiliar. Interest arose. Soon vocations were created; tasks were assigned and disputed among the various sub-leaders. A small hierarchy was formed, engendering several jealousies—as desired by Pons, who wanted to divide even further. As evasively as you please, via a series of historical allusions from which he was careful to dissociate himself, he began to inoculate certain select minds with the insurrectional germ. Success: after only a few weeks, a schism fissured the union nucleus. Soon tired of pampering this newborn entity, a fringe of radical peasants impatiently advocated hard action, against the grain of a legalist slough. Around the two Aw brothers (who for all intents and purposes incarnated these harder tendencies), they heatedly debated three increasingly urgent objectives: immediate abrogation of Jouvin's decrees; departure of the couple in short order; and reinstatement of the old system, of which the indispensable, discreet, and well-liked Duke constituted the cornerstone. The younger of the Aw brothers insisted less often on this third demand—a fact that never failed to irk Pons, for whom all this meant some exhausting days.

Late in the evening, after a glance at the starry sky, he found it restful to consult his blueprints, his photographs of old astronomical instruments. One of the Duke's hopes, if he managed to stay on, was to build such an instrument for himself alone, at the edge of the jungle. It would be a simple gnomon, a tall thin triangle made of brick, a giant sundial, easily constructed. But bricks were expensive east of Malacca. What to replace them with, wondered Pons. All these questions comprised his usual routine, took up all his time, kept his mind off his former life.

No more than Jean-François Pons did Charles Pontiac dwell on the past, and thus each one thought very little about the other. Still, they had known each other well, had been on friendly enough terms despite their love for the same Nicole; they had even developed a mutual esteem. Charles was now accustomed—and had been for some time—to living without fixed abode. This asceticism presupposes a method. While he was quite capable of sleeping under bridges, on the grates of the metro, and in doorways, emergency exits, service entrances, and cellars, he had nonetheless secured nocturnal access to public establishments: offices, libraries, and museums that he toured at leisure, pondering the exhibited works by the light of his Zippo.

So Nicole Fischer searched for them in vain. They had loved her too much not to disappear—one to become a Duke and the other to wander, neither having shown any prior inclination toward such destinies. For some twelve years, each was to know nothing of the other two. Then came the thaw; they sent news now and then, scraps of news. Pons, as much as possible, renewed contact with his sister, keeping abreast of Paul J.'s progress, of his growth and his dreams. Nicole received a photo of Java, on the back of which Jean-François summarized in fifteen words his life in all that time. Much later there was a manila envelope, postmarked at the central post office on Rue du Louvre, containing only an address in Levallois, in Charles's hand, in pencil. But it was too late; she no longer felt like answering. She did not see them again.

Charles, for his part, noticed her once, in the metro—she in the nearly empty first-class car, he from the platform of Picpus station (a pretty good station: regular public, easygoing personnel, paucity of officers in blue). He was in the company of colleagues, behind whom he quickly hid until the train had disappeared. The colleagues had looked at each other, surprised: ordinarily Charles wasn't very emotive, very demonstrative. His calm more often inspired their respect, a slight respect tinged with fear and incomprehension, though he had always proven thoughtful, even of rather good counsel. Once, the Duke, too, had felt the same kind of fear toward Charles. This was the basis of his esteem.

· 9 ·

2

NOW HERE'S Justine Fischer in a grey room. The young woman is sewing a white seagull onto a grey sky. She is leaning over her handiwork, sitting in the middle of a large bed covered with synthetic zebra and bordered by lurex cushions. The bed takes up almost the whole room; the window overlooks a square in which a dozen evergreen trees grow, next to a dozen others that look dead. Night still falls early. Two pieces of furniture flatten along the walls like chilly rats, out of reach of a lamp wedged precariously against the bed.

Justine Fischer will turn thirty when the days get longer. A heavy sun always weighed on her birthdays, forcing the cake to be squeezed into the refrigerator. We cannot see her face behind her curls, nor her body beneath an ample blue thing. We see only her hands; her red nails as they draw graphs; her cigarette ash as it traces a Martian alphabet in the shadows.

Justine shared 750 square feet with Laure on the fifth floor of a white stone building. At first this was to be a temporary stay, the fruit of an arrangement. It had become the campground of sultanas on holiday, who found themselves not so badly off in the middle of the desert, not too far from an oasis, surrounded by light, useful objects within easy reach on the carpet. Outside, past the trees, spread a diorama of glassed-in lofts and little shops in the bottom floors of other buildings that dissolved into the falling night. Headlights wound around the square like electric eels, searching for a crevice in the parking-meter rock. The windows were yellow quadrangles and white rectangles, frames containing other frames. On television, a large, indeterminate machine spewed brightly colored balls.

"I got the eleven," Laure lamented, "and I almost got the twenty." The TV set was small, portable, and crowned with a V-shaped antenna; interminable extension cords trailed behind it. Laure carried it into the kitchen where the ice cubes jumped from their rubber tray. Then they shivered in the gin, heading toward the door of the grey room. Laure opened the door.

Justine was still presiding over the pieces of fabric she had bought that very morning at Reine's and Dreyfus's, at the foot of the Montmartre funicular—large, all-inclusive stores, stuffed with every imaginable kind of cloth, with women to match: round brunettes with gold ornaments, dry striped blondes, satiny beige over neat yellow chignon, fluorescent adolescents. Laure had gone with her, and then they had come home together, buying on the way some flowers and veal near the Khmer restaurant that eats up the corner of Rue de Prague. Next they had passed in front of the boxing gym and the police station, the latter guarded by a wooden booth containing a live policeman.

They were childhood friends, even though they hadn't attended the same establishments. They had met far from school, during a field trip organized by the Villemomble Magic Club, and at first they hadn't liked each other one bit. They drank a little gin before going out and tidied the place up a tad, with their gin glasses trailing behind, leaving wet rings all around the room. Laure donned her fur and Justine a hat; the stairway carpet muffled their high heels. At twenty-five minutes to eight they walked with a brisk step, in the brisk air, to see a film starring Richard Widmark.

3

THIRTY YEARS earlier, they had torn down a failed bis-
cuit factory in Rue Jules-Verne, which cleverly runs parallel to Passage Robert-Houdin. In its place they had built a small
residence in the style of the times: five stories with wide balco-
nies bounded by curved tiles, furnished with washer-dryers, featuring a badly mown courtyard bordered by a row of studio
apartments. Between the latter's French doors, water leakage had
smeared dark stalactitic forms on the cracked plaster. Bob lived
there.

So here's Bob, and Paul has come to visit him. Bob's place has
a northern exposure: when the sun is strong, you can see it coat
the facing wall the whole day through, more or less ricochet off it,
but you never receive it directly. The studio is exempt from this
erosion, as if virgin, deprived of its spotlight, in the perpetual
shadow of the sliding door nearest the courtyard. It's fairly calm.

"I quit," said Paul.

It was fairly calm, not counting the numerous members of the
family upstairs who started shrilly insulting each other at the crack
of dawn, threatening to get it over with once and for all until well
into the night, all accompanied by a din of chronic frying and

flushing. "Let's quit the whole thing," said Paul. "The Italians was the last time."

"It went pretty well," Bob recalled, "with the Italians. It went really well with the Italians."

"And what did we get out of it?" wondered Paul. "Three cents, and in hot water with the Belgians. No, no. What's that guy's name again, the little guy?"

Some people also found Bob little; some people found him dry and peevish, nervous like certain musicians, certain mechanics. Only when absolutely necessary did he remove his leather jacket full of slant-cut pockets. "What do they call him?" Paul insisted. "You know, that little crud who's always hanging around Van Os?"

"Toon's nothing," said Bob. "Van Os is the one who counts. He likes you, Van Os."

"That's what worries me."

"He must envy you," speculated Bob. "That Van Os isn't at peace with himself. You can tell. He tries hard, but you can tell."

Paul shrugged his shoulders while prowling around the studio, hands in his tweed pockets. Paul changed clothes more often than Bob. He was taller and richer, and still other details set them apart from one another: their tastes in food, their perception of colors, the woman they would never find. Still, they had recognized in each other an alter ego; they used the same expedients, frequented the same margin—a badly lit, scarcely comfortable margin, to which one might even cling at times, one's feet then dangling in unison over the void. They had met at a costume party; Paul wasn't disguised as anything, Bob went as a camera.

Paul lived on profits from the family printing plant, Bob from stunt work for television. Sometimes they also smuggled little items: souped-up motors, hi-fi's, small weapons furnished by Tomaso. This arms traffic did not exceed the parallel supply of collectors, recreational marksmen, and petty malefactors. As such, they had helped Van Os out of a jam when *he* was but a petty malefactor, newly installed, in a modest and irregular situation. But Van Os was becoming more prominent, hospitalizing too many bank tellers, rousing the living forces of insecurity. Paul and Bob, worried about this new development, preferred not to deal with him anymore. While Paul was trying to persuade Van Os that their weapons source had dried up, Bob, unthinkingly, in a fit of compassion, had practically donated two Swiss Parabellums to an Italian couple in desperate straits. Van Os had learned of the set-up, become upset, then had calmed down, but kept trying to get his guns. He was becoming insistent. That was how things stood at the moment.

A kind of bar isolated the kitchen from the rest of the studio. Paul skirted around this installation, rinsed a promotional beer mug covered with peeling decals, filled it with water, and contemplated the grassy alopecia through the windows. Bob stored tires there, sometimes many tires, which vexed the co-ownership. Paul set his glass down without having drunk, picked up his coat, and headed for the door.

Paul J. Bergman, who was midway through his life (if all went well), walked out into Rue Jules-Verne and up to his Mitsubishi Colt. Following the one-way streets, he circled several rotting tenement buildings to take a southerly direction. On Rue de la Fontaine-au-Roi, four large black men were pulling a large, black, dead goat from the trunk of a small burgundy Renault. On the Colt's dashboard, the dials and meters said that all was well. The digital clock displayed 6:00, and the radio emitted some Buxtehude, then some Joe Pass, which was muted for an instant so that a silky nearby voice could confirm that all was well.

The Mitsubishi crossed the river via the Pont-au-Change, got caught in the coldness of Rue Danton before vainly seeking a parking place near the Odéon Theater, and was finally reduced to slinking into an underground lot. Had one been searching for Paul, one would then have found him eating raw fish in a Nipponese establishment on Rue des Ciseaux. He often lunched and dined alone now, since Elizabeth had left six months ago, at any hour of the day—often uncooked things, as if solitude induced a resurgence of barbarism.

A short while later, the falling night finally hit ground. Over the boulevard the sky was a purplish leg striped with varicose clouds. Paul wandered aimlessly; his eyes met those of the mannequins in their shop windows. We have no reason to believe he had planned to enter the movie theater. Sixty people were ahead of him: couples who were looking for each other, finding things to say to each other, or kissing as a last resort; loners buried in their newspapers; little monosex clusters, like the two girls next to Paul, including one stunning blonde wearing a man's hat. The procession waited, shivering in place like a caterpillar, each member lending a little ear to the bordering conversations, then turning a whole face away when a young Anglophone with green teeth, twelve strings to back him up, came to spit a little too closely that the time he loves best is the morning when he and his beloved walk in the park, among the peacocks, under the pink stars. The beloved followed behind, offering a timid cup into which some divested themselves of their yellow change.

The blonde with the headgear leaned toward the brunette in the fur, who didn't have any cigarettes either. Feigning nonchalance, Paul held out his open pack of Senior Services. The young woman accepted, smiling measuredly, exhaling a thank-you with another smile, a ghost of the first, leaving Paul to search his pockets for matches. But she had her own lighter, gold, shaped like a water tower, which she flicked while turning away, to signify that they would take this no further. Then it was time. Everyone came in out of the cold, squeezed in next to each other facing Richard Widmark.

They saw him play his part, then eyes shone under relit neons. They emerged from the auditorium as if from sleep, haphazardly, mouths dry and thoughts fleeting, loitering and taking themselves for someone else. Paul more or less followed the young woman in the spectatorial flow, using her fedora as a buoy. He managed to end up not far from her, stopped before the stills under glass as if he wanted to reappraise the film.

She and the brunette were conferring; their discussion was none too audible. As Paul tossed a prudent glance at the hat, its wearer swept him with a haughty stare that offered no encouragement. His shoulders drooped, but just then, in a clear voice, she announced her plans to go see Richard Widmark again in a movie house at Les Gobelins, next Tuesday, same time. Very soon afterward they disappeared at the end of Rue Christine, to his right. Paul remained in front of the theater entrance until it had swallowed the audience for the next showing. He examined the left end of the street, which was empty, and then the sky: beyond the streetlamps it was totally black. You could see nothing in this blackness. But that nothing seemed very near.

4

WHEN THE SKY was like this, it sometimes meant rain. When it rained too much, the water rose in the tributary bed, the canals, the gutters; it invaded the banks of the river and the express lanes that ran alongside it; it chased the men and women with no permanent address to street level, and the rodents to mud level, their little eyes surging coldly, tousled fur revealing pallid skin, long snout split over the ridge of their teeth, which were yellow and red with an impure blood.

But it hardly rained that night. The bridge dwellers stayed put under conglomerations of cloth and cardboard, feet wrapped in newspaper. There were, for example, three of them near the Pont Alexandre III: two, hugging, formed a heap of sleep; the other rested in an oblong bin made of small wooden crates with a green plastic tarpaulin over it, striped with dried mud and tar. Out of this mass stuck a pair of threadbare light-and-dark-blue sneakers, sometimes animated by the toes they contained. Their owner coughed, scratched himself in his stall, causing its walls to tremble, then slid out on his back, feet first. He was already dressed in grey nylon pants, a chocolate-brown turtleneck sweater, and a fur-lined olive parka with a string-belt at the waist and a removable hood—good solid worker's clothes, the kind you see in farmers' markets. Frayed without being torn, only superficially dirty, these clothes looked better as soon as the upright Charles had adjusted them, tucked them in, smoothed out the sloppiness. They immediately took on a certain style.

Charles Pontiac kept up his appearance. When he was dirty he went (for lack of a better opportunity) to a metro station better policed than most by the men in blue. These latter brought you without too much violence back up to the street, to a bus like any other except that it was iron grey, its windows were opaque, and they checked your identity. Then they took you to the Nanterre poorhouse where they showered and disinfected you and gave you a meal; you slept; it was a chance to meet people. But Charles was satisfied with only a few intimates, including that torpid entanglement next to whom he occasionally slept. Though he was normally based in Saint-Ambroise station, his other habits led him to the Saint-Martin canal to see Vidal and his cannibals, and there was also Madam Gina de Beer in Brochant. A number of these journeys were accomplished in solitude, Charles having access to individual shelters that no one else shared. And besides, we know what that kind of life is like: in the morning you recover from the night before, then you look for some coffee. It's a whole ordeal, followed by the matter of breakfast; by the time that's settled, you've spent your day.

Charles had become a man with short, dry brown hair, rough red skin, a thick red neck, and fat red-and-white knuckles. He bent toward the river and dipped in a hand that he then passed over his face, keeping his mouth shut tight, snorting hard through his nose. He wiped himself off on his sleeves and spat several times while heading for the stairway. No one at street level: at this hour no one had any reason to be out in the dark and cold. Charles glanced back at his peers pressed into the yellow side of a streetlamp, then began to walk.

He crossed the Seine under the bridge's gold-leaf ornaments, followed the quay up to the Louvre, through whose gates he passed; day broke over the miniature Arc de Triomphe that squatted there, a pretty little object that made you want to take it home with you. He passed through the new section of town toward Boulevard Sébastopol, then through the outskirts of the Marais toward Place de la République, whose allegory found itself caught between perpendicular scaffolding like the figure of a molecule. After absorbing a bit of Rue du Faubourg-du-Temple, he arrived at a complicated intersection, muddled at the upper end by a lock, downstream from which the canal slipped underground. All day long barges passed by, contemplated from the isolated square by loafers leaning on the bust of Frédérick Lemaître. Leaving the lock where they changed level, they sank into a reach which the boulevard covered over from there to the Bastille. The canal, some sixteen hundred yards long, then became a tunnel flanked by quays, ordinarily closed to the public by barriers and barbed wire. But Charles Pontiac was not your ordinary public: he stepped over the barriers, penetrated into the gallery. Charles was a man of the underground. Night had barely ended and he wanted to return to the darkness; he wanted to return to his friends.

5

Now it's Bob who has come to visit Paul, in his next-to-last floor of a high-rise in the fifteenth arrondissement, overlooking the Seine. From the depths of a red couch, in front of a picture window facing east toward the skyscrapers of the thirteenth and their stifling vertebrae, Bob intermittently tosses out topics of conversation. But Paul, once more in the grip of melancholy, tosses none of them back, doesn't even answer. Despite Mrs. Perez's best efforts every Tuesday, the domicile's neglected state reeks of Elizabeth's absence. On the walls, faded quadrilaterals attest to pictures that she has not left behind. Paul often fights this absence by going often to small evening get-togethers that he is often the last to leave, having lost consciousness, alienated his conscience. At best, he might feel himself dazedly being led away by a kindred soul with a scarcely credible forename; tumble too early from a bed that means nothing to him; find his apartment especially cold on those mornings, like a reproach; fall into the red couch: we know what that kind of life is like. All day long his sadness multiplies, relaxing just enough by evening for him to go out again—a cycle of sorts, under whose pernicious influence Paul no longer even answers his friend. So Bob gets up, his efforts being vain, and goes to lean against the window: hey, there's an airplane in that leaden sky. Oh—no, it's not an airplane.

"I told you," Paul nonetheless sighs, "about that girl. The one I saw at the movies. In the movie theater, let's get that straight, a real live movie theater. A real live girl."

Bob doesn't react. "A real girl," Paul insists, "that's what we need." Bob shrugs one shoulder, looks at the city crushed under all that lead. In the final account it was only birds that looked like airplanes, a volant flock maintaining its visible initial against the watermark clouds. They are migrants heading east–southeast, who want to cover almost six thousand miles as the crow flies. Heedless of the dangers inherent in their enterprise, they rush headlong past Joinville-le-Pont without once deviating from their path. First they distinguish no sea beneath them save for a bit of Black, after having followed the river that runs into it, having even touched down on the banks of same to take a breather, to extract several Roumanian earthworms washed down by a shot of Danube, to survey with undaunted pupil the local hoopoes and herons who vociferate in their special Slovene. Leaving Eastern Europe behind, steering toward Mount Ararat, they fly over the remains of the arch in which their forebears once took shelter; then mullahs and then brahmans will see them head off toward the Bay of Bengal and will interpret their passage.

Long is the crossing of the bay, and so they will have to rest periodically on the reefs, the flotsam, the rigging of a ship passing in the night. Off the Nicobar Islands, for example, they will take advantage of the MS *Boustrophedon*, a small cargo vessel some 150 feet in length, complacently sailing under the Cypriot flag after having changed name and home port eight times. The ship, manned by a regulation crew of six, is equipped with radar, a direction finder, sonar, and an ultra-short-wave transmitter thanks to which Captain Illinois communicates with the coastal stations.

It's a versatile freighter, this *Boustrophedon*, built to transport all kinds of merchandise and endowed with a single large hold, which simplifies loading operations. Ostensibly effecting a round-trip to the East, its itinerary is not subject to prearranged stopovers like that of an ocean liner. It drifts from port to port, wherever a given cargo leads it, delivering bananas to London or wax to Trivandrum without batting an eyelash. This time it's 3,000 barrels of a tar-like substance destined for Surabaja.

It is three in the afternoon. The captain stands on the upper deck. His old cerulean eye scans the Prussian blue horizon, over which the islands tipped that morning. There is a flat calm; the sea is an empty phonograph record of which the cargo ship would be the center hole, Illinois's eye the stylus. Yesterday the vessel skirted the Malacca peninsula, having cast off three days earlier toward the Christian West, its hold stuffed with rubber, palm oil, and tin. All seems peaceful on board, but it's pure appearance; in fact the sailors are grumbling under their breath about the conditions they have to endure. The food, they find, lacks abundance and freshness. At that point, who could be surprised when, a bang having rung out aft, two men rush toward the dead migratory bird, argue over the lukewarm thing, but apparently reach a compromise since together they carry it to the kitchens. The captain delicately turns away from this scene, preferring to revert to his oceanic inspection. Distraught but soon forgetful of their mourning, the birds have resumed their exhausting flight, already far from the vessel, as far away as possible, in the direction opposite its wake, straight toward Malaysia.

6

THIRTY Malaysian peasants were dozing off on parallel benches, before a dais where two of the whites facing them dozed more comfortably in their armchairs. The peasants sported the traditional work accoutrements: blue rag knotted over the loins, sometimes embellished by a strip of cloth slung across the shoulder. Scarcely more vigilant, Chinese foremen watched over them—it's a frequent occurrence in Malacca for the Chinese to climb the social ladder with more agility than the natives. The white man who was not sleeping read figures, lists of figures and percentages that an interpreter rounded to the nearest decimal. This took place once a month. It was customary. The peasants had to be silent during the hearing; it was all that was required of them, in return for which they received a bonus of one-twentieth of a Malaysian dollar.

Seated to the left of Luce Jouvin, Duke Pons raised an eyelid. One long wall of the room was pierced by windows through which he saw the rows of hevea plants growing beyond the latex factory; the heat produced limp waves that deformed the vista of bushes, as if under the influence of a breeze unlikely in this season in this part of the world. On the opposite wall, tall mirrors romantically eroded by mould doubled the quantity of locals, while the ceiling fan subtracted a little humidity. Pons had jury-rigged this fan eleven years before from the propeller of a De Havilland Vampire fighter plane that had crashed in the jungle in the middle of a raid around 1953. He had discovered the wreck swarming with crawlies, rodents rubbing shoulders with each other and even criss-crossing the helmeted skeleton gripping the controls, the top joint of his index finger welded to the ejector button. The Duke had belatedly shuddered for Nicole Fischer's fiancé before starting to remove the propeller.

Pons wore almost sixty years under a greenish-black sweatshirt that was stained and torn at the shoulders. He was tall and dry; the gaze above his neck was dry. Raymond Jouvin, on the other hand, sweated profusely while reading the figures, and Luce Jouvin slept behind large sunglasses, slept while intermittently snoring, slept in her cretonne printed with faded flowers, although theoretically it was she who presided over these monthly meetings. It seemed that the audience was beginning to chafe under the weight of this institution: the peasants whispered, elbowed each other, sniggered in their pidgin. A recreational atmosphere threatened to corrupt the proceedings.

"Do something, Raymond," the Duke hissed, leaning across Luce, whom a dream made moan at that very instant. "Say something, you see how unruly they're getting. Pretty soon we won't be able to keep them in line."

First Jouvin, then his interpreter looked at Pons with indecision. The interpreter was a Negrito from a tribe near the Siamese border. His skin was dark, his hair had gone white, his good will was fading. Jouvin's hesitation, which interrupted his accounting, allowed for the formation in the back of the room of a more distinct movement, in which the Chinese did not join at first. In measured tones, one of the peasants had just launched into a little speech. Jouvin pedagogically tapped the edge of the table with his fingers—in vain. Careful to echo the boss's slightest nuance, the interpreter did the same with the tips of his fluted nails, producing no effect other than Luce's startled awakening, the lifting of her heavy eyelids under all her diopters.

Luce had a large, wide mouth containing a disproportionately voluminous tongue; no doubt it was tiring always to keep one inside the other, and so Luce occasionally had to let this tongue out, the way one stretches one's limbs or walks the dog. She ran it over her thick lips, swollen like chapped tires, then grumbled something for the interpreter's benefit. Happy to be relieved of his translation duties, the latter blinked, smiled, disappeared, and returned carrying a metal goblet whose contents Jouvin did not care to identify. He turned away, whereas Pons leered at Luce with teeth agleam. Profiting from these excesses, from the diminished lucidity that was their natural consequence, the Duke had ventured five or six times toward those exceptional mucous membranes, which downed the contents of the goblet in one gulp, and which then articulated: "What's with him, what's he want?"

"It's always the same ones," Jouvin observed. "What's his problem, Jean-François?"

"Hard to hear," Pons pretended. "I can't make out all of it."

Gradually the entire room had turned toward the fiery-eyed orator, whose black hair yielded blue glints. His loincloth hung like any loincloth, but tiny semi-precious stones embedded in the front of his incisors denoted an attempt at style. His bust was also tattooed with eagles, pansies, and abstract designs, including, on his shoulders, chevrons that were perhaps coincidental. He was a long youth with a long face punctuated by a small nose and narrow ears, whose lobes had been elongated by polytheistic charms. When he spoke, his peers listened. Even the foremen under Kok Keok Choo, indifferent at first, ended up tossing several diphthongs back and forth. Then looks were exchanged with the locals, and soon everyone was heatedly commenting on the younger Aw's peroration. Only his older brother watched him in silence, resembling him like a first draft, a fuzzy photo. While he shared nearly all his brother's ideas, the elder Aw restricted himself to more custodial action, preferring to check off the absentees at union meetings, collect the dues, write up the minutes and his little brother's speeches in his literate scrawl.

"There they go, now the Chinese are getting into the act," noted Jouvin. "Do something, Jean-François."

"But what's he want?" reiterated Luce.

"The same old story," went Pons. "Working conditions, no big secret. Hours, salaries, that's all they care about."

He moved his hands apart. Jouvin frowned and knit his brows while leafing through the account book, keyboarding numbers on his calculator to give the young Aw's recitative some backbeat. He tossed back his elbow, urged on by his demonstration:

"This business of salaries, you see that we can't. Let's say two percent, sure, all right, I won't even count the charges, and that comes to. That comes to, that comes to," he sniffed, extracting a soft white particle from the corner of his eye, "of course we can't. We'd lose."

"Be tough," approved Pons, "stand firm. Don't give in. You understand" (he pointed one finger toward his other finger), "we give them this much and immediately they" (he pointed to his entire forearm).

Disorder in the room swelled. Luce cried for somebody to do something, somebody do something.

"It's a bit late," said the Duke, "they're worked up now. Or at least, we'll see. Berhenti," he called out, "berhenti."

This must have meant something like stop—and, Pons having some influence over the Malaysians, the elder Aw gestured toward his younger brother, who braked abruptly, parking his speech on the roadside of his consciousness. "Hey now," continued Pons, avunculo-vernacularly, "hey now, hey now." The locals turned obediently toward him; curiously, it was the Chinese, normally the better disciplined, who prolonged the commotion for an instant.

The Duke created a diversion by announcing some minor technical improvements: from now on, they would broaden the use of anticryptogamous pulp, and as of tomorrow they would double the first crew of syringe-men. Instead of the old sheet-metal barrels, they would now employ a tanker-truck to shuttle back and forth to the coast, from where the rubber would slip to Le Havre—a French port, Pons reminded them—on a boat over whose destiny presided Captain Illinois—whom you know, Pons reminded them, whom you respect. He also repeated the announcement of his upcoming departure, the date of which was not entirely set, in a week or two. The peasants noted this news; shortly afterward the meeting was adjourned.

Shortly after that, the Duke immersed himself in the white light and in air that was thick as strong coffee. Three hundred yards separated the Jouvin villa, the site of these monthly conferences, from his assigned bungalow. Two rooms: in the corner of the larger one, a telescope trained its powerful lens toward a hatch cut in the ceiling, which Pons opened on clear nights. Having studied the sky until late the night before, he had gone to bed without closing the trap door; photons, diffracted on the suspended pollens, now poured through, crushing the dust to the floor.

He sat at a work table shoved into another corner, tried to make headway in the letter he had begun—the first after a long silence, very delicate to compose. Written the previous evening on a square of paper, four lines awaited their sequel. Pons preferred to crumple them, took another sheet of paper, wrote My dear Nicole (crossed out), Dear Nicole (crossed out), Nicole, crumpled again, then looked at the table itself. Moved several objects on it. Managed only to convolute the disorder.

There were much-reread books, or partially reread—as indicated by a more sustained tan line running the length of the front edge; an equal number of magazines, more or less licentious, more or less unstapled; cans of Tiger beer, pencils, scratched sunglasses, three cotton handkerchiefs loaded with various secretions; and then expired documents, obsolete tickets, and lighters without benzine and watches without batteries, stamps and toothless combs beneath the photo of his nephew that no longer stayed put in its frame; there were also two dirty dice worn out by craps, an aluminum tube containing eight opium seeds, keys rusting together under a stainless steel alloy, spare change, string, bottles of Tiger beer, an iron box containing two iron boxes containing a rubber bulb prolonged by a putrid hose, as well as other things with no name, things to which one cannot put a name, except maybe a spindle of catgut. Pons did not look at all this without feeling some small pleasure, along with a minor discouragement that couldn't kill the pleasure. And so he yawned peacefully, but could not finish this movement since someone was calling him (Duke, Duke Pons) from the other side of the trap, above his head. He raised his eyes.

"What should we do, how should we do it?" asked young Aw.

These two questions are equally distinct in Malay. Pons promptly examined the surroundings: finding it virgin of witnesses, he allowed a brief confab.

"Be tough," he said, "stand firm. Don't give in. You know," he added, raising a finger, "you let 'em do this much and—"

"Yes," said the younger man.

"Scram, now. They'd better not see you here."

Once the trade unionist had evaporated under the sun, the Duke could resume his yawn and bring it to term. Then he walked toward the telescope, in passing folding down a quilt on the dubious sheets. Squeezed against the eyepiece, his eye saw only a slightly brownish, slightly painful whiteness, furtively crisscrossed by blurry stains. Intrigued, Pons focused the lens: it was nothing but those same migrant birds arranged in spearhead formation, pursuing their rectilinear flight in an east–southeasterly course, next stop Java.

7

T HE DUKE wasn't the only one interested in celestial bodies. "In this neighborhood," Bob told Paul, "you'll find a
number of specialists who not only watch them and assess their
position, but also calculate their influence over our common fate.
You go see them when you're unhappy, or confused."

Now, Paul was feeling utterly hopeless. He was a man alone
since Elizabeth had gone, a man who couldn't stay at home in
the evening, who moped around forlornly in the countdown of
twilights, killed moments of silence with men like himself, and
paid lukewarm visits to friends' homes: warm homes regularly
repainted and vacuumed, pastellized with windowshades and little girls' cheeks, mellow vegetables and calming roast beef, sparkling china, fresh aromas and velvety scents—whereas the solitary eats (if he eats at all) his rice without appetite from the pot,
his sardines from the can, standing on the carpet amid the stains
and the dustballs. Paul's sorrow, the sorrow of a man abandoned:
his life was purgatorial, a tundra without horizon, which he
crossed indefinitely, without raising his eyes for fear of puddles.

"You can't stay like this," said Bob.

It was another very bad Tuesday for Paul, who was huddled in the corner, glass in hand, in the studio on Rue Jules-Verne, sitting on the edge of the worst armchair. The worst armchair vomited whorls of rust and green straw, shreds of rotten jute.

"Relax," said Bob, "look how uncomfortable you are."

Paul contemplated the surface of the colorless liquid in his hand: an ice cube turned slowly inside the glass, like an aging monk wasting away in his cloister.

It often happened like this since Elizabeth had tendered her resignation. Paul buzzed, Bob opened, Paul entered, Bob went down to buy something to drink at the Arab market. Later, when Paul was in no shape to return home, he slept on Bob's couch, a five-foot-long parallelipiped that they extended with a sheet of foam rubber rolled into a spiral. The mornings after, Bob filtered the coffee in the kitchenette, closed off by a plastic accordion above the bar.

In the evenings they spoke little, eyes dimly on the television, leafing through magazines that weren't outdated enough. Bob sometimes put on a record, generally old-fashioned easy listening; Tennessee Ernie Ford or Georges Ulmer spun in the dust. Now the day was ending, no doubt the evening would quietly pass as usual. Or so Bob thought. But no, Paul glanced at his wrist: it was almost seven o'clock. He got up, revived the coat thrown over a chair.

"Where are you going?"

Paul didn't answer; Bob was a bit worried. A little bit disappointed, a tiny bit annoyed. He mustn't show it. He leafed and leafed—without looking at Paul, who tied his belt with a decisive knot and limply wished him 'night as he headed for the door. Through the grubby windowpanes one could see the darkness hurled onto the lawn.

While Bob dialed the numbers of friends, of almost-friends, who served as tire patches in his social life; while his disappointment mounted as the numbers didn't answer, people already having gone out to chase other tires; while he wondered why he shouldn't spend an evening alone at home, in fact, why shouldn't he go to bed early like everyone else since the best sleep occurs before midnight, why not *him* for a change; while he then admitted the vanity of such a project, recognized that in less than an hour he'd be hanging around the back of a club full of stand-in tire patches; while all this was happening Paul started up his vehicle, then crossed the city once again, heading south. This time he transected the river via the Pont d'Austerlitz, followed Boulevard Saint-Marcel toward Les Gobelins. A café of large proportions served the crossroads. Paul entered, settled near the windows through which a movie theater was visible, and ordered a bottle of dark beer. Not fifty feet from where he sat, a very young man born in Liège and hidden behind a pillar ordered a light beer on tap. Driving an old, modest, overheated Fiat, as far from the Mitsubishi as Guinness can be from Schlitz, this youth had been following Paul, unbeknownst to the latter, since Rue Jules-Verne. It was half past seven.

At fifty minutes past, Paul got up and crossed the street toward the cinema. Without joining it, he inspected the waiting line, a cousin of the one from the other day. He waited near it, then stood alone for a full fifteen minutes after the blackness had swallowed it up. No one. Stationed behind a small van, the young man coldly watched Paul. He was a small, frail young man who never smiled, a small young man who didn't remind you of anyone, except perhaps Elisha Cook, Jr., in his early days. He took shelter under a twill coat that was much too large for him, whose sleeves, which could have held eight of his arms, covered everything but ten fingernails gnawed to the blood. He called himself Toon and it seemed he was afraid, or maybe he wanted to inspire fear. He appeared antagonistic, internally raging at being no more than himself in his ample garment, far from the measurements he would have preferred. When Paul finally walked away from the cinema and returned to the huge bar, this individual recrossed the street as well, from another angle, after a short delay. He waited until Paul had reclaimed his seat, then entered, reclaimed his own, and concealed himself behind a wide-open copy of *France-Soir*: following people evidently constituted part of his professional functions.

Paul, idle, ordered another Guinness, then another after that, but no more. He had to get up three times, first to buy cigarettes and go downstairs for a pee, then to call Bob, finally to call Bob again and pee a second time. Each time it was only a mediocre need to pee, and each time Bob wasn't home. Returning from his third voyage, Paul swiped off a table a copy of *France-Soir*, a twin of the one from behind which he was being watched.

Shortly before ten o'clock, this periodical having been picked to the bone, Paul returned to the cinema, still followed by the aforementioned Toon. They took up positions again: Paul still didn't join the forbearers waiting for the next showing, who constituted a line by agglomeration. Finally, this time without her hat, the object of his anticipations appeared.

She was clad all in grey: pigeon, mouse, pearl, iron; she joined the line. Paul let several couples get in behind her before joining it in turn. Those from the earlier showing came out blinking, as if emerging from a grotto; the others replaced them. At the tail end of the tail, Toon entered the auditorium against his will: to this young individual the movies seemed a flat art, a flat custom; he always saw, behind the action, the stretched screen that supported it. A handicap, of sorts, possibly the effect of a malformation. It was the same thing with television: he saw only the tube. The woman in grey had taken a seat in the front row, right in the center. Paul settled in at about the eighth row, enough to the side to keep both her (in rear-three-quarters view) and the screen in his field of vision; Toon sat down in back to watch everyone—and, if need be, the film.

Which soon hit cruising speed. To his surprise, and for perhaps the first time in his young life, Toon almost immediately forgot the existence of the screen; he even forgot his surprise, so prodigiously did he identify with the rebel leader. Paul, on the other hand, too distracted, periodically squinted at his watch without making out the time, the irregular waves of technicolor cancelling out its phosphorescence without being bright enough to light the dial. Then the film ended—happily, it seemed. After the final panoramic shot and the return to light, its theme music continued a bit, injecting a small bonus of fantasy into the lives of the dazed, a transition between pure fiction and irrevocable reality, sonorous extra helping, annex to the lie, sugar-coating of the pill of truth.

The three real actors left the auditorium, among the crowd of real extras, in the inverse order of their entrance. Having quickly recovered from his emotions, Toon immediately positioned himself in the vestibule to watch Paul, who turned toward the grey young lady, his banging heart holding the banging door for her as she went past. Paul inhaled deeply, then joined her, came up close to her, too close, leaving no room for ambiguity. "Excuse me," his voice caught. She looked at him with startled eyes of blue-grey enamel, decorated with gold sparks on the circumference of her pupils, like the solar corona during an eclipse. Again he rasped:

"You don't remember me?"

8

"SHE SAID NO. Doesn't ring a bell. That's what she said, but I'm not entirely sure she's— Would you mind not snickering?"

"I've been there," said Bob, waving his hands above his head as if to ward off a squadron of flying insects. "Man, have I been there. So then what?"

Then Paul had tried to commend himself to Justine's memory. He had alluded to the film from the evening when she'd been wearing her hat—especially certain scenes that, to his dismay, she seemed to have enjoyed less than he—without daring to mention the hat itself. He had suggested they go somewhere to get something, but she had pleaded friends that she had to meet somewhere else. It was a casual rejection, without haughtiness; Paul had not felt too let down. She had seemed quite willing to jot his phone number in her leather-bound address book with copper clasp, which she sought at length at the bottom of a large bag chock-full of objects. She had even agreed to give him hers, her own phone number—although in a murmur that barely made it past her red lips, and without revealing her name. She hadn't thought to make up a false name; she just didn't want to tell him her real one, go figure.

But a week had gone by without her phoning Paul, whom we again find lonely and unkempt in the hollow of the same armchair, in the same dark corner of Bob's studio. His feet are resting on an incomplete collection of *Penthouse* magazines. One hand clutches the edge of the bar, on which a collection of former mustard and anchovy jars squats. Some of these jars are chipped; others have not yet shed their labels. Rings of alcohol have become sticky, hardened, tarnished. The bar is affixed to the wall at a right angle, but the juncture remains unfinished; without a protective coat, the plaster appears naked, powdery. It isn't complete, it isn't clean. At Bob's, almost everything is like this. Paul's face expresses one part renunciation, two parts bitterness, with a dash of hidden self-satisfaction. He looks at his glass, at the bottom of which, in its tall translucent courtyard, the ice cube has resumed its slow course, like a jailbird at recess.

"It doesn't make any sense, I don't even know her name. I know her number but I don't know her name." (Paul now ponders, at a distance, his left thumbnail.) "I can't call her in these conditions." (Paul gnaws at the nail.) "It doesn't make any sense."

"You can't stay like that," Bob repeats. "Don't you want to see someone?" (Paul shrugs while spitting out the crescent of nail.) "Come on, let's go see someone."

Scornful of the sempiternal tarot, disdainful of the crystal ball in which the beloved does the dance of the seven veils like a Chinese fish in its jar, Bob knew several neighborhood specialists in rare techniques, experts whose practices would have become extinct were it not for them. The most recent crop of Africans, for example, a fresh load on the divination market, commanded a network of hieratic sales reps—men of large stature wearing enormous, light-colored boubous and leopard-skin toques, distributing business cards in well-traveled crossroads. Bob had broken the ice with several among them, who had all spoken of a certain Mr.

Brome, the ultimate Marabout, the most extralucid in his field. "Let's go see him," suggested Bob. Paul was always willing to let someone take care of him.

Mr. Brome was out, said to be visiting his brother-in-law, who was not at home either. In the kitchen of a next-door neighbor of the brother-in-law's, four plaited subjects were quarreling in Tukulor idiom; Bob went to reconnoiter. Paul waited alone in a narrow living room with red-and-green wallpaper and orange carpet, with an equally vibrant bedspread on the sofa. A large television was perched on a table made of metal tubing and smoked glass. On the table's lower shelf, a primitive VCR displayed a patina of sticky dust—except on the control buttons, which fingers had polished into gleaming ovals, shiny as fresh licorice.

Paul sat on the sofa, flipped through the pile of cassettes at the foot of the table, read the labels without recognizing a single title, a single name, without even understanding all of them. He chose one of the cassettes at random and slid it into the belly of the machine. Abruptly the half-rewound tape brought forth a love scene under coconut palms, many coconut palms, an incredible number of coconut palms, their branches limply swayed by a syrupy zephyr. Bob returned from the kitchen, resting his conversation-clouded eye on all those palms. "Come," he said, "let's go."

Outside the dusk asserted itself. On Rue de l'Orillon other Africans walked; their teeth tore off small bits of night that they chewed like gum, like cola. A green collar phosphoresced around the neck of one, the forehead of another was cancelled by a line of pink Band-Aid. None of them knew where Mr. Brome had disappeared to. At the corner of Passage Piver, Bob remembered a geomancer of his acquaintance named Bouc Bel-Air, met at the local grocer's, who practiced his profession on that street. Shall we go? "Wait," said Paul, who had stopped in front of a shoe store. "I really like those," he said, indicating a pair on display. "I like that kind. Don't you?"

Bob winced at the model in question: its instep was decorated on either side with a kind of lapel, like a collar, which gave the laces the appearance of a Texan string tie, knotted, as if around a neck, at the base of the ankle. They went into the shop. The salesgirl was humble, shy in a lavender blouse, friendly in a resigned sort of way. Paul plunged his foot into the shoe, which at first seemed too large, then too small, although still too large at the same time. Tested, each adjacent size accentuated one of these defects without entirely managing to eliminate the other. He tried on, several times, all the half-sizes in both directions, uncertain of his discomfort, without being able to call on any witnesses other than his own feet, and the feeling of loneliness engulfed him once more. He raised his eyes toward the footwear specialist: Touch my foot, he begged, just the tip, does it seem all right? Am I comfortable in them? She had neither the will nor the desire to answer. He gave up. They disappeared into Passage Piver.

Bouc Bel-Air was an average man who lived cleanly in small lodgings. He wore the same clothes as anyone else, although his beard and hair were plentiful, almost perpendicular to his skin. All across his cheek, parallel to the arc of the jawbone, this beard showed a long trans-Amazonian gash with several lanes: the tines of a small fork or the claws of a medium-sized lion. No wooden tables or chairs were to be found here, no piece of heavy furniture. The furnishings consisted of rather outdated camping equipment, smacking of salvage: a folding bed, chairs made of tubing over which stretched heavy fabric with faded stripes, in diluted colors, pocked by use. The geomancer greeted his guests around a table of blue plastified hardboard, its circumference streaked with the memory of cigarettes. Then he retreated into what must have been the kitchen, in which they could see a metal ice box, a butane burner on a cadmium-plated steel stand, and a pantry covered with nylon netting. He returned with a bottle and three dented aluminum measuring cups; they drank. They drank in silence, after which Bouc Bel-Air considered Bob interrogatively.

"It's for him," said Bob, indicating Paul.

So Bouc Bel-Air turned toward Paul, seemed to study him a moment, then leaned toward a tub of sand sitting on the floor near the table, similar in all respects to the commodes that serve for the exoneration of cats. "The principle," he said, "is as follows."

He lifted the heavy tub, placed it on the table, and equalized its blond surface with the tips of his fingers. "The principle is as follows," he repeated, removing from his pocket a thick plastic bag from which he poured half a dozen buck-shot pellets into the palm of his hand. He examined them, made them jump in his palm while reiterating that the principle was as follows, seemed to hesitate as to the best way to outline this principle. Then he apparently renounced his didactic views, for all of a sudden he made his projectiles leap onto the miniature private beach.

Instantly, a perfect silence filled the apartment. The external world itself—most immediately represented by Passage Piver— observed same. For several seconds a cluster of children disturbed it; one of them cried distinctly that that's how it is, Pascal, that's how it is.

Bouc Bel-Air contemplated the sandy pellets one by one, then the totality of their configuration. Paul and Bob watched him lead his flat palm over the arrangement, move it around as though he were taking measurements in the air, and open various compasses with his fingers, on which he then seemed to be counting. After this he leaned back a notch as if to get a better perspective on the matter, all the while carefully massaging the exterior, then the interior, of his nose. Finally he stood and walked into the other room. They heard him run water from the tap, drink, gargle, and blow his nose between his fingers, which he then rinsed. "The hell's he up to?" whispered Paul.

Bob did not explain how the other had just scattered the pellets, formed the figures, defined the horoscope; how he now had to reflect actively, return, as if to the source of a river, toward the axis of a whole range of partial deductions. He simply muttered, "Shut up, you'll break his concentration."

Bouc Bel-Air reappeared from the kitchen, wiping his hands on a blue dishrag. "It's very clear," he said, reclaiming his place before Paul, who threw Bob a mildly worried glance.

"It's clear," he repeated. "I just have to verify."

"You're not sure?" ventured Paul in the sustained silence.

"I'm sure," said the other, "I'm sure. It's just that my confidence does not exclude a certain monitoring."

With a sure hand he groped under his chair for a thick booklet full of minuscule numbers crammed onto poor-quality paper, which must have constituted a kind of stellar calendar. He leafed through it, jerkily, glancing at the spaces separating the buckshot, then closed it again; unwilling to part with it entirely, he finally slid the book between his seat-cushion and his seat. His body leaned farther forward toward the geomantic tableau.

"It's completely clear. Everything will come in twos, always more or less in twos. This is what will happen: you will meet an energetic man, with greying blond hair, wearing glasses. Glasses, Mars in Aries, don't you see. He should ask you, wait a moment."

Already more detached, Bouc Bel-Air adjusted the joint of his thumb and forefinger over two pellets, then over two others, comparing the spaces by raising his fingers to the level of his half-closed eyes: the lab assistant before his test tube, nodding a professional skull.

"To take part in something," he completed. "Something like an investment. Involving tools, it seems. Machine tools. Naturally, at this degree of precision it can always—"

Evasive gesture, like garage mechanics and surgeons. But even so, Venus in the fifth house theoretically meant smooth sailing ahead. As to determining when this meeting would take place, one could not. The heart of the matter, furthermore, did not lie there.

"Where does it lie, Bouc?" Bob wanted to know.

"The heart of the matter lies not in the facts," said the geomancer, "but in their consequences."

"So then," asked Paul, "what should I do?"

"It is my belief that this man . . ." Bouc uttered after reflection, "you should not accept his offer (I'm simply telling you this, you can of course do as you like). It seems to me that it would be better to decline. I could not say why, however."

"Nothing else?"

"Another man," assessed Bouc Bel-Air. "I see him as being closer to you, older than the first, thinner as well (did I tell you the first one's thin?), also tools."

"All right," said Paul, "so I decline."

"No," said Bouc, "this time you go along with it. It's what I recommend, naturally it's up to you to see. Strictly a personal opinion."

He traced in the air a gesture more expeditiously rounded than the others, as if he were signing a discharge. "What about love?" said Paul. "Let's hear about love now." Bouc Bel-Air stared at his knees. "Right," Paul said. "Do you take checks?"

9

CHARLES SPENT the following night in the Jacquemart-André Museum, which overlooked an almost peaceful stretch of Boulevard Haussmann. It was one of his favorite shelters, a guaranteed sojourn, although not so comfortable or well heated as one might expect: the bedding consisted of a long, overstuffed settee, which was very hard, covered with dusky rose satinet, and highly slippery, like a sausage made of soap. Gripping the armrest, burrowing his feet under the other armrest, Charles jammed his massive body against the back but loosened his hold as soon as his body grew drowsy, at the opening credits of his repetitive reveries. And so he fell, then got back up on his bed, gripping harder, until the first hypnagogic images sent him back to the foot of the sofa. Loath to tie himself on, Charles therefore knew only the beginnings of sleep, incipits of dreams whose incompletion he never regretted.

He always got up early. At around four in the morning, abandoning his struggle against the settee, he came to life from the depths of his indifference. He exhaled deeply while sitting up, touched his damp forehead, slipped on his shoes by feel, tied them by instinct in the dark, then stood and pulled out his Zippo, which lit an area one yard round. For several minutes he traveled the network of the great dark rooms, holding his lighter tightly above his head. Paintings floated by, portraits that were immediately snatched back by the shadows and that he scarcely looked at, except, for an instant, Fragonard's *The New Model*. Apart from these canvasses, the galleries abounded in all kinds of art objects in their fragile glass cases, objects of all sizes, particularly small ones that Charles could have taken and sold, thereby procuring a better life for himself; but the idea hadn't occurred to him, or hadn't stayed long enough.

Circulating like this among the works of art, the black-and-yellow glow flickering at the end of his raised arm, Charles himself became a good subject, a perfectly plausible artistic motif. He entered a gallery at the dead end of which a heavy tapestry, weighed down by heraldry, concealed an iron door. From another pocket he pulled two keys, wed by a bit of dry rubber band as brittle as dead grass. One of the keys turned out to be too flat and too small; the other was a rudimentary skeleton that managed to open only two locks out of five of a certain kind, among them the one in the iron door. The door led onto a lawn that muffled his footsteps; then a gravel path circled the museum all the way to the outer gate. Charles scaled the gate.

Under the first threats of daylight, Boulevard Haussmann remained calm and clean. Garbage collectors were already passing, charged with putting the finishing touches on the scape, preparing the way. Around a green vehicle that advanced in spurts, a leather-gloved crew pirouetted while lithely projecting the scoriae into the crusher. Charles did not grace them with a glance. Despite his profession, the negative state of his profession, he was not spontaneously drawn to refuse. He followed the boulevard toward Rue de Miromesnil, hands thrust in his pockets. Alongside the Zippo and the keys, said pockets harbored two yards of hemp twisted into figure eights; two yards of metro tickets in a roll; five dice; a Swiss army knife with three well-sharpened functions; eleven francs and thirty centimes in small change; and three aspirin tablets in a metal case. In the zipped inside pocket of his parka, Charles also possessed a fake-lizardskin wallet containing one hundred francs folded into an identity card. This same one-hundred-franc bill, which Charles had not touched in four years, was a kind of insurance policy rather than real money. On the identity card, to the left of his absent smile, was written Pontiac, Charles-Frédéric-Marie, born in Verdun fifty-six years earlier, five-foot-five, distinguishing marks: corrective lenses. But there was no trace of eyeglasses, an unnecessary luxury, in Charles's effects.

He did not count the six or seven chimes ringing from a nearby bell tower, which stood out more and more clearly against a pale sky with pinkish overtures; anyone other than he would have been delighted by this beautiful perspective. After the garbage men there was not much happening, not many people on the boulevard. Then things picked up a little near the Villiers metro station.

Charles's was one of the first trainloads of workers, heading from the northeast where people slept to the northwest where they labored, in an atmosphere streaked with toothpaste and tobacco, ink and new gossip, sheets and sweat, soap, aftershaves akin to brandy. On reddened eyes heavy eyelids blinked, sometimes drooped. Over resigned shoulders, Charles deciphered the headlines without digesting their significance; his reading was mechanical, barely connected with his consciousness. He got off at the last stop, Pont de Levallois. By now the rooftops were sharply delineated in the daylight; the sun made shimmering patterns on their zinc surfaces.

In the town of Levallois, Charles took a street called Madame-de-Sanzillon. Along it the buildings shrank, blackened, sometimes deteriorated to the point of crumbling, belted by fringes of earth from which giant weeds proliferated, terrified at their own growth, genetically unaccustomed to such permissiveness. At the end of the street to the right, all cramped, two stories stood one above the other, the windows of each barred by a rotting plank, the absence of door leading onto an intimacy of grey rubble, grey ash. Through the gashes in the roof, daylight diffracted a blunt grey. A senile barbed-wire fence ran in front of the house, concluding in a gate where a bit of iron wire held a white metal mailbox bearing two surnames (Vidal, Pontiac) painted dark.

Charles could have lived in this house, taken up permanent residence, but actually he had only slept there twice. After making sure that the place was indeed abandoned, he had inscribed those names on that mailbox—appropriated with his little key from the outer fence of another abandoned house, this one in a street far too busy to do the trick.

He went twice a month to Rue Madame-de-Sanzillon, opened the box; nothing was ever there except brochures stuffed in by a hasty, ill-remunerated hand. Having accumulated enough in two weeks to obstruct the recipient, the latest tracts overflowed through the slot, stopping it up like a clogged latrine. Charles uncrumpled them, skimmed their contents, recrumpled them, then tossed them into the water of the gutter, in whose currents the compact little bundles waddled hesitantly toward the first sewer opening. Nothing in this standard fare of service offers, subscription suggestions, sparklings of discounted objects, and cyclical civic exhortations had anything to do with Charles, but this did not bother him. Levallois every other week was a breath of fresh air, a little change of scene; to see the contents of the mailbox was the only social punctuation in his peripatetic life.

It was still early in this eccentric quarter; there was no one but a melancholy old dog rummaging through a torn bag, throwing Charles discreet glances as if suggesting that he come rummage with him. Charles unlocked the box swollen with reply coupons; it opened, grating with relief. As he summarily sifted through the promotional wad, he perceived the atypical corner of an envelope—an authentic envelope destined for private use, surely sealed with the help of veritable human saliva, posted with a real stamp glued on a bit crooked through excessive realism and cancelled in Chantilly (its Forest, its Castle, its Racetrack). Even the address was handwritten: the handwriting of a woman, of a slightly mature woman, a well-heeled mature woman, elegant, nervous as an electroencephalogram. This real letter was unusual. There was no mention of a return address on the upper left-hand corner; the postmark bore witness to the fact that it had been mailed six days earlier.

It was unusual, yet Charles's heart beat no faster than normal. No emotion colored his face and his hands did not tremble, his fingers did not become tied in knots in their haste to rip open the envelope. He stared for just a moment in front of him—precisely nothing—then toward the sky, then toward the dog; no doubt his mind was in motion. The dog must have sensed that something abnormal was happening, for his glances shaded over with caution, with tact; he even pretended to forget the man and to devote himself entirely to the bag. Charles slipped the letter into an inside pocket, then reclosed the mailbox, which he patted with a distracted hand as one would more likely have done with the dog, as if to reassure oneself of the old dog's presence, console this good old doggy for having fallen yet again into the same hole.

Periodically verifying the presence of the envelope in his pocket, Charles got back on the metro, changed lines at Opéra, ended up at Gare du Nord. There, without hesitation, he broke his hundred-franc bill against a round-trip ticket to Chantilly, asking for the special train + bike package. He had not been on a train in so long that he felt like taking full advantage of it. During the entire trip he remained standing next to the door of the car, his hand clutching a vertical bar, his glance shifting from outside (private houses, factories, wasteland; cemetery adjoining the pork factory; residences, fallow sports fields on which mismatched reds and blues faced off) to inside (few people in this direction at this hour). But these glances were not enough to afford him a truly global view, a total perception of the railway; something was missing, had escaped through an undetectable crack. Only then did he open the letter and read it.

At Chantilly he traded his bicycle voucher for a Batavus semiracer, a lightweight, camomile-colored apparatus without sidebags, equipped with a large, intimidating gearshift. He walked the bike away from the buildings, waited to be alone before straddling it. After several sinusoids he gained control of the machine, and very quickly he was pedalling without difficulty: the science of the bicycle, the inexpugnable equilibrium of the bicycle must have been engraved in a very archaic sector of his brain, a kind of airtight strongroom. Charles wheeled on, never feeling the cold, keeping well to his right even though alone on the forest paths. The air, heavy with tree scent, parted around him, a boiling bath endlessly renewed, bearing and reviving childhood memories. Scattered along the path, tiny black twigs broke under his tires, snapped with a dry softness like the collarbones of small animals.

He pedalled for three miles in the direction of Senlis, running alongside a greyhound track, setting foot on the ground when he had to cross a main road. After three more miles he crossed a bridge suspended over the highway, and after the Espionnes crossroads there was a pond. Charles skirted the pond and followed a stretch of two-lane with heavy traffic before turning right onto a new path.

Topped by white angels, the pillars of a gate marked the entrance to a road leading to a private residence. Were it not for these two angels, miniatures of those on the Ponte Sant'Angelo, equipped with all the accessories (robe, reeds) of the crucifixion, nothing would have distinguished this entrance from a million other entrances; someone had not forgotten, in the letter, to mention this landmark. The residence itself was a large construction with purple-brown Anglo-Norman half-timbering on a bed of weeded gravel, raked, furrowed like purée under a fork by numerous sets of tires—although now there was only a Ford, the sort of large, blue, banal Ford that you see all the time.

Charles looked for a place to prop his vehicle, but the nearest tall tree was too far and the wall of the house too white. He tried to lay it on the gravel, endeavoring to arrange it delicately, gracefully, but there was always a wheel jutting clumsily; the handlebars raised pinned, suffering arms to the sky. Vertically serene, gleaming with balance, the bicycle, once recumbent, could adopt only bizarre, disharmonious postures, like a fractured corpse. Charles rang the doorbell.

It was a fresh-faced sexagenarian with a Russian accent, his short pointed beard smartly groomed and perfectly aligned with a narrow ivory tie, who took so much time to answer. He rubbed his dry hands together. "Charles," he warbled, hospitably rolling the median r.

"Boris," said Charles. "Everything going all right?"

"It's comfortable," said Boris. "Fresh vegetables, radiators, makes for a change. Hygiene. I miss the outdoors, but I couldn't take it anymore. How's Vidal?"

"Same as always," answered Charles. "He says hello."

"No, I just couldn't take it anymore," grimaced the other, pointing to his legs. "Arthritis."

In point of fact, Boris seemed rather unsteady on them. After an inviting gesture he limped down a corridor tiled in black and white, on the surface of which his oscillating advance called to mind a deranged chess piece: mad king, drunken queen, or knight off the deep end. Charles followed straight as a rook, right as an angle. "And how's it going with Nicole?"

"Nothing much to report," Boris allowed, opening the door to a small bronze-green salon. "A little tight with her pennies, but I can't complain, and besides they're nice. She won't be long. The young miss is upstairs, there's a guy with her. I'll go tell her you're here. Come in. You know the young miss?"

"No," said Charles.

The salon was furnished with reproductions of antiques, and some genuine antiques. Bills on a writing desk attested to the fact that accounts were settled here. Charles rapidly tried out the armchairs, preferred to remain standing near the fireplace, looked at the objects arranged on the endtable: two crystal roses, two cervidae in spun glass, three real roses in a crystal rhyton. Boris reappeared:

"I'm eternally grateful," he confided. "I feel pretty good here, all things considered. Without you, this arthritis, I don't know where I'd be."

Climbing the stairway, Boris used the entire width of the steps, lurching from one ramp to the other. On the first floor he rolled his finger joints against a closed door, then entered without awaiting a reply. Charles entered behind him: a man his age, a woman half that. Charles identified the young woman without ever having seen her, using his memory of her mother as a guide. He recognized the man as well: Gazol, a fellow from the Café Perfect crowd who had also dearly loved Nicole Fischer thirty years earlier. Gazol still had a large chest, to which an abdomen now added a third dimension. A scent of aromatic herbs emanated from him, like an aftershave made from pizza. Charles Pontiac greeted him with a brief glance, then turned toward the young woman standing at the window, behind whom a willow wept.

"I came immediately," he pointed out.

"I know you," smiled Justine, "I've heard a lot about you."

Charles bowed his head without smiling back—he couldn't. From outside came the sound of a motor: luxurious purring, pairs of tires voluptuously sculpting the gravel, not without an arrogant languor that let one imagine mahogany veneer on the dashboard, perhaps even a minuscule bar in back.

"There's Mother," smiled Justine.

1 O

TWENTY MILES to the south, Paul still stands alone in his overbright apartment. He moves from one room to another, finds these rooms uselessly white and numerous, sees nothing. These paintings on the wall mean nothing to him. Mostly they represent things: a Caterpillar tractor in action; an alienated elephant, out of its biotope. But there is also a small abstract gouache (1959) by Gaston Chaissac. Since Elizabeth's departure, some of these paintings are no longer there at all. In their stead pale squares and rectangles house a lonely hook, or a couple of slanted nails straddled by a thread of dust. Plants beneath the windows struggle in their pots against neglect, against the concept of death. Time expands, the void beckons. A transistor sputters help! in the kitchen, but the silence merely looms all the larger, cranks up a notch, crushes its intimidations.

Late to bed, Paul had been late to rise, at first without memory of the night before, which he was then able to reconstruct in scraps, using traces found on his clothes, in his clothes. Molecules of L'Heure Bleue near the collar of his jacket, a cloakroom claimcheck in the left pocket neighboring an entrance pass, in the right a nasty parking ticket—clues. On the low coffee table in the living room, a note in unfamiliar hand indicated the whereabouts of his vehicle. It could in fact be seen at the base of the high-rise, properly parked between two markers. No doubt someone had driven, undressed, laid out, then left Paul alone in his bed, but he was unable to identify the parties responsible for this initiative: in the ambient sourness of curdled alcohol, the remains of fried neurons blocked access to his memory. The Heure Bleue possibly meaning Claire, Paul tried to call Claire, but the first time it was busy and after that there was no one home.

Then Paul made coffee in the white kitchen, standing before the row of culinary enamel and stainless steel, scrubbed every Tuesday by Teresa Perez; the only thing he ever made there was coffee. With the dark liquid balanced at the end of its handle, he moved into the bedroom: too large. The unmade bed too large. The useless roll-top desk.

A photograph on the desk depicted Elizabeth smiling, Paul less so, posing together before black-and-white flowers. Someone had cut it to separate the protagonists, then Scotch-taped it back together without excess meticulousness, so that the two were no longer at quite the same level. Paul turned toward the window. On the other side of the void, leaning out a window of the neighboring high-rise, an elderly man aired a dog that he hugged against his chest, their eyes plunged in the same direction. Ring of the telephone.

Van Os.

"I hope I'm not interrupting anything? Have you got something for me?"

Van Os had been much too timid at the beginning; no one took him at all seriously. Through Tomaso, Bob and Paul had procured him a Tokagypt in fairly good shape, which wasn't bad. But they had furnished the weapon only as a kind of trick encouragement, anticipatory consolation for the vanity of his enterprise, like an expensive box-calf schoolbag for a young dunce, for the ugliest girl on the beach a mink.

"Still nothing," said Paul in a toneless voice, "I already told you. There won't be any more."

Then Van Os had begun making his way in the world; bought himself a car, then two; recruited people; banished his timidity. His early successes rendered him a bit more forward, and even his lieutenants tended to act familiar. It was very annoying.

"That's very annoying," he said. "We should get together in any case, I want us to have dinner. Wednesday okay?"

"Difficult at the moment," Paul scratched his head. "Complicated."

"Problems? You have to let me know when you have problems, if I can be of service. I can do you a lot of favors, you have no idea."

"That's very decent of you."

"Yes," admitted Van Os, "I'm very decent. I'm not mad at you anymore, you know, about the Italians. Let's see each other on Wednesday, you'll tell me your troubles, we'll see what we can do."

"Really, I can't," exhaled Paul, "it's a special case. It's personal."

"I understand," went Van Os solemnly. "Still that business with your wife. But these things pass, you'll see."

The photo began to tremble in Paul's hand, who only then noticed that he hadn't let go of it. He put it back on the desk, not without violence, turning it face-down with some effort, as if it were glued to his fingers.

"You're already getting over it, in fact," the other man continued in a soft voice. "I sense you're getting back on your feet. You're meeting people—that's good. That young lady, the other night, very pretty from what they tell me."

"What are you telling me, what do they—"

Van Os dodged, apologized for the interruption. "Too bad about Wednesday," he lamented, "we'll do it some other time." He would phone again tomorrow, the day after tomorrow, to see how it was going. "Think of me," he pleaded before hanging up.

A pause. The dregs of the coffee pot are lukewarm on the drainboard; Paul finds a long-necked bottle of pale ale in the fridge. Too cold, too frothy, but Paul drinks half a glass in one gulp, a little of which drips onto his stubble from the day before. He shuts off the radio, returns to the bedroom, puts his glass down next to the overturned photograph, not far from the telephone which has just performed its first role of the day. At this altitude no noise can be heard; one is encased in silence as if in a headcold. Paul contemplates the telephone and vice versa: the household instrument is anxious to yip, to bark anew; sitting on its throne, its tongue slightly hanging out, it implores Paul with all its digits, yanking against its cord.

Call who? Paul dissects his address book. Names followed by numbers pile up as if on the base of a monument to the dead, an infertile field of honor bristling with lost intimates, friends of an evening, former girlfriends who would despise each other. There's always the number of the young woman in grey from the other evening: go for it. Someone picks up the receiver in the distance.

"I'd like to speak to someone," ventures Paul, "but I don't know her name."

"How very annoying," assesses Laure in turn.

"But I know her voice. It's not your voice."

"Yes," Laure says amiably, "I don't think I'm the one. She isn't here."

Who else? There remains the eternal Bob, last resort, desperate measure and spite of better judgment. The delighted receiver nearly hyperventilates when Paul phones Bob, for a while lets it—six times, ten times, sixteen times—ring. Then he gently hangs up. Rises, goes to throw the bottle down the garbage chute, listens to its pings diminish the length of a thirty-story shaft. Consults the hall clock, pulls another Martin's from the fridge. Doesn't open it right away, places it on the coffee table in the company of an ashtray, a novel by Day Keene, and the television remote control. Falls into the red armchair, presses the remote: sports, men who throw, run, jump, fall down. Then everything repeats in slow motion.

1 1

MEANWHILE, they had not yet left the table in Chantilly; Nicole Fischer dusted her coffee with low-calorie sugar substitute. Nicole Fischer hugged a pouting Pekinese named Baby Love, which drooled slowly while projecting corporal glances onto those present. Nicole Fischer wore a tailored suit with grey-white squares shot through with burgundy threads, and lizardskin shoes. Today, Nicole Fischer was a pale woman with light-blue eyes, translucent fingers, and nostalgic features. Maintaining her looks required an insane determination, an outsized energy, a care similar to the one she took every morning in gathering and teasing her platinum hair into an ovoid bouffant that rose from the crest of her narrow skull, tipping slightly rearward, like a football propped lopsided in the heavy field before kick-off.

Charles, seated next to Nicole, softly shook his head when she turned to him. Across from them, Gazol examined his empty plate. Justine, at the foot of the table, studied Charles with calm interest, gentle curiosity. Baby Love, finally, snuggled up in angora, raised a crafty eye on the world. Its drool abundantly dripped down its hairs, but stopped just at their tips, without ever soiling Madam's garment; they must have trained it well.

"It's about Jean-François," Nicole announced. "I asked you to come because of him."

Where is he, what is he doing, what has befallen Jean-François, faithful friends would have cried out. None cried out. Gazol twisted his mouth and gripped his nose with two fingers; Charles lowered his eyes. "You *do* remember Jeff," said Nicole, making memory vibrate in her voice (how they had loved that voice, once). "He wrote me."

"What kind of trouble's he in?" Gazol said abruptly.

A laugh rose from her, scarcely altered—that sharp-toned laugh they had loved, too. "No, no," said Nicole, "no trouble at all. Just a bit of help, it doesn't seem like anything serious, he thought of us. He's thinking of us, that's all."

"I've had *my* share of pain, you know," Gazol reminded them after a moment, "but I wasn't a pain about it. I managed all alone. We're all alone, Nicole, we take care of things alone, you understand. I had problems too, you know."

Charles did not evoke his own, which were readily apparent. Focusing elsewhere, his eyes met Justine's.

"Would you have helped *me* when things weren't going well?" continued Gazol. "And besides I still do, have problems that is, so are you going to help me? What are you going to do for me?"

"Of course, Vincent," claimed Nicole, "you just had to say so. You only had to speak up."

"You can't do anything for me," went Gazol, bowing his head and deflating his thorax.

The exchange carried on a bit longer, degenerating; it progressively became stripped of arguments, was soon reduced to a raw antagonism. Charles, no longer listening, studied the remnants of foodstuffs on the table. The sound of a chair pulled him from his distraction: Gazol had just gotten up, breaking off all discussion. Sorry, Nicole, wish I could, but no, no way. Charles instinctively got up as well. Everyone seemed embarrassed; there was silence and no one moved. The women remained seated and the men standing, as in the paintings of Fantin-Latour. Then Gazol departed and Charles sat back down. "So you're in?" went Nicole. "You accept?" Without answering he drew toward himself a saucer regarnished with charlotte. Shortly afterward, Justine showed him to his room.

It looked out onto bushes, trees with birds on them who squawked in the sharp cold. The cream-pink wallpaper depicted marquises under parasols and on swings; yews and wells; fool hares. Two paintings: an ancestor, a flat landscape. A bronze Heracles grappled with a lion of Nemea on the chest of drawers. Justine left, shutting the door behind her, and Charles sat on the bed. It needed a bit more light, all things considered; it was still the north, after all. Justine returned with a change of clothes and bath towels that she distributed among the drawers. "Would you like anything else, do you need anything? A radio, something to read? A newspaper."

"No," said Charles.

He had gotten up again, not knowing what to do with himself; the tips of his fingers struck him as idle. He lit a lamp, which scarcely threw any more light on the room; he switched it off. Baby Love passed by the door, raging feebly.

"Thank you," said Charles.

Justine turned to him, smiling rapidly. "It's at the end of the hall," she said, pointing to the towels.

"Good," said Charles. "But the bicycle? What do we do with the bicycle?"

1 2

_____

A T THE SAME local time, every day it was the same thing:
Jean-François Pons lunched late on a bowl of stir-fried noodles in a red sauce, washed down by a lukewarm Tiger. He was
alone at his table, shut away at home during the heavy afternoon
heat. These pallid noodles, dead fish floating on the current of a
toxic mud—the Duke ate them without looking. He flipped
through his dog-eared magazines, turning each page after having
wiped his fingers on his overalls.

Every morning was the same: Duke Pons rose before dawn to
supervise the sapping of the heveas, which every day were tapped
a little more deeply to extract a maximum of liquor, following the
theory of reaction to injury as elaborated by Parkin in Colombo in
1900. This practice required extreme care; the finicky squadron of
Chinese foremen had its hands full trying to ensure that precisely
half a millimeter of bark would be stripped from each trunk,
under a sky and a sun that grew increasingly brighter, increasingly
heavier. The morning, then, was spent reopening the plants'
wounds, after which everyone retreated to his allotted shelter: the
agricultural laborers returned to their outbuildings, about whose
condition the Aw brothers were never late in voicing an indigna-

tion, and the Chinese rejoined their own lodgings, scarcely more spacious although better ventilated, less prey to an infinite variety of insects and bacilli.

The Jouvin couple generally remained cloistered in the villa, except for Raymond's occasional mute appearances on the terrain, when he jotted unfathomable things in the hollow of a notepad; or Luce's much more enjoyable sallies, when she showed up too drunk and made-up, and zigzagged among the shrubs, gesticulating tunes by Line Renaud, clucking intimate invitations to the great joy of the personnel until the prompt intervention of Raymond, who would come running in his socks from the villa and firmly, breathlessly lead the poor fat creature stumbling away in her badly buttoned flowered dress, on crooked heels.

In the afternoon, the furnace appeased, they returned to the fields to gather the latex that had sweated into cups affixed to the trunks. Pons then had to supervise the raw material's transportation to the factory, then the stages of its treatment, not to mention the maintenance of the machines, the arbitration of conflicts, and the sometimes strained relations with the small planters' cooperatives.

Three P.M.: outside there was a great dry light. Duke Pons scratched his scalp with a moist finger while leafing through a magazine imported from Northern Europe—someone knocked on the door. Pons closed his magazine, scowled at the wall clock, a gift from the foremen five years earlier: a panda beat the time every other second. Someone knocked again—pinned to the door was an old front page of *France-Soir*, all yellow, entirely taken up by a photograph of a demonstration, during the Cold War, in Paris: in one corner, young and already very bony, one could make out the future Duke. Pons called to come in.

The elder Aw entered furtively. More intellectual, less charismatic than his brother, he served as the latter's scrupulous shadow, his eminence grim.

"Oh, it's you, Sam," sighed Pons. "Sit down, I'll get you a beer."

While the other set his awkward body on a stool, the Duke went to extract two Tigers from the icebox.

"We won't have time," Aw Sam said softly. "We have to go see my brother. He wants to talk to you."

Pons scowled anew, plunged one of the bottles back into the blocks of dirty ice, opened the other, and took a long swig before turning back toward the Malaysian, pointing to the window as if it were thundering—don't you see what it's doing out there? Insects were in fact rushing to take shelter from the thick heat; they drummed against the mesh of the mosquito netting. The Duke drank some more, then hiccuped. "Okay," he said finally, "I'll get my hat."

Some three hundred yards farther on, beyond the grid of rubber plants, the multi-tiered forest swelled monstrously, deploying a gross excess of species. The Duke followed the elder of the Aws between two rows of shrubs, in an ochre corridor of crazed sand and clay, toward an area that was absolutely green. Everything was green in this favorable clime: first a nuanced, multiple green, exploited to the fullest, unfurled to the point of encroaching on its related colors, its uncle brown, its cousins yellow and blue; then, once beneath the cover of the trees, the gamut regrouped ferruginously around basic dark.

Aw Sam led the way, pushing aside the branches of thickets, sometimes holding them for the Duke to prevent their whipping back. Almost immediately they were in the bosom of the forest primaeval, completely virgin of any clearings and scorched spots, untouched by pewter prospectors. Jean-François Pons came here only rarely of late, for the infrequent rendez-vous with a lost pig or a day-laborer's wife. But this latter sort of expedition excited him less than in the early days. He had lost the habit; now he fairly balked to find himself forced into it.

"Hey, Sam, what are we doing?" he protested once. "Where are you taking me?"

And that imbecile keeps pushing through the ferns without worrying about the mud, those large, almost uninterrupted muddy puddles—are we going to keep walking like this for long? Pons felt a stab of worry when he remembered that his feet were clad only in ordinary sandals, made of translucent plastic, the kind that the peaceful hunters of Western limpets wear.

"Wait, junior," he called out in a blank voice. "Leeches. Wait, leeches."

Everyone knows that leeches are uniformly distributed over the surface of the globe, grow in any climate, on any base; one, for instance, was attached to the right foot of Duke Pons, who protested nervously, openly, scrambling to find a cigarette in the depths of his pockets. He lit it, took two rapid puffs, then dug it into the soft body of the vampire worm, which began to squirm slowly before coming unstuck. The Duke took two more puffs for himself before they resumed their walk with greater caution, Aw Sam endeavoring to find Pons fordable passage. Crossing a fog of insects they advanced into the forest; they skidded their way up its moist belly, holding tightly to the branches. Thirty yards above them, the uppermost foliage formed a humid arch, jagged like an old sponge. Still thirty yards beyond that the tops of giant trees were braided in the lacework of intertwined vines, a network of cables diffusing a light a thousand times refracted, diffracted in the heart of the green system. And the sun occasionally drilled a path through this labyrinth to go rest its beam, as if at the circus, on some wild beast, some monkey surprised by the infrequency of such an event, caught unawares, missing this rare occasion to perform a little routine.

After twenty-five minutes of walking, they reached a clearing coated with hibiscus and rhododendrons, spotted with polychromatic lichens, occupied by five seated men leaning against the trunk of a dipterocarp. They were heavily engaged in extracting, for the purposes of eating, the seeds of the large tree's fruit, fallen among red flowers. The tallest of the five smiled and stood at his brother's approach; the red gems set in his incisors gleamed in the emerald air.

Aw Aw, younger brother of Aw Sam, with a gesture bade the Duke be seated. Pons declined with another gesture, wary of the reptiles around the orchids. "What's all this nonsense?" he grumbled. Aw Aw smiled without answering. His person inspired a complex comradeship, which made you regret distrusting him all the more. To hide his discomfort, the Duke examined his arm, where, for the last few instants, a different discomfort played—a high-caliber mosquito that he crushed. The insect spewed another touch of red as it exploded.

"So, what's going on," grated the Duke. "Let's hear it."

"We're going underground," the younger Aw bluntly announced. "Everyone's ready, the conditions are ripe. I'm heading off with these men to prepare for the big moment. We're waiting for the big moment. When?"

"I've written," said Pons. "I'm expecting an answer, be patient. There are still a few points we haven't settled."

The distribution of power after they had seized it was yet to be negotiated, for example. Pons, who firmly intended to keep at least his status as manager, found himself caught short. He wouldn't have thought things could go so fast, nor even imagined the end of the process—in the same way one becomes used to a pregnancy, almost forgetting about the inevitable outcome.

"Weapons, for instance; we haven't decided about weapons."

"That's true," said Aw the younger. "So when?"

He continued to smile unperturbed. The semi-precious stones in his front teeth gleamed an instant with increased brilliance, as a light on a dashboard signals an emergency, and the Duke got a bad feeling.

"I'm taking care of it," he said, "I'll take care of it. I have to write again. Tonight."

"Are you sure?"

"I know what I'm talking about, junior."

"Excuse me, but are you sure about your supplier?"

"Sure I'm sure," the Duke exploded. "It'll take several weeks, perhaps a month, but it's as sure as can be. I'm going to France, in any case, I'll be able to take care of it better there."

"That's good," said Aw Aw.

The Duke saw himself up against a wall, gnawed by discouragement: now he really would have to take care of it. He avoided the Aw brothers' glances, turned his own toward their men. Squatting beneath the immense tree, two Negritos commented on the exchange in hushed tones, in their unfindable language; one of them squeezed an imaginary trigger with his index finger, the rest of his hand closed onto the hope of a grip.

"All right," concluded Pons, "I think everything's been said."

An hour later, his feet in a tub of vinegared water, half a toothbrush glass of gin in his hand, he again called to come in after another knock on his door. This time it was the interpreter.

"It's the captain," announced the interpreter. "He's just arrived."

"Oh, for God's sake," the Duke invoked in vain, emptying his glass to grab a towel. "Tell him I'm coming, run quick."

Captain Illinois stood in the center of the little factory in the company of Raymond Jouvin. The heat had forced the seaman to remove his woolen jacket, as well as his cap, which turned limply at the end of a chunky finger. It fell from time to time, occasionally upside-down, and you could then see the interior circumference of the lining, the ruin of a leather ribbon kept company by a faded silk bow. Huffing and puffing, the captain picked the cap up, straightened while squeezing out his beard, and with an immaculate handkerchief sponged his forehead, striped red by the headdress. His cheeks were red, his small eye still blue. The Duke, out of breath, joined them in the coagulation room.

"Pierre-Yves," he exclaimed.

"Hoh," the skipper's vocal chords vibrated warmly.

They grasped each other by the right hand, using the left to clap mutual shoulder blades. Ledger in hand, Jouvin contemplated this ritual from the depths of his shirt. "Shall we move on," he said cautiously when the rhythm of claps began to wane.

For him, every visitor was yet another opportunity to cover the factory while emitting numbers. Leaving the coagulation vats behind, the husband Jouvin preceded the captain into the subsequent rooms where one pressed, washed, and cut the coagulate into thin sheets, which one then dried and smoked in a special chamber reeking of creosote. Sparing himself the pleasure of entering, the duke threw glances at the busy workmen and gave them different kinds of smiles, depending.

The captain was in tears by the time he left the smokehouse. Without interrupting his recital of figures for an instant, the affectless Raymond made them continue all the way to the packaging area, end point of the chain of production. Later, in the warehouse, leaning against the elastic wall, they agreed that the stock would be loaded that very evening onto the plantation's new truck; by the next morning the latter would reach the coastal station where the *Boustrophedon* had dropped anchor. "We'll see each other again at dinner," said Jouvin, "to sign the papers." Then he went off, looking busy. As there was a little relative coolness in the warehouse, the captain put his hat back on, using both hands.

"What's new on board?" Pons inquired politely.

"Everything's okay, all's well. Although the men get edgy from time to time, I don't know what's eating them. To each his own, eh?"

"When are you coming back, Pierre-Yves? When's the next shipment?"

From his uniform Illinois pulled a robust notebook, bound in thick cardboard and held shut by a large rubber band, which he leafed through for a few moments before showing Pons a page: the date, printed somewhat crookedly in light blue, would occur forty days later.

"That could work," said Pons, "that could still work. You coming back empty?"

The naval index, weathered like an old bookbag, dropped two inches down the page where the words *spare parts, grain, wine* lined up in a large, rounded hand that was almost too legible.

"Will you have a little space left over? It wouldn't be for much, about a dozen crates. Seven or eight cubic yards."

The captain pondered, then nodded.

"Good," said the Duke, "I'll be there in any case, I've got to make the trip. Then I'll come back with the cargo. I'll take care of the whole thing, the loading and everything, won't be a bit of trouble. We'll see each other again at dinner?"

The mariner wandered off into the sunlight, jauntily throwing his jacket over his shoulder, adjusting his visor over his short, healthy hair, swaying in his dirty trousers. Pons followed him with his eyes before returning to the fields.

That evening, after dinner, Pons had returned to his bungalow, in whose two rooms he paced for a moment. He was bitter. His heart was laden with an annoyed sadness that the ridiculous dinner had only heightened: Luce who dozed off by the time the salad came, Jouvin boasting of his futurology, the captain and his limited vocabulary—the Duke had been bored rigid. He attempted once again to straighten up his table, on which the remains of his lunch stiffened, where the pages of the magazines leaning against the wall sagged like the wings of dead birds. He washed a few dishes, then sat down before his plans and photographs of astronomical gardens.

He had lost himself in this, dreaming of his gnomon which would be, yes, on a Haussmann-like scale. A number of gauges would surround it, full of gradations and dials on which its fallen shadow would produce many meanings. Inspired by Jai Singh II, it would be one of those gigantic narrow braces, pierced by alveoli, such as have been found in several towns of northern India over the last two or three centuries. A stairway would indent its rigid hypoteneuse, which would be oriented toward the Pole; Pons would scale it every day, every night, to conduct numerous readings. The form and cut of his project, the possibility of climbing upon it, all this procured an ever-renewed exaltation for Duke Pons, who saw in it, yes, the ideal trace that one could leave of one's passage on the earth. There remained the problem of raw materials, at which he made several passes, as he did every evening, before sending it back to the bullpen along with other pending questions. Pons was in no hurry, Pons had time. No doubt he would finish his days here, of which nothing foretold too rapid a conclusion: amoebas work slowly. He closed the folder and stared at the wall before him.

Alongside the photo of his nephew at thirteen (leaning against a plane tree, little Paul J. tries to smile but he appears unwell, convalescent), there was one of a device (Rashivalaya Yantra) built by Jai Singh II; a postcard sent from Bayonne in August 1953 ("Dearest Jeff, it's very sunny here, I've seen a whole bunch of people from last year, you must remember Gerard, he was here last year, it's really very hot here, all my love, Lili"); and a polaroid of a woman (wearing precious little black leather) met during a business trip to Singapore. All this was held in place by blue-headed thumbtacks.

Pons's eyes rested on the photograph of the boy. His hands felt around on the table, pulled toward him a pad of airmail paper. The matching envelopes came with it, then a pencil took off from its white iron base. The Duke raised the pencil, immobilized it in a fixed point above the pad; his blurred glance had returned to the memories teeming within him. Then he began to write. The date in the top right-hand corner. Dearest Paul.

13

A S U S U A L , Bob is wearing a leather jacket and faded jeans. He has put on black boots with slanted heels and some very large Italian shades, and he has gloved his hands in kid.

With rapid steps, he approaches a window protecting indistinct jewels. He lowers the jacket's zipper by a third with a clean motion and pulls out a large hammer, which he smashes into the storefront just about at center, producing an ardent explosion of vitreous matter, a joyful *tutti* of drunken cymbal players at the end of the corporate banquet. Fat triangular shards make an avalanche on the asphalt. Some of them, prismatic, fleetingly decompose the daylight; one, too sharp, has just nicked the leather crust of his left boot.

Although access to the jewels is by now assured, Bob continues to hammer furiously at the tiniest splinter of glass, as if he had it in for their very transparency. Paul stares at this uncomprehending, never having seen his friend in such a state.

"One example among thousands," enunciates a serious male voice, "to illustrate the theme of today's discussion."

We see this serious male; his jaw is square, his teeth detartared. He turns to his left, to his right: with us today, Jacques Terrasson,

Gerard de Broche. We see them in their turn. One—Terrasson—ripens under the spotlights; his heart beats too fast beneath royal blue, but he admires himself for being there. Paler and shinier, de Broche also seems more bored; he casts a condescending eye on the bit of crocodile containing his foot.

In the adjacent studio, a young lady in slacks signals to Bob, who immediately stops pounding. He approaches, hammer in hand—she keeps some distance between them. At another signal, he follows her into an office, where the young lady hands him a form; Bob enters his name, his bank account and social security number. After he leaves, the discussion gets underway for the housewives' benefit: can one really speak of perceptible deterioration? "Perceptible isn't the word," Terrasson chokes. "You shouldn't say *perceptible*." Letting the matter drop, Paul pushes a button on the remote control. Were there more people he knew on the other channels? And while we're at it, the girl in the grey fedora? No, it's a story about clones.

An inventor builds men in his image. These latter help him in his work, which consists in producing further doubles of himself. Although this process, naturally, soon flies out of control, all is peace and harmony in the lab. The scientist gets along marvelously with his doubles, until the day when one of them, seized by a legitimate identity crisis, claims that *he* is the scientist, the other being only one of his clones who has tried to usurp his civil status—Paul soon got lost in the endless repetition of these illusions. He was sitting in the red armchair. A tray before him held a glass of white wine and a white plate under cold meat with red ketchup on it, along with a squirt of very bright, very strong yellow mustard that made Paul's eyes water, muddling the storyline of the TV film even more.

Then he paced around the apartment again: even for two it had been too big. All the windows of the opposite high-rise were closed save one, through which the retiree was still exposing his brown dog to the air, hugged to his chest, the animal's paws sharply outlined against the aluminum window frame. Paul knew that farther to the left lived a skinny unmarried woman, fifty years old, maybe forty-five, not much to look at but friendly enough. Every Sunday morning she played loud music while pedalling, with conviction, on an exercise bike attached to the floor of her living room, her large mouth split in a panting smile over long sorrel incisors, the accordion fluttering in pearly gobs through the open window.

Then the bedroom again, poop during stormy nights when the wind made the high-rise tremble. Paul stood like Illinois himself in the days of Cape Horn, recommending his soul, devising a course of action to get them out of there. But today the weather was like oil, it flowed like cold oil. The telephone was asleep, there was nothing to do here. Passing through the bathroom, Paul grabbed a bag of dirty laundry from the closet.

Later he engaged in minor operations in the kitchen—rinsed a glass, heated water for a fleeting idea of tea, verified the expiration date stamped on the lid of a divorced yogurt. The washing machine ran through its cycle click by click, vibrating in varied rhythms, from sensual prewash to furious spin-dry, during which the frenzied apparatus growls and trembles, stamps its feet and threatens. The rotation of its entrails becomes unbearable; it yearns to escape, to rocket toward the sky, smashing holes in the ceiling, the successive ceilings; to whirl across the kitchen destroying everything in its path, as when a vivisected ox, bellowing with pain, breaks its bonds and demolishes the operating block under its thrashing weight, chrome tweezers and scissors twirling in its flesh signposted with red gauze. The fury of washing machines on the one hand, the placidly alternative hum of refrigerators on the other: kitchens are corrals full of wild and domestic machines, huddled around stoves where waters boil for tea. Paul surveyed his livestock, a lonely cowherd crossing the salt desert.

Someone rang at the door; it was Bob rubbing his hands together on the landing, his leather jacket still zipped up to his ears, two sugars in his tea, not too warm out, what's new, things don't seem to be going so hot. (He drained his cup.) Let's go out for a bit, get some fresh air. It'll do you good.

He hadn't removed his jacket; he called the elevator. "Have you thought any more about Bouc Bel-Air?" Paul slipped something on, leaving his mechanical herd to snort untended. "What he told you the other day?" Bob persisted. Paul buttoned up. His mouth, about to open, was beaten to it by the elevator door, which revealed a car crammed full of pregnant women. They remained silent all the way to the ground floor.

The door opened onto the lobby, in the center of which, like the original person-cooling-his-heels, stood the aforementioned Toon, he of the chubby if not downright puffy features, with the nasty face of a former child who's miffed at not having grown to full height like everyone else. His chrysalis remained his overlarge, overlong raincoat, from whose overtightened belt a Niagara of pleats flowed down to his ankles. A floppy hat shaded the soft abutments of his face like a plotting of contour lines. He walked up to them, the hands in his pockets jiggling keys and spare change. His knuckles cracked vindictively among the jangling of alloys.

"Lucien wants to see you," he said in a high-pitched voice, with a movement of his chin.

He indicated the light grey of the street through the glass doors, past the angel- and butterfly-fish winding among the bubbles, the begrimed neons; he studied the air beyond the protective glass of the giant aquarium. Three hundred yards away stood a jacked-up brick-red Lada 4 × 4, whose rear window was decorated with a green sticker inviting you to visit scenic Waterloo Park. At the wheel, Van Os watched the three men grow larger in the surface of the rearview mirror.

Toon and Bob slid in behind, Van Os having designated the death seat for Paul—a corner of whose raincoat got caught in the slammed door. There was a lot of noise in this car full of men: the radio was turned up full to the police band, which relayed the mobile brigades let loose around town to the administrative headquarters. Calmly the lawmen summoned each other to various scenes of the crime or to sites of minor news briefs. Their transmissions were gnawed by static crackles and gurglings that occasionally buried the remarks, making them unintelligible, forcing the functionaries to repeat them louder. Van Os put a finger to his lips and turned to Paul: he seemed to be welcoming a latecomer to his box, program in hand, right in the middle of the larghetto. Paul couldn't understand a word of what the cops were yelling at each other.

Lucien Van Os was long-boned and dressed in sand-colored clothes, with a nose like a stem, an almost pointed Adam's apple, and a scarcely loosened tie; he might have been mistaken for a leukemic Randolph Scott. Under the pale skin you could easily distinguish the skeleton of his hand, of his wrist, around which a fat watch with twelve functions played loosely. His yellow-and-white hair shone on his temples and the back of his skull; its gelled grooves faithfully preserved fond memories of the comb. His high forehead shone as well, and his hollow cheeks abounded in dental gold. While listening to the radio he chewed one stem of his glasses after the other.

The ear being just as able to adjust as the eye, Paul finally caught the thread of the police band conversations. They were running down the list of local epiphenomena: cyclist fractured at Gare d'Orsay, crazy old lady on Rue du Commerce, strong smell of gas near Javel. Van Os seemed to lose interest; he lowered the volume and studied Paul.

"Things going better? You didn't sound so good on the phone the other day. You should call me when things aren't going well. Come see me at the hotel, it'll take your mind off things."

His voice, at once deep and sour, throaty and sugared like the sound of the bass clarinet or the taste of grape juice, carried easily over the lapping of the short waves. Paul tugged on his raincoat, in an attempt to free the trapped corner.

"Have you thought about it?" Van Os continued. "Do you think you could find me something?"

As the corner wouldn't come free, Paul contemplated his hands with an obstinate air.

"I don't do that anymore," he said. "I told you. I don't want to do that anymore. Anyway, there's nothing left, I no longer have any contacts. Why don't you try someone else?"

"That's a load of crap," judged Toon behind him. "Sure there's nothing left. They've got all they want, you bet."

His own voice squeaked like the siren of a little tugboat in the grey air. Paul stared through the window of the 4 × 4: few people in this street; not much potential help, in case.

"What does he know about it?" Bob intervened. "What do you know about it, huh?"

"Yes, shut up," Van Os said to his lieutenant, "you're an idiot. He's an idiot. You think it's easy to try someone else? You have no idea. No, deal with me, please. I know what things cost. I know the value of things and I pay."

Toon put a respectfully chubby hand on one of his boss's collar-bones, just as a more hurried, more hierarchic voice came from the Hertzian chicken coop fastened under the dashboard. "Listen to that!" he said. The voice gave details of a shoot-out in front of a bank branch office in Vanves. It exhorted all available colleagues to rush over and join in.

"It's Henri," went Toon excitedly, "they screwed up! It's Henri, they got caught in the shit!"

Van Os promptly activated the starter. "You see," he said, "the importance of being well equipped. Well" (the motor revved), "I won't offer to take you along. Think it over," he added, leaning to open the door on Paul's side, liberating the asphyxiated raincoat. Four seconds later, the four-wheel drive of the Soviet-built model made its reddish mass shrink toward the southern suburbs.

"You see," said Bob, "exactly as Bouc had predicted. He's the one, did you see? The glasses and everything."

"I saw," said Paul. "By the way, what were you up to before in my TV?"

"Oh," went Bob, "it's the assistant producer of the show, she's a friend. They were looking for someone to smash something, so I offered. You saw that too?"

14

WHEN A bad dream awakens him this time, Charles, frozen in his cold sweat, doesn't know where he is. For several seconds he worries about the soft, damp surface on which his body (normally scant prey to nocturnal terror) lies. He stretches out an arm in the blackness. The tips of his fingers meet a lampshade, descend the length of the stand, find the switch: Chantilly. His memory returns. He grunts, retrieves from beneath the lamp a book open face-down. Charles reads several lines, then is astonished to feel drowsy again so quickly. He turns off the light and falls back asleep, curled up in the knot of sheets.

He was still asleep when Nicole asked Justine to take care of him that morning. She had to go out rather early; Charles might not be up yet. "You explain it to him"—she breathed a centiliter of smoke from the tip of her lips—"you know as much about it as I do."

From inside a scant grey silk robe with a giant ideogram on the back, Justine looked at her uncoifed mother in wrinkled lace. Between them loomed a mound of toast, surrounded by every-thing needed to smear thereupon, but these they did not touch. They barely touched the lapsang suchong that continued to smile placidly in its cups, more and more coldly after they had left it. Nicole had gone off for a long hour of boudoir; Justine went out, shivering, to look for cigarettes in the Austin. In the mornings there were still cold, cutting little nips in the air, and the car interior was scented with leather, wood, vetiver, and Turkish tobacco. The young woman quickly reentered the house; in one bound she climbed two steps bordered by two more white angels (vinegar-soaked sponge, nails) bathed in dew, beyond which the Austin was wavily reflected in the French doors, under the aerated foliage.

Later, wearing a velour sweatshirt and cobra-skin pants, Justine returned to the dining room where Charles was slowly breakfasting. Standing near him, Boris watched; he disappeared almost immediately. Charles raised his head. He had redonned his clothes, which in the meantime had been washed and ironed. He gave off a discreet aroma of detergent and lotion.

Justine repeated everything Nicole had said about Jeff Pons, of whom Charles kept a tender, narrow-shouldered memory. They agreed on certain dates, a port town; Charles refused the money, then Charles took half the money. As he was leaving the Fischer villa, his glance fell on the tall Boulle grandfather clock in the foyer: on its flanks two Cupids, held on by copper leaf and watched over by a black angel armed with a sickle, indicated eleven-thirty. At five-thirty, Charles found himself back in the heart of the Bois de Boulogne, shortly before the closing of the Jardin d'Acclimatation.

As everyone knows, you can find all sorts of rides there: little road, railway, and airport circuits, packed with mini-creatures remote-controlling weary nannies through the amusement network. Each ride is flanked by a solid construction that serves as both cashier's window and storage place for the equipment— shovels, rolls of tickets, PA system. These were conceived as model houses in miniature, sometimes decorated in Bavarian style, or Basque, or Breton—pinnacles, whitewash, thatch, or rafters, depending. The arrangement of these cottages forms a mini-city where two confirmed gendarmes, barracked in a grey regulation fish tank, attempt to enforce the law on pedal cars.

Charles had occupied nearly all of these shelters on one summer's night or another; the park was a residence easily entered. The operators quit their work post after closing time without leaving anything valuable in their lodges—not anything, in any event, that justified the installation of a lock beyond the capabilities of the wandering man's simple skeleton.

So they were about to close; the children firmly gripped the seats of their vehicles, countering their mothers' exasperation with a passive and gyrating resistance. Finally, given the hour, each one dismounted his ride and departed. Charles had hidden in a clump of trees bordering the Enchanted River, on which flat boats floated without oars, powered by the perpetual movement of the water alone. Through the leaves he saw the slackly attentive uniformed guards; their whistle blasts herded the little creatures toward the exit.

When silence had been restored, Charles, shut in the park, inspected the familiar cottages, especially that of the Express Railway where he had fixed up a cache under the register. He removed four tiles that held in place without mortar, like the pieces of a puzzle; under them lay an envelope of thick, old plastic, like solid oil, where the opaque and the translucent vied bitterly. Leafing through the passport Charles came across his image, felt no solidarity with it, then folded his identity card back into its pouch.

Later he strolled through the empty park in search of dinner. Not far from a cluster of idle rides, two garbage cans proved to be reasonably well garnished with remains of sandwiches and cookies, whose soiled edges Charles eliminated, wrapping the rest in an almost virgin paper napkin. Having even discovered a can two-thirds full of flat soda, he settled into a little green airplane relaxing at the end of its mechanical arm. This space was tight, and Charles bent his knees against his chest, on either side of the minuscule steering wheel, his potpourri of scraps balanced in front of him on the vehicle's gleaming nose. He chewed slowly while watching the sky darken.

He fell asleep behind the funhouse mirrors, then left the amusement park well before opening time. It was a weekday, and few would show up to be amused. Near Porte d'Auteuil pensive children hurried, their schoolbags bouncing against their shoulder blades. After a half-hour's walk, Charles stopped in a calm little street before two floors full of ivy, separated from the sidewalk by a low fence and twenty square yards of rose bushes.

Charles pushed open the gate, rang at the door, and Gina de Beer came to let him in: pink lips, three rows of pink pearls around her neck, the happy smile of a rested widow; her eyes and teeth produced an elegant sparkle, her saliva was no doubt sweet.

"It's you," her smile widened. "Come in."

Warm, tidy living room, pierced through with mirrors, spotted with flowers in an odor of wax; frames of gold-plated wood contained watercolors of no particular importance. An open door in back revealed a slightly unmade bed. Charles folded his parka over the gleaming backrest of a chair. "I'm not interrupting anything, am I?"

"Put your feet up. You look tired."

"No," he said, sitting in the chair, "no."

"Something hot, perhaps? Would you like to take a shower? I'll run you a bath."

"I'd like that," said Charles, "although I already had one yesterday."

"It's relaxing," said Gina de Beer, "it'll relax you. Make yourself comfortable. Put your feet up, I'll be back in a second. If you're thirsty, you know where everything is."

He wasn't thirsty. He listened to the water running at the other end of the apartment, from where the fragrance of bath salts soon drifted, followed by Gina's voice calling him. He stood up, disappeared; the water stopped running in the distance; the living room was empty. Silence. Gina de Beer returned, crossed the living room toward the bedroom, whose door she closed behind her. Long silence. Charles neither sang nor whistled in his bath; he reappeared in the living room dressed only in a large, very clean pair of undershorts, still showing the creases of the iron at the hips. He walked toward the bedroom and opened the door. Undressed on the half-made bed, Gina de Beer was leaning toward the lamp, draping a scarf around the shade. She turned and pulled up the corners. "Would you close the door," she smiled, "if you don't mind." Charles was sitting on the other side of the bed. He ran a finger between his toes where it was still wet. He looked at Gina de Beer. Sweet little embarrassed laugh of Gina's, "What's the matter, don't you want to?"

"Of course I do," said Charles, raising himself just enough to slip the undershorts off with his thumbs.

"Wait," she said, "would you mind shutting the door?"

After lunch, Charles asked Gina to collect several belongings that had been left with her. The secret of his fairly good appearance was that he actually owned a few changes of clothes, which she gladly took to the laundry between visits. On the other hand, he refused her offer of suitcases, briefcases, or trunks made of exaggerated leather. A little bag would do just fine, a little canvas shoulder bag that Gina dug up at the bottom of a closet, all bunched up, all resigned, having lost all hope that anyone would ever want to put anything in it.

"All your things," worried Gina. "Are you leaving?"

"Perhaps," Charles said, throwing the strap of the fulfilled bag over his shoulder. "A few days."

"You're not coming back," she suddenly flared up. "That's it, isn't it—you're not coming back."

"Of course I am," said Charles softly. "Hey, Gina, of course I'm coming back."

The posters had changed in the two weeks since he'd last been to Saint-Ambroise metro; new promises curved along the station's vaulted walls, but the chest hadn't moved. Charles, coming by subway, spotted it immediately at the end of the platform, even before the conductor had begun to brake: a large padlocked chest serving as a toolbox for the line repairmen. Two persons awaited the train. Two others awaited nothing: a woman as close to thirty as to sixty years of age, asleep under a rumpled quilt of empty or near-empty plastic bags; and a young man fallen from brilliance, nodding on his bench, ballasted by a blue-black flask that he gripped in the hollow of his hand. Ether whitewashed the air with harsh aromas, which made the pair of patrons in the warm bosom of their second-class car jump.

The latter having returned to its burrow, Charles crossed the platform toward the large chest, where he stored several other possessions: two packs of damp cigarettes and two large cans of food without labels, institution-size. The first in his pockets, the second under his arm, he shut the chest and retraced his steps, passing by the young man enclosed in his anesthetic bubble. He stopped near the woman under the bags, leaned over her, touched her shoulder.

"Ghislaine," he whispered.

Ghislaine raised her lid over a fixedly distrustful eye, striped with polychromatic lines. From his pocket Charles pulled one of the packs of tobacco, which he held out to her along with a can—peas, I think. The marginal's eyelid did a rapid back-and-forth

(Charles was unable to tell whether this denoted connivance or a neurological disorder), then Ghislaine nabbed the presents with an instantaneous claw, with the rapidity of an insect. She shoved them into one of the bags and her eyes again became fixed. As if closing them for her in death, Charles passed his hand softly over her face before exiting into the fresh air.

The street-level shops had just reopened on Faubourg-du-Temple and it smelled violently of fish, ham, exhaust, cheese, and bread dough, in a slightly less fresh version of that morning. Charles crossed the intersection toward the profile of Frédérick Lemaître: as usual, loiterers, backs leaning against the actor, followed the evolution of a barge through the canal locks. After the canal it would take the tunnel up to Arsenal, where the channeled water caught a last fleeting glimpse of daylight before throwing itself into the river. Charles took advantage of the lockkeeper's absorption in this spectacle to hop the fence and fake his way past the iron door barring access to the subterranean quays.

Within moments the entrance was but a milky stain behind him, a wan point of light suspended in the dark, scarcely reflected by the tar-like water whose lapping seemed, through echoes, to emanate from everywhere. Soon another point of light appeared in the opposite direction, mobile and orange, tainted by red and a little white; it smelled funny. Between these two points reigned a blackness that deformed the distance. Charles groped his way along, staying as far as possible from the edge, brushing the wall with his hands, scraping himself on the sharp rubble until the orange was just ahead, along with the funny odor.

The latter emanated from a muted fire around which four people huddled. Brown light and greedy shadow played on the hollow faces; the division of sexes was not readily apparent. Charles recognized the sleeping Vidal by his green cap—supposedly taken from one of his victims, a nameless sailor on whom he had then allegedly fed—as well as by the SNCF towel forever knotted around his neck: he was the head of this savage faction of outsiders. A blond fellow near him tensed, sensing the approaching shadow; once he had identified it as Charles's he dropped the heavy object he had just grabbed. A woman turned.

"Charles," said Jeanne-Marie. "You've got a new pair of pants."

"An old pair I had mended," said Charles. "Here are some peas, I think."

Jeanne-Marie took the can and began rummaging in the pile of rubbish on which the quartet had settled. A heap of volcanic appearance: the fire at the bottom of the crater heated a black cauldron without handles, from which the odor rose. The disjecta were of very diverse origins; it was difficult to imagine their trek to such an out-of-the-way part of town. She displaced them in search of a can opener. Charles finally handed her his Swiss army knife. Vidal half-opened his eyes.

"Charles," said Vidal. "You've brought a can."

"Peas," repeated Charles, "I think."

"Beans," corrected Jeanne-Marie, emptying the can into the cauldron. "They'll go well with the meat."

Charles sat down near a man named Henri, who lay a little behind Vidal. Being one-legged, this man slept. "I've also got cigarettes," said Charles, patting himself down.

"That's nice of you," opined Vidal, " 'cause we don't go out much these days, you know. We get by for the food. Visitors," he added, indicating the canal.

He snickered. The blond started to snicker as well, but Charles remained skeptical. With the help of a bent iron wire, Jeanne-Marie stirred the contents of the cauldron, dredging up things that she deposited on a piece of wire mesh. They helped themselves. Charles, like the others, chewed his thing, which evoked no precise animal taste: neither fish nor fowl, it was mainly reminiscent of burnt tire, burnt plastic, burnt wet cardboard, of other non-putrescible refuse consuming itself flamelessly. Charles doubted it was really human flesh; it might simply have been remains of the poorest quality, saved in extremis from a junkman's trashbin, which several days' cooking had rid of their miasmas along with their identity. Vidal snickered anew while spitting out a tough little fragment.

"You go by the mailbox?"

"Nothing for you," answered Charles, "but Boris says hello."

Each of them, having taken a second helping of vegetables, leaned back to digest. Henri the unijambist was still asleep. The blond tossed some pebbles into the water. Jeanne-Marie came nearer the hearth, unglued the mildewed pages of a magazine, then leafed through the pretty people and practical advice for laundering in low temperatures. The fire lent the faces a pale, reticent glow.

"Can you stay awhile?"

"Just tonight," said Charles. "I've got things to do tomorrow."

He took three of the dice from his pocket and they played 421, using flasks of rotgut to keep score. They spoke a little while playing, spoke of the world as if from within a cave, until Vidal showed signs of fatigue. As he stretched loudly, Jeanne-Marie came to snuggle against him, and the blond against the unijambist. Charles went off to sleep alone, apart from the anthropophagi.

He awoke first, flicked the Zippo. A hodgepodge of cold and lukewarm stenches rose from the entwined bodies near the hearth. Charles picked up Gina's little bag, which had served as his pillow, slung it across his chest, and began walking toward a point of rising daylight. Dropped through sealed grilles along the central divider of Boulevard Richard-Lenoir, pale columns of light spattered large stains on the surface of the underground canal. At the tunnel exit, large, empty yachts, baptized *Clipperton* or *Wanderlust*, lined up along the Arsenal boat basin; there was even an *Abigail's Daughter* for sale. Charles sat down on an emergency lifebuoy to read the sign in its entirety: the boat's description, price. Then he skirted the captain's office, heading for the last of the canal's nine locks. As always, he took the passageways restricted to authorized personnel, hanging over the dirty water in which floated continents of bloated polystyrene, empty bottles, innumerable somethings old. A slight sourness hovered over the boat basin; it smelled a tiny bit like the sea, the yachts having no doubt brought back a few molecules of salt and iodine caught in the tar, absorbed by the rope.

Passing the Institute of Forensic Medicine, Charles returned to the river, which he followed upstream to Port de la Rapée. Shipments of raw materials waited there to be loaded on board: bricks, tubes, fencing and tiles, synthetic rubber and river sand, thermal insulation, lime cement next to acetylene, argon. Blue trucks carrying orange cement mixers and red trucks with white cement mixers were parked in a line, not far from yellow Fenwick and green Clark fork lifts. A triple row of sleeping barges, named *Francine* or *Mekong*, hoisting the torn flags of oil concerns or brands of beer, were chained to the dock. Cabin windows overloaded with green plants revealed familiar objects: toys, underwear, pots and pans, full ashtrays. Charles made sure that everyone was still in bed. Several cars zoomed along the one-way road bordering the Seine; moist eye behind cloudy windshield, the drivers were inattentive. Charles crossed the port, inspecting the piles of crates, sacks, motors under tarpaulins, heaps of things arranged on palettes. Against each load leaned a black-painted board, indicating in chalk its nature, its destination, the name of the barge, and the time of departure. Noticing a heap of gravel big as a Volkswagen, leaving for Le Havre at nine o'clock, Charles thought a bit, then turned, and discovered a bundle of plastic tubing in all sizes. He felt in his pocket for his knife.

He cut off twelve inches of a tube one inch in diameter, then climbed the heap and began to tunnel into it. He burrowed in like an insect, careful not to overly modify the spontaneous arrangement of gravel, to preserve its heap-like profile. He sank down until only his head was visible. With one hand he stuck the straw in his mouth, then began to pedal while pivoting, screwing himself into the gravel, disappearing within it, the other end of the tube jutting discreetly into the open air.

At six in the morning, as every morning, everything was the same on the waterfront to this man living closed in, buried in raw materials. A light wind cellulited the surface of the river, rocked the skeleton of a dead leaf, pushed a bit of dried paper into a puddle, raised dust with a little sand. Charles occasionally moved, breathed too heavily, then heard several stones tumbling as if within him; he found that the time passed slowly despite his familiarity with empty situations.

It must have been close to nine o'clock because the gentle motor of a Fenwick could be heard: the lift conveyed the pile on the pallet toward a crane the same color as itself; the crane gripped the merchandise and lifted it through the air toward the hold of the *Anthrax*. Two pigeons fluttered around, squawking, yielding to a seagull who had right-of-way. Aside from air, the pipe conducted toward Charles's interior the amplified noises of the maneuver, the cries and overlapping shouts under the rumblings of gravel; he perceived all this, in his great padded robe for live burial. The pallet landed lopsided on the barge's flat bottom and brutally vomited part of its contents: his air-line cut off, the wandering man thought himself lost. There again, although on a tighter rhythm, the thing seemed interminable—then the heap recovered its heap-like balance. Charles sighed with relief, so heavily that he lost his own rhythm and inhaled wrong; it was painful to keep from coughing into the tube. He regained his composure all the more quickly in that they were right near him, onloading other raw materials that, at first, made a clear sound. Then came something like sacks, no doubt very heavy ones, which fell to the ground with the sound of a suction cup. Then someone closed the hatch, and darkness invaded the tube. A few stifled noises filtered through the moveable deck, unintelligible statements, accents; Charles waited for them to start up the engines. As soon as the latter were purring, the wandering man shook toward the surface of the pile, undulating and swimming in the stone with all his limbs, biting the tube very hard, emerging from the gravel in stages, like his forebears from silt.

He ran his hands over his face for a long time. He massaged his ears and his neck, plunged deep into the rolled collar of his shirt. He rubbed his hands together thoroughly, then rubbed himself all over, lingering on his ankles, a long time on his knees, a long time on his shoulders, then he resumed rubbing his eyes; he found it a little difficult to stop rubbing. It was still very dark. He had to force himself to stand still, eyes wide open in the blackness and the diesel, rediscovering the rhythm of his breath, shivering as if naked.

Finally, come round, Charles emptied his pockets of surplus gravel down to where his personal effects were, starting with the Zippo. Zippo: all around, in fact, where sacks and ploughshares, fat new ploughshare blades in blue plastic film, which had rung so clearly shortly before. Dispersing its vapors into those of the fuel, the Zippo felt at home, olfactorily speaking. Charles dusted himself off a little more with one hand, running it over his body. It was not hard to find a plank among all the other planks, which Charles dragged next to the gravel. Sitting on his feet, leaning against the heap, he stood the lighter on the plank and pulled all his dice from his pocket to attempt a series of figures in three tosses. He immediately rolled straight sixes, just as the *Anthrax* began to move in a westerly direction.

15

A T T H E Subang airport, the wait had annoyed Pons. The heat concentrated in the asphalt caused everything at its surface to tremble in a sticky will-o'-the-wisp, and the Duke began to melt at both ends before freezing under the air conditioners; his sweat, gluing his shirt to his skin, began evaporating in deep, slow shivers. Wrapped only in cotton, he made sure to change in the Boeing's exiguous toilets, doubling thicknesses in preparation for Paris: in too much wool he was thus bathed at Charles-de-Gaulle as well, in the waiting line for taxis. He was tired; the notions of sleep and day intermingled, slid over those of space and cold; his knees hurt. He was surprised at being tired, too tired to be surprised at not being more tired. Pressed against the conveyor belt, he had had to wait a long time for his luggage. The same bags kept parading by, except for his. Sometimes they were thrown on askew; their jutting corners smacked into his fragile knees. Once Pons nearly fell over.

Later he steadied himself against the door of a taxi, having had to load his own suitcase into the trunk. On the way, the northern suburbs progressively stood out: different, of course, from the memory he kept of them, surely different, parts had surely changed that he wasn't able to see, wasn't able to distinguish from the other parts. The taxi stopped near Maubert-Mutualité, in front of a hotel lodged in Pons's memory.

It still existed, faithful to its image, equally faithful to its lease, having added no new stars to its rating. The room looked out onto a dog sleeping on a plaid blanket, at the back of a fairly well-lit courtyard under hanging sheets. Pons opened his suitcase, closed it, stretched out on the bed only to get back up immediately, elbows at right angles, I'll never be able to sleep. The brushes at the bottom of the case, the soap; the Duke left the hotel twenty minutes later. The air currents in the street coolly dried his scalp. He stopped in Place Maubert at a Vietnamese grocery, the mangoes and the cashier already reminding him of home; then he cut over to the Seine. But like the northern suburbs and no doubt like those mangoes, the river seemed cockeyed, ill-synchronized with his recollections. Looking upon it Duke Pons felt no satisfaction, not the slightest emotion, not that much nostalgia. Later, sitting with a glass of white at a café near the Cluny, it was the same for the wine: neither like nor unlike what he remembered, no better than any other. It's nothing, it's just fatigue. Jet lag.

Women, still covered, passed by on the large sidewalk. The Duke shivered a little; he was reluctant to get up and plunge into the cold city. Near the hotel, this café was a free, protected zone, a transitory area, like the foot bath preceding a swimming pool. If it weren't for the chill edge in the air, Pons would have dozed off. After another glass of wine—a little better than the first—he stood and headed surefootedly toward a post office that he knew to be there; no reason for it to have moved from the corner of Rue Danton. Apparently Pons's skin had not eliminated all the tropical humidity accumulated in its pores, for a thick fog condensed on the glass door as soon as he entered one of the downstairs phone booths.

"It's Jean-François," he said. "Excuse me? Fine, I'll hold on."

With a patient index, Pons traced figures in the condensation, a chair, a profile, while Boris ran helter-skelter after his mistress. Finally the latter's voice came on the line, and Pons crushed the receiver to his ear. "It's me, Nicole," he breathed. "Jean-François."

"Oh, Jeff," she exhaled.

"Went fine," said the Duke, "yes. Not much, a little. Not right away, first I've got to. And then I want to see George. I know, I know, me too, me too. Tomorrow. Me too, yes."

He hung up, thought for a moment, electrified the chair with a mechanical zigzag before returning to bustling street level. Shortly afterward, tucked into the furry seat covers of a Datsun taxi, he discovered the riverside roadway heading downstream, running beneath an outcropping of hieratic facades sculpted in grey iceberg. The Allée des Cygnes on his right, concretizing the river axis, was still decorated with the same figurines—a couple, a nanny, a reader on a bench—that one finds in old toy shops. The taxi slowed on Quai André-Citroën at the foot of a thirty-story tower with yellow facings, striped with picture windows, caught between two other towers, white and tan. Pons opened the car door and raised his face toward the building tops. There were similar ones in Singapore, which he'd like to see when they got old; would he see them when they got old? He left that question behind in the taxi.

Along with the aquarium and the plants, the high-rise foyer was decorated with geometric wall lamps and bas-reliefs in yellow metal and smoked glass. Pons read the names, the numbers of the apartments on the gilded mailboxes. His lips moved soundlessly. In the elevator he found himself squeezed against the mirror in back; one of the pregnant women had donned light earphones that crackled in the total breathy silence of the machinery. They exited one after the other with their cargo. Pons, checking his image in the mirror, continued his ascent alone to the penultimate floor.

Behind his door, Paul was watching a program about mountain fauna: the doorbell made him stiffen in his chair; the marmots froze onscreen. He got up, lowered the volume, and opened the door. Let's skip over the surprise and Bouc's prophecies: the other was there, framed by the doorjamb, still the same. "Ah." Paul said whatever came into his head. "I knew you'd come." The Duke, his glance conveying a waggish dignity, said nothing. "Come in," added Paul after they hadn't embraced. Pons let himself fall into an armchair, sighing, making the leather envelope sigh under him, turning his grey-seamed face toward Paul:

"Did you get my letter?"

"You'd like something to drink," Paul assumed, having at his disposal something to drink.

"That one'd be fine" (Pons indicated the yellow label), "a little more. Little more, little more, little more—stop. You've become a good-looking guy," he stated, raising his glass. "That's good. I see things are going well." (He drank.) "Thirty years, right? You were like this." (He levelled his hand appraisingly in the air.) "That makes you how old now?" (He drank.) "You ever hear from Albert?"

"Retired," summarized Paul. "They found him something. Something, you know, for when you retire, but seems it's okay, he's okay, they say it's really okay. They go visit him now and then."

"I see," said the Duke. "And little Monique?"

"She went back to George's mother's," Paul said wearily. "After the funeral."

"When did George's mother die?"

"No," sighed Paul. "George."

"Ah," went Pons. "So George is dead?"

"Some kind of fall," explained Paul, "three years ago."

Pons drank.

"It's a loss," he declared afterward. "It's really a shame. I don't understand why no one let me know. You could have let me know, it's family after all, dammit. You had my address. Especially for George."

As Paul expressed in a single gesture the idea of distance in space and in time, the Duke observed a minute of silence, drinking to George's memory in little sips, between which he looked at what remained in his glass.

"Nobody else?" he verified. "Nobody else has . . ."

"I can't think of any," said Paul. "Well, Janine, but you know."

"With Janine it was inevitable. And how are *you* making out?"

Paul's arms swept from his chest to the decor, the way an actor politely designates what is not himself: stage left Gaston Chaissac, stage right the unimpeded view.

"You seem okay," said the Duke, "you must be okay. So, did you get my letter?"

To the best of Paul's ability to summon them, his memories of that letter were but scattered miscellanies in which the affective jostled without method against the meteorological, the ethical against the geopolitical, the autobiographical against the astral as if in a laundry bag. With, it seemed to him, many quotations from memory, exclamation marks and ellipses, unclosed parentheses, and questions left fallow. Such disorder reigned in it that he had not really paid attention to the final envoy (essential envoy from Pons's point of view, everything preceding it being only garnish; but this very fact made it a bit too circumspect)— mannered allusions to necessary exchanges, to business matters that Jean-François wanted to settle with his people, squatting on the native soil. In this letter Paul had preferred to see only sentimentally insomniac elucubrations from the old colonial drunkard: Jean-François Pons was that absent relative from whom they would get nothing, whom they would never see again, who was so far gone that he no longer even figured on the family announcements list. And now here was the Duke, as healthy as you or I, come back from the realm of the dead to pour himself another whiskey.

"I mentioned a business matter in the letter, do you remember that?"

"Of course," said Paul, "that is, not all the details."

"One thing, first," said Pons. "I know this is your specialty. Don't feed me any stories, don't deny it. I know this is precisely your specialty."

He outlined the Malaysian situation, the state of affairs at the plantation. Very soon they got down to logistics. Paul understood what Jeff was going to ask him ten seconds in advance; he immediately grimaced, pretended not to understand, tried to protest.

"One thing," Pons reminded him, raising his finger. "Don't feed me any stories. It's George who told me this was your specialty. He wrote me. He was worried about you, old George."

"It's over now," Paul said. "I don't do that anymore, now."

"But you know people. I need enough for fifteen, you see," Pons ordered, rounding his arms in front of him as if for a cake. "Let's say twenty, better to think big. Solid stuff. Not too heavy, not too complicated. You know more about this than I do."

Speaking in the conditional, Paul inquired in a pouting, pained voice about the specifics, including the technical and military competence of the eventual users. "Rudimentary," admitted Duke Pons, "and purely theoretical." In the evenings, at the back of the shed, the elder Aw ran his flat index over washed-out alcohol prints of plans, for the benefit of the fading locals. He also handed out pamphlets from time to time, but the guys didn't give a fig for pamphlets.

"Assault rifles," hesitated the Duke. "It seems they're the best. Of course, I don't know anything about it myself, it's the kid I told you about who told me about them, the other guy's brother, energetic boy, things in his teeth" (he drank), "he's the one who told me about them. Does that sound good to you, assault rifles?"

Paul reeled off the names of the various models, names known to other specialists, as familiar as Heinz for ketchup.

"I'm not following you," said Pons, "but that sounds good to me. Okay, about twenty of those."

"You can't get them just like that," Paul observed.

"Never hurts to ask," said Pons. "On top of which, I'll also need somebody, an instructor of some kind. To teach them how to use the stuff, can you think of anyone? You'll see how pretty it is over there, especially now. It's all green."

As Paul, immobile, stared at the Duke without answering, the latter preferred not to develop this point immediately; they would have time to come back to it.

"All right," his nephew finally said, "I'll try. Of course I'm not promising anything. Frankly, I'd be amazed, but I'll try."

Pons nodded. A fright shot through Paul.

"Where are you sleeping?" he worried sincerely. "I mean, do you have a place to stay?"

Pons scrawled some numbers in the margin of a newspaper. "As of tomorrow," he specified. "Until then I've got nothing but time." He tore off the bit of paper and held it out to Paul, holding out his empty glass in the other hand. So it was that Pons now wanted to rise from his armchair and found it difficult. But he finally extricated himself from the octopus-like hold, then crab-walked to the picture window, flattened his open hand against it and looked at the exterior that hadn't really changed, all things considered; still hadn't really changed. His glass hung at an angle from the end of one arm.

16

HERE'S Justine again in her grey room. Outside, white clouds filter the daylight trailing behind them—cold light of scialytic neon, falling equitably on all things. The cries of recessed children rise from a nearby schoolyard; pigeons leap like obese grasshoppers, undaunted among the cornices, window rails, and rooftops.

Justine stuffed enough clothes for a three-day absence into a large duffel bag. She wasn't paying attention to what she was doing, dissipated her efforts in a string of little annexed actions that constantly distracted her from the large bag. Leafing through a book before putting it back on the shelf, she discovered a photo between its pages, stuck the photo under the frame of the mirror in which she judged herself for an instant, changed her sweatshirt at the conclusion of that examination, lit a Gitane, immediately stubbed it out, then lit a Benson & Hedges that would consume itself alone on the edge of a chest of drawers. She walked through the apartment, returned from the kitchen with orange juice in a very fat bottle. She drank carefully from the very fat bottleneck, one hand in her hair as if to support her head, her shoulder leaning against the studio door: Laure was working in a tempest of cloth and stacked patterns that unfurled at the foot of the sewing machine.

"I'll be back on Tuesday," Justine reminded her, "Tuesday evening. Do you want some?"

"What about that guy?" said Laure, taking the bottle.

"What guy?"

"The one who keeps calling. What should I tell him?"

"You don't know when I'm coming back, and don't give him my name. Call me at Mother's if he gets too pushy, but don't give him the number. I'm not really looking forward to going to my mother's."

But off we go: One hour later, having taken the northern highway at top speed, Justine arrived at the house in Chantilly. Shouts emanated from the green salon, where Pons was painting for Nicole several portraits of Malaysian life, his femurs crossed toward the fireplace that Boris had just replenished. He stopped speaking at the young woman's entrance, looked her over uneasily, and started to rise.

"It's Jeff, it's Jean-François," Nicole said to her daughter before walking into the foyer to instruct Boris—through the doorway one could see the domestic grappling toward the second floor in a disjointed diagonal, lugging the large duffel bag behind him.

"I've seen a photo of you," Justine said. "I remember."

"Wear and tear," Pons pleaded flirtatiously, "I'm unrecognizable. The tropics age you."

Nicole returned, then Boris reappeared, signaling that dinner was ready whenever they were. Justine was the first to leave the salon. "Beautiful girl," breathed Pons. "She takes after you. She looks just like you."

At the table he showed himself to be jovial, fairly indifferent to the issues that motivated his trip, the object of which he seemed to have lost sight of somewhat. Boris served, compromising above their heads the future of the gravy boats, avoiding tragedy by miracles. "What's with this guy?" Pons asked between lettuce and casserole. "Is he sick?"

"A friend of Charles's," said Nicole. "He lived like Charles, you know." (Pons raised his eyes heavenward.) "He decided he'd had enough. Did you notice he can't stand altogether straight? He was looking for something. A rehabilitation, of sorts. He's good-natured, clean, he gets along well with Mrs. Boeuf."

"Ah," went Pons. "And how *is* Charles, by the way?"

Nicole shot a glance at Justine before not answering.

"I have to tell you. I spoke about you, you know. The crowd from the Perfect, you remember? I see some of them from time to time."

"I don't follow you," grumbled Pons.

"If you need some help," she said. "So I thought—I asked them."

The Duke brought forth his cold adventurer's smile, distantly bitter, for which too few opportunities arose.

"They came out in droves," he accurately supposed. "But I don't need anyone, don't need them."

"I have to admit that apart from Charles . . ." Nicole hesitated.

"I liked Charles and I feared him," continued Pons in the same tone, "but that rat's life of his. I don't see how he could help me much."

"Fine," went Nicole, not daring to say more.

"You didn't tell them too much, I hope. This business, I mean, if it gets out we could be in deep trouble. I could be in deep trouble, over there. Speaking of which, I have to call, find out what's been going on in my absence."

"I'd prefer," said Nicole, "that you used a public phone. The rates per minute, I'm sure you understand."

"I understand," Pons darkened. "Right. But I'll take care of this by myself. I've got contacts in Paris, good contacts. Very good contacts and everything's going to turn out fine."

Forgotten for a moment, that prospect put some ballast in his movements, his thought processes. This recall to reality made him stop talking and lay his knife on the edge of the plate, lift his glass without bringing it to his lips, stare out his window: softened by the curtains, the trees scratched the light with their pruned nails. Silence arrived with its inhabitants: a dialogue of muted barkings; musical carhorn on the road; game show from the kitchen where each day the encyclopedic Boris never ceased to amaze Mrs. Boeuf; trio of sparrows in the skies; tractor solo in the distance; ringing of the phone in the salon. Justine stood up.

"Of course," said Nicole, "everything's going to turn out fine."

Justine crossed the foyer, then the green salon, and picked up the phone: Hello, she said.

"Hello," ventured a man's voice that Justine recognized immediately.

"It's you again," she said, her tone chilly; to hear her you would never have known she was actually smiling. Brief pause, then the voice went excuse me, I think I have the wrong number, another pause, then the line went dead.

At the other end, Paul J. Bergman was not smiling. He hadn't recognized Justine, did not remember her well enough save for her eyes; the hostile greeting of a stranger did nothing for his spirits at that moment. Annoyed, Paul reread the numbers scrawled on the scrap of newspaper by Pons, who had no doubt made a mistake—ravages of alcohol on the memory, after a certain age. Just to be sure, Paul dialed them once more, more slowly; this time the line was busy.

"No," Laure was in fact telling Justine, "he didn't call. I wouldn't have given him the number in any case. You must be mistaken, it couldn't have been *him*."

Him called back five minutes later. The line was no longer busy. It answered immediately; the same female voice said hello, less assured; you still would not have felt any smile coming from within.

"Could I speak to Jean-François," Paul said quickly, full of urbanity, as if nothing had happened. "If he's there."

Another brief pause; Justine pulled a bit of lower lip between her teeth. "Just a moment, please," she said, before gently setting the receiver down on the leather blotter of the writing desk and reluctantly heading back to the dining room. "It's for you," she told Pons, who promptly rose, whisked the sleeping napkin from his lap, and hurried to the salon with a martial stride. Justine took her seat, looked at her mother. "His contacts," she said. "Who are they? He said, you know, he had contacts, did he talk about them?" But Nicole was dreamily gnawing at a crumb: contacts, she finally reacted, what contacts.

As he crossed the foyer in turn, the Duke got hold of himself. After only several hours in Chantilly, the urgency of his mission risked becoming dulled in Nicole's warm company, round and soft like a cushion in which one had, nonetheless, left several pins. This opportune call snatched him from the jaws of repletion, from that hothouse torpor that threatened to engulf his consciousness. In one stroke, the telephone reestablished his hold on the world of his virility; he charged toward it, breathing heavily, his back straight. He recovered his strength.

"That you, kid?"

"I wanted to let you know I'm seeing a guy."

"What kind," went Pons. "What kind of guy?"

"I called him last night. He might have something for you, he'll have to see. I'll have to see. I just wanted to let you know."

"Perfect," said Pons, "keep me posted. Here, there's" (he lowered his voice), "here, where I am, there's this absolutely stunning babe, I wish you could see her."

"Really," said Paul. "The one who answers the phone?"

"Mmm," suggested Pons. "I'll introduce you if you like."

"Yeah," said Paul, "maybe. She struck me as a bit strange."

"Paul, how's it going with the girls?" The Duke suddenly felt like exploring the subject. "Do you see them often? Do you see them enough? I'm saying this because—" (Alone at the top of his tower, Paul J. Bergman let out a joyless laugh.) "It seemed to me that you—"

"Have you recovered from the trip?" asked Paul. "Are you getting the rest you need?"

"I was tired this morning," the Duke reminisced, laying a hand on his forehead, "but I think I'm fine now."

"Be sure to get all the rest you need," said Paul.

17

IT WAS without pleasure that Paul had called Tomaso, without pleasure that he arrived at his shop. The shop stood in the middle of Kremlin-Bicêtre in a commercial artery, which was relatively feverish at the end of the afternoon, plainly tachycardic on Sundays when, under their canvas shelters, itinerant merchants of old and new scurried about. At the halfway point, Tomaso ran a discount appliance store, featuring machines of recent vintage but that were afflicted with some defect, which a reduced costliness hoped to absolve: ill-closing freezers; hyperactive convectors and toasters; dented televisions with disconcerting labels; and accessories such as custom telephones (not federally approved), Taiwanese tea services (with one member amputated), or pairs of stainless-steel napkin rings (You and Me engraved inside). Tomaso, who dealt in all this, was a small man, deceptively thin and wrapped in a grey smock. A beret of excessive proportions flapped above his translucent ears, encroaching on his heavy eyebrows, squatting on his head like a bird of prey about to take off and whisk the salesman from the ancestral floor.

Paul parked in front of the empty shop. This emptiness suited Tomaso, who did not encourage his fellow men to buy appliances that they might want to return and complain about later; his fellows having no other reason to address him, his profit margin existed only theoretically. Tomaso's real dealings, the ones from which he derived his considerable revenues (unscented by the feds), were concluded in hushed tones with well-dressed men, among the fallen gas ranges and dryers. Humble, draping their shame in cancelled price tags, these downgraded machines witnessed auctions for their rarer, more precise, and more murderous sisters, much better maintained, much too good for the likes of them.

To reach this point—leaving aside a natural aptitude—Tomaso had simply met the right man at the right time, the man who had introduced him to wholesalers and let him use his diplomatic pouch, at first. Then things had started moving by themselves: under his discreet home-appliances cover, Tomaso had continued to profit from arms traffic, even after the right man's violent demise. In this domain, the routine consisted of supplying the parallel network of amateurs, but it also befell him to play the middleman in large markets opened abroad, in sales of P-27 bazookas, M-52 mortars, M-59A cannons, AGL rockets, Super 530 missiles, M-1 magnetic mines, M-2 magnetic mines, and even once an AMX tank. After laundering it, Tomaso put a part of his money in stones, changed it into houses that he neither let nor lent, that he visited only occasionally. This money piled up; at times it let itself be wagered in large amounts at the racetrack; but Tomaso would never have bought a horse, for instance. This money was under his wife's reasonable care, and also served as the sole support of their son, Gerard, a good lad, completely unproductive after thirty-nine years. This money dissolved in long thermal cures for the three of them. Tomaso did not feel that he was enjoying this money as he would have dreamed: too old at the time of his meeting with the right man, too anchored in a discount salesman's way of life, he had not managed to rid himself of his network of habits, replace it with a more urbane network. So this money accumulated, principally in Switzerland, with a bit of working capital set aside for life's daily needs.

He was doing the cleaning, dusting off his wounded goods, when Paul walked through the door, activating two bells separated by a diminished fifth.

"Mister Bergman," Tomaso rejoiced. "How are things, what's new?"

Paul gave the standard answer—not bad, no better—returned these questions without warmth, then explained what had brought him there. He had the feeling of playing a part, without much wanting to play it, while he outlined Pons's concrete problem, suggested possible solutions. Citing Kalashnikov, he wanted to know what the other thought of that prescription. The discount man's head cocked to one side, his entire beret blowing off course in the movement.

"Yes. For this kind of operation," he recommended, "I would consider something a bit more flexible. Reduce your number of heavy parts, don't you see, compensate with your handgun. Of a high caliber, naturally, it's all a matter of proportion."

"Possibly," said Paul. "Do as you think best."

"Yes," continued Tomaso. "I had someone last year, sort of the same problem. That was my advice to him, he did very nicely by it. In any case I don't carry that model you mention, but I've got some good Herstal at the moment. The caliber is practical, it performs well. It's Belgian, very reliable. A pleaser."

"Do your best," repeated Paul. "It would be good to have it by next week. If you're overstocked at the moment, I can send some people your way. Van Os, for example, is desperate."

"I'd rather not," said Tomaso. "Mister Van Os, well, I prefer not to do business with him. I have my old regulars, people I can count on, it's quiet, they know how to behave themselves. Of course, I'm not saying this about your friends. For you I'd do this any time, Mister Bergman. I do it because it's you."

"That's very kind of you," opined Paul. "How much is that little radio, over there?"

"I wouldn't recommend it," grimaced the discount specialist. "I'd gladly give it to you as a gift but it's no gift. The stuff I've got here, you know" (he made a gesture to signify junk). "On the other hand, if you're looking for good merchandise of this kind, I have a colleague—I'll write you his address on this piece of paper."

After Paul's departure, Tomaso left his shop without locking the door behind him. A cafe stood 300 feet away: at the bar he allowed himself a cognac to celebrate the new sale, downstairs he telephoned to honor it. It was the first slack period of the afternoon, following the return to offices and workshops. A man standing alone by the cash register consulted *Nice-Matin*, which a geezer straight out of the westerns skimmed over his shoulder, mashing a pipecleaner between his brown molars, spitting through his absent canine. Cut off from the world by a smoked-glass partition, a rather shameless heterosexual couple stared at each other without emitting a single word, giving all the signs of a humble and perfect contentment—the male partner moved his head a bit from time to time, to shift perspective. Tomaso returned to his post at the counter, facing the bartender stooped over the rinsing rack. He was a pale bartender with fine hair, anxious eyeglasses, rolled-up sleeves, a gold signet ring bearing his initials, a gold chain bracelet inlaid with his first name (Jean-Claude), and a gold-plated watch, professionally waterproof.

"Did I tell you about the one with the dog?" he wondered.

"Yes," went Tomaso in a skeptical voice.

"I heard about another one, even more disgusting."

"Another dog?"

"This one, you can't imagine what she does," the bartender supposed bitterly. "But let me tell you."

"No, no," said Tomaso.

"She comes on Wednesday, every Wednesday. She stays exactly one hour and you know what she does? A small bottle of Vittel, and then she looks at guys, can't keep her eyes off guys. It's all she does."

"Incredible," admitted Tomaso. "Does she look at you, too?"

"I'm the bartender," the bartender reminded him, elliptically.

Tomaso downed his cognac in one gulp, exhaled noisily from the bottom of his throat, then went out. In the street, the proportion of the crowd and its composition corresponded to that of the bar: little traffic, little noise; two cars passed calmly, followed by a strident young man on a motorscooter, his red helmet ripping the sullen air. Tomaso was calm in his heart. "Damn," he thought, and this heart began to beat a little faster when, returning to the shop, he recognized the back of a man who had entered during his absence, leaning over a display case near the smaller appliances, dressed in a vast overcoat whose flaps undulated at his slightest movement like a canopy. In front of this back was the hollow chest of Toon; behind the shaved occipital his eyes devoured an array of pocket calculators. One after the other, Toon handled them, tried to terrorize them by perverse operations of the square-root-of-minus-one type. The young Brabantine was obviously doing his best to derange the little circuits, gloating with method, the way he used, as a child, to pull the legs and wings from insects. Tomaso tried to regain his calm: Toon couldn't have overheard his conversation with Paul. He coughed.

"Mister Toon," he said, "how are things, what's new?"

The other turned his head without responding. "What's new," he finally said in turn, curling his white lips over a crooked line of yellow enamel.

"As you see."

"I don't give a damn about what I see," said Toon. "I don't believe in it. Still nothing?"

"Alas," moaned Tomaso, "it's become very difficult. There's no more turnover, so to speak. Always the same, don't you know— demand exceeds supply and prices go up. It discourages trade, circulation stops."

"All right," said Toon, "all right. How much do you charge for those little calculators, there?"

"Choose one," smiled Tomaso. "On the house."

Two blocks away, Van Os waited in the 4 × 4, listening to his favorite short-wave program. "Car one-thirty-three," crackled a male voice, "what is your position?" "Seated!" shouted a hilarious chorus, amplified by the metal walls of the paddy wagon. Van Os did not smile, being too used to the recreational rites of the forces of order. Toon tapped his fingernail twice against the window, and Van Os unlocked the door. "So?"

"So nothing," said Toon. "I can't figure out if he really doesn't have the stuff or if he's jerking us around."

"Of course you can't, you're an idiot. Your skull is a hollow box."

"Then why don't *you* go," protested Toon. "You'll see."

"I can't," Van Os clouded over, "I know he doesn't like me. He's afraid of me. He's wrong."

"Even so," objected Toon, "he rented you the house in Craponne last summer (it was nice in that house), he didn't give you any stories when it came to renting the house. He never rents, usually."

"Yes," said Van Os, "that's just what I mean. It's because he's afraid of me."

They took the beltway up to Porte de Sèvres, and from there headed straight to Quai André-Citroën via Place Balard. "So send Plankaert, then," Toon continued to protest, "you'll see."

Van Os pushed his glasses back up his nose: "Plankaert is ill, you know very well he's ill."

There were some people on the quays, owing to the hydroplanes on the river. Their bright colors stifled under ads, the hydroplanes pushed arcs of beige froth around two buoys; the people watched. Toon would have liked to watch, but Van Os signalled him to keep moving, as they were heading for Paul's high-rise.

At the very top of his building, Paul was watching the hydroplanes, giving his brain a rest, when the doorbell rang. No doubt Pons already, anxious to hear the latest. He took out a precautionary bottle, which he placed on the low table before going to answer: Van Os. A second of suspense. Van Os entered, followed by Toon who avoided Paul's eyes.

"You're drinking alone, Bergman?" worried Van Os, pointing to the bottle. "That's not very smart, eh?"

"I was expecting someone," Paul specified.

"We're interrupting something, of course." (In turn, Paul pointed, interrogatively, to the alcohol.) "No, thank you, but if you have some coffee."

"The machine is broken," said Paul. "It's clogged, it doesn't work anymore. Hard water."

"Too bad," said Van Os. "In any case, I don't really like coffee made in machines, it's better from the old-fashioned drip pots. You should try it. You have the Cona, for example, which isn't bad. Of course it's a bit delicate. I prefer the good old Italian model, you know, the kind you unscrew from the middle. There are little individual ones that are really quite good. I'll just sit for a moment, we won't be long."

Paul sat down after him. Toon remained standing, at first behind his chief as befitted his status; then he backed in a scarcely perceptible progression toward the window and the hydroplanes. Paul searched for a reply to the coffee pots.

"So," he came up with, "did everything turn out all right, the other day at Vanves?"

Van Os's hand flitted near his temple, shooing away the skirmishes of world history:

"It was nothing, nothing major. Some people I don't usually work with, acquaintances. But we help each other out, you know what it's like. We give each other a hand."

He removed his glasses, deposited his breath on them, then wiped them meticulously, without looking, his eyes squinting toward the reproduction of a painting on the wall entitled *Seven O'Clock in the Morning*: at the corner of an empty street, behind the nearly empty window of a closed shop, a pendulum clock in the middle of the picture in fact said seven o'clock. The painting was principally light blue, light green, white. Greener foliage shivered to the left, under a much bluer triangle of sky. "It's pretty," said Van Os. "Have you thought about what I told you?"

"No," said Paul, "I mean, yes, that is, there isn't anything, absolutely nothing. You can't find anything at the moment."

"That's true, you can't find much. It's rather worrisome. You're not the only one I've asked."

"I can imagine."

"Nobody has anything. Not Dufrein, not Omar, not even Labrouty. You'll tell me to try Chonnebrolles, but there's no way to get hold of Chonnebrolles. No one seems to know where he is. Nothing at Tomaso's either. Do you know Tomaso?"

"I don't think so," Paul gulped. "Nor the others, for that matter. Except Chonnebrolles, of course, but only by reputation."

"It's troublesome," said Van Os. "It's so very troublesome. I'm so in need of materials at the moment. My stuff is too low-caliber, you can't do a thing with it. You're not feeding me a story, at least?"

Paul shook his head.

"It would hurt me if this were all a story," pursued the other, staring at his hands with a hurt look. "I'd take it very badly. We have always had, you and I, a relationship based on trust. It would hurt me very badly. It would be very bad."

Paul was shaking his head in the other direction, perpendicularly, when Toon cried out: one of the hydroplanes had just spilled, its pilot now splashing about under his helmet in the virus-rich water. "Whoa, look out, guy!" escaped from Toon. Van Os smiled with tender pity, jerking his thumb toward his right-hand man.

"A child," he said softly. "So impulsive, so unaware." As Van Os was unfolding his bones, Paul stood up after him. Toon regretfully detached himself from the window.

"Be seeing you," said Van Os. "Call me. Promise you'll call. In any case, I'll stop by again."

They left. Let's see them to their car: "I've had enough of that guy," expresses Toon, "I've had enough of following him, I sure have. That girl from the other day, on the other hand, I haven't seen boo of. And yet he seemed really big on her."

"All right," says Van Os, "continue to follow him. And try to watch the girl as well."

"What the hey!" Toon becomes indignant. "Do you know how much work that means?"

Their vehicle starts up. We'll let them go. We return to Paul, who has closed the door soundlessly after them, put the bottle back in its place in the cupboard; who stands near the cupboard for a moment, still, with nary a thought for the hydroplanes. When the telephone rings again, Paul remains near the cupboard. He listens to it ring—it'll tire itself out. On the contrary: it ups the ante; the sour rings streak the air before Paul finally decides to move. Holding the instrument by two fingers, with its cord trailing behind, Paul answers while walking toward the window. It must be Bob. I knew it was you, Paul is getting ready to say, guess who was just here.

But no, it's Justine, who still doesn't reveal her name; this time Paul recognizes her voice at once. It's unexpected. She wants to meet him, that's very unexpected. She suggests a day, a time, a café. "Yes," says Paul, "I'll be there. Of course. I'll be there, with all my heart."

1 8

INNUMERABLE, astoundingly varied are the rings of tele-phones around the world. You can hear it for yourself without ever leaving home; all you have to do is call a foreign country. Immediately several different dial tones follow in rapid succes-sion. When you telephone overseas, you even hear for an instant the noise of a given ocean, as calm as a beast stuffed with second thoughts. Then it vibrates somewhere in the distance; you hear the reflection of a ring faded by space, pale like the photocopy of a photocopy: it's enough to get an idea, enough to know that, depending on the climate in which it's interrupting something, the telephone rings in different ways, following multiple rhythms. Contrary, for example, to our long green shrillnesses, English instruments proceed by binary series of brief brown buzzings, Finnish ones crackle without nuance in purple, and the Malay-sian variety distills interminable whitish jingles, invertebrate, al-most transparent.

From the other end of the globe, their echo wormed its way into the ear of Pons who, taking advantage of Nicole's absence, was trying to reach the elder of the Aw brothers. The enterprise was risky, given the surveillance exercised over there by Jouvin, and here by Boris—Pons had first made sure the latter was busy in the garden. Two lines relayed the plantation to the world-wide telephone network; as one ended at the Jouvin villa, the Duke had dialed the number of the other, which shivered on the desk of the little accounting office adjoining the factory. It must have been close to midnight. Watching his prostrate spouse out of the corner of his eye, Raymond Jouvin was no doubt verifying the marks he had drawn that very morning on the bottles. Pons hoped to get the night watchman, an excellent Temoq won over to the cause of the Aw brothers and entirely devoted to his person.

After five or six jingles there was an audible connection, followed by a beeping of pointed waves; a silence in brief suspension; then an imposing background noise, Niagaraesque, enfolding an almost inaudible interrogative coming from very far away, as if from the other side of the waterfall. Having recognized the drawling Temoh accent, the Duke shouted several words of identification. He had to shout them several times, but then the night watchman's joy was extreme, voluble. Pons had to shout some more to interrupt him; he covered the receiver with his cupped hand, threw worried glances toward the door and the windows. After that he had to get across the idea that he wished to speak to the elder Aw. "Of course I'll go see," the Temoq finally said. "I'll go see if he's there." From so many thousands of miles away, Pons heard the clank of the receiver thrown down on a desk, then silence filled by that torrential clamor. This was taking more time than planned, and threatened to drag on forever if they had to wake Aw Sam. Carrying the telephone as his nephew had, the Duke walked to the window, inspected the garden: Boris was nowhere to be seen among the shrubs, over which rapid little clouds, playing kickball with the day star, chased somber stains in fast motion.

Meanwhile the night watchman pushed through the openwork

door, then through a mosquito netting stippled with minuscule fly specks, and headed into the reddish night. Two thousand square feet of trampled fallow land separated the accounting office from the peasants' barracks. A solitary tapir bolted, and the watchman recoiled before the sacred animal's passage: everyone knows that contact with its flesh gives you a good dose of leprosy on the spot. Collapsed on their mats, the agricultural laborers were for the most part asleep. Among the insomniac contingent, three made fat steel tops hum; three others, leaning side-by-side against the dormitory wall, smoked while passing around photographs of women endowed with large behinds and very large breasts. Squatting near the window at the rear of the building, a dish of porridge at his feet, Aw Sam reread Lenin's *Report at the Second All-Russia Trade Union Congress* (January 20, 1919), in its Malay translation published by Foreign Languages Press, Peking. He raised his eyes over the rim of his spectacles, lifted them toward the watchman who leaned over, balancing a lantern at the end of his arm. "Duke, Duke Pons," the watchman whispered hoarsely, jerking his thumb over his shoulder, then straightening his pinky to symbolize the telephone. Sam jumped to his corned feet and ran toward the door.

The watchman dawdled a few moments with the top-spinners, then left the barracks, standing awhile on the threshold in the warm air, loving it that everything was so calm. Toads and flying frogs projected their bitter injunctions over by the swamp, supported by a *tutti* of beetle-violins. A stock of mosquitoes bustled about at tree-level, pierced by nightjars in hunting formation, their wide-open beaks haphazardly snatching up large families of suspended insects. On the other side of the courtyard delimited by the low factory, the watchman could see Aw Sam hunched over the telephone, framed yellow against black by the accounting office window.

As the wire at the other end was too short for Pons to carry the phone to the salon door, he had had to leave it a moment to go open, verify the absence of ear or eye at the keyhole. The hall was deserted. He ran back to the writing desk and grabbed the receiver, in which the elder Aw was fretting in a hesitant voice. All this took an inordinate amount of time; Pons began to sweat.

He outlined the situation: everything was going as planned, the weapons would surely be delivered to him soon, later in the week he'd confirm the date of his return. The elder accepted all this with soundless nods. It would be a good idea, the Duke specified, to intensify the men's preparation; everything would happen quickly from now on. They hung up in synchrony.

The hallway was still empty. Back up in his room, Pons vainly sought rest on his bed. He felt excited, strong with an overflow of unsated impulses, pierced with nervous needles that the ambient silence honed sharper. He got up, changed to go out in jerky, disorganized movements that tortured the seams of his clothing. At the foot of the stairs he called Boris, who immediately loomed from an undefined part of everywhere. Pons contemplated him suspiciously.

"I'm going to Paris," he said. "I have to go to Paris. Can you drive me to the station?"

A little later, a train was leaving in fifteen minutes; an hour later, Pons hailed a cab in front of Gare du Nord. This time the driver was a frail man, evidently tormented; his defeated face reflected the ascendancy of unpleasant thoughts on his mind, hateful thoughts on the boiler room of his soul. Silence in the vehicle, which angrily defied the yellow light at the corner of Boulevard Poissonnière. The Duke, feeling increasingly hot under the collar, lowered his window a little—is that all right? Without answering, the driver turned sharply off the Pont de Grenelle onto Quai André-Citroën, then braked violently at the foot of the high-rise with yellow facings. Pons handed him the money cautiously, like a peanut to a gibbon; the other scratched his palm as he took it. Shortly afterward the Duke cooled his heels at Paul's door, rang in vain.

Paul was not there because Justine had agreed to see him, fixing the site of the meeting not far from her home. Naturally very early, Paul walked down Rue du Faubourg-Saint-Antoine between shop windows stuffed with furniture of all styles. He paused briefly at number 53, from where the Bastille statuette no longer seemed to be perched on its column, which at that point the buildings hid completely: it appeared to walk on their roofs, dance on their chimneys, on their zinc, exhibiting in its flight round buttocks beneath spread wings. Everyone knows this; people often stop at number 53.

She had consented to have tea with him in a café on the square. Paul entered; the decor was fantastically impersonal. He sat without removing his coat, watched the walking world on the other side of the window: a distinct minority seemed triumphant or even satisfied; some laughed nervously; others held their foreheads. After having followed Paul from Quai André-Citroën, Toon the invisible had settled behind his habitual daily, in an unoccupied stall at the other end of the establishment. The narrowed eye of the young Belgian subject widened when Justine appeared; Paul had half-risen, hesitating between smiling or not smiling.

Since this was their first actual conversation, it was mainly exploratory: touching on many subjects without probing very far, they conducted a pointillistic tour of the horizon, principally through references—he liked Matisse, she preferred Lermontov, both knew Ahmad Jamal. Killing the fine arts below them, they moved on to geography—abroad, seaside—then to history, including childhood, from the origins to the modern world, with people they knew hardly or not well, and certain ones they had in common. We notice that Paul spoke more. Although without allusion to the far-flown Elizabeth, he gave more of himself, without even daring to ask Justine her name. She listened carefully to his voice: it was a dead ringer for the one on the phone the other day, you really could have mistaken one for the other. Perhaps she had come only to verify this coincidence, since she soon stood up. Toon's eyes reappeared above the headlines. Justine looked at Paul, smiled without holding out her hand. I'll see you again, he suggested, he implored. Alas, she was so busy at the moment, work, the upcoming shows, but they would surely call each other. Soon. She disappeared; he stared into his glass. It was quick.

It had almost been as quick as Duke Pons's ride across Paris at the same time: some fifteen stops separated places Balard from République via Line 8, which is dark purple on the subway maps. Pons's head felt cold again as he returned to the fresh air of Rue du Faubourg-du-Temple; he continually ran his shining hand through his hair, wiped it on his clothing while scaling the commercial street. At the top to the right, he verified the address fished out from the bottom of his pocket, and rang. Hearing nothing, he knocked. Someone opened. Someone looked suspicious.

"I'm Jeff," declared the Duke, "you must be Bob. Paul said he told you about me."

Bob said indeed, remained on his guard. Shortly afterward, his back against the door, he contemplated this new personage circulating around the crowded studio. "It's a little like my place," said Pons, "you can feel that it's lived in. The problem with Paul's is, it's empty. Sure, it's got everything you need, but it seems empty." He toured the images on the walls, weighed several objects. "I've come to hear the latest (may I sit down?), you must know all about it."

Bob confirmed this: within the week Tomaso would supply the stipulated items, which they would store in a safe place—a private parking garage at Place Beauvau—before transporting them to Le Havre as soon as the ship arrived; then they would see what was what. "When's the boat due in?"

"On the twentieth," answered Pons. "Should be in around the twentieth."

This was to overestimate the abilities of the MS *Boustrophedon*, which was presently stalled in the middle of the Arabian Sea, some six hundred miles south of the Gulf of Oman. They had just crossed the Tropic of Cancer, but were sweating too much to register this passage. The vessel was showing signs of fatigue. Three days earlier a leak had sprung in the engine room, followed last night by the beginning of a fire resulting from a breakdown of the oil-cooling system. Almost immediately it had extinguished itself; the watertight compartment had played its protective role, and neither water nor fire had been able to spread to the hold, crammed with eminently fusible and combustible materials. The repairs would take a little time, and they had already lost enough of that the day before yesterday, making temporary repairs to the first damages. Via the Yemenite station, the captain had dispatched a cable to Le Havre, where the port authority had duly noted the expected delay.

While Lopez the helmsman, assisted by sailor Gomez, busied himself with the oil-cooling system, Illinois updated the ship's log in his quarters located above the engines. These quarters were limited to one room, at once wardroom, salon, and sleeping quarters. It was hot on the edge of the tenth parallel, and the skipper diluted his sentences; in the circle of the porthole, a slice of empty sky-blue weighed on a slice of deserted navy-blue. As the motors were still, the clanks of tools pierced the silence, rising from the engine room, seasoned with Cartagenan curses. The captain closed the log and stretched out on the brown canvas-covered settee, bordered by a bookcase whose shelves contained the ship's library: fewer adventure stories than professional works, such as the bound collection of *Ships, Ports and Shipyards* magazine. Opening one of these volumes haphazardly, Illinois tried to rally his attention to an article entitled "The Mechanics of Breakage as Applied to Metal Fatigue"; then he laid the open tome over his eyes and tried to rest like the three other crewmen, temporarily off-duty, stretched out on their tiered bunks at the other end of the vessel. That was how things stood. Day drew to a close.

"Would you care for some ice?" asked Bob when night had fallen.

"Let's not be so formal," Pons protested, "we don't have to be so formal. So, don't you think it's a little empty at Paul's? It's too neat, you don't know where to sit. Does he ever see any girls?"

"Some ice?" Bob repeated, pouring.

"No," said Pons, "but you should tell me. I'm sure he doesn't even go out. That boy seems sad, he wasn't like that before—when, when, that's enough," he said, pulling his glass back too abruptly. "Shit. No, leave it, it doesn't stain, it'll dry all by itself. So, what's he so sad about?"

Bob conjured up the memory of Elizabeth, then the departure of Elizabeth. "Ah, I didn't know," Pons commiserated. "Poor kid. All alone." Bob reassured the emotive uncle: Paul certainly went out with girls, he went out with several girls, he went out with them often. "Careful," warned the Duke, "too many isn't good either." Another glass and they got down to confidences—heavy ground in which the Duke became mired, his tongue bucking like an old clutch. Ideas, then the absence of ideas; recollections and memory gaps jostled against each other; anecdotes cancelled by laughter concluded in snickers that dragged on too long after the punch line, as if by preignition. Then Pons suddenly nodded off, with clearings of the trachea that sounded like the breakdown of a connecting rod. Bob tucked him a little deeper into the armchair, threw a blanket over him, and went out, leaving a single lamp lit.

He had still not come home when Pons opened his eyes the next morning. After a great effort to identify his surroundings, he found himself alone again, with no prospects other than Chantilly. At Gare du Nord, squadrons of Parisians working in the suburbs crossed their opposite numbers in a muffled milling of rubber, crepe, and leather, under the polyphony of fresh perfume, fresh sweat, fresh toothpaste and tobacco, in which a few early notes of calvados dissonated. From Chantilly station, a taxi took the Duke to the villa.

"Jeff," Nicole's voice nabbed him as he was discreetly crossing the foyer toward his room; his nickname cut harshly through the air. He awkwardly entered the green salon. Nicole was seated behind her desk, bills before her eyes, pen in hand; the stems of her glasses, joined by a chain, were buried in her rolled mohair collar.

"You made a phone call," she said without transition.

"What," went the Duke. "Oh, yeah, I know what you mean, I had to make two or three little calls. Why?"

She didn't answer. The Duke thought it best to elaborate.

"Two to Paris, I think, but one guy wasn't there. And then another guy I knew back when. College, you know, hardly somebody I met yesterday. He's living in the Mayenne now, near Evron."

"You called *there*."

"I don't know what you mean. Oh, yeah, I know what you mean," Pons repeated. "No, not at all."

"They don't speak Chinese," she said, "in the Mayenne. You were speaking Chinese. You called over there."

Not Chinese, the Duke refrained from pointing out. Malay. And the best Malay. The State of Johore, where the plantation was located, was known as the region where they spoke the purest dialect, the freest from regional accents, from non-native influences. It's a bit like the Touraine for a Frenchman, or the Midwest for Americans.

"Oh, all right," he admitted, "it was an emergency. I had to call, really, what's the harm? Five or six minutes, of course I'll pay you back."

"Not five minutes," Nicole distempered coldly, "and you know it. Boris kept strict count by his watch."

"That sonofabitch Boris," muttered the Duke.

II

19

CHARLES HAD already been in Le Havre for two weeks, but the city did not displease him. He had settled not far from the freight yard, in a shack where the railway men stored worn materials—rusted or burnt-out signals, lights. Several years earlier, one of them had nailed up a block calendar embellished with an ad for a brand of girdle; it stopped being current on March 11th. Charles had fitted out a corner in which to sleep, sometimes in which to eat in the evening, heating a can over a low flame.

He spent his days on the port. He watched the sea and ships, the freighters. Few men in his condition were to be found there; most of them spent the winter in Paris, waiting for the return of warm weather before invading the seashores. They were usually chased off by the longshoremen, but Charles helped once or twice with the maneuvers and they let him wander the docks of the merchant port. Sometimes crates fell, breaking apart; sometimes they were badly resealed after inspection; Charles then helped himself moderately, consuming the bananas on the spot and keeping the canned goods for later on.

He began to miss the company of women five days after his arrival, but he didn't know anyone in Le Havre. Still, late one afternoon he saw someone sitting on a bench on Rue Lord-Kitchener, a bag of groceries beside her. Hair in a bun, without makeup, she was not very pretty at first glance, all the more so since she was breathing too heavily, a hand on her chest. She must have been a bit younger than Charles, who stopped in front of her. Are you all right?

She seemed surprised, gave him a quick little smile, almost like an apology. She pointed to the shopping bag, then her chest. "I'll help you," said Charles.

"No," she went hurriedly.

"Have no fear," said Charles, "I don't expect anything in return." She shook her head no again, but with a slightly inquisitive air. "Then I'll be going," said Charles. "My apologies."

"Wait," she puffed, "I'd like that very much, but wait a minute."

He sat on the other end of the bench, separated from her by the shopping bag. She seemed to be breathing more easily; he asked if she was ill. "It comes over me from time to time," said the woman. "Are you from around here?"

"No," said Charles.

"I think we can go now," she said. Charles picked up the bag.

She lived farther away than he would have thought. On the way, in the dusk, she pointed out the courthouse, the sub-prefecture, city hall, the prison, the birthplace of Frédérick Lemaître. On blue signs Charles read the names of the streets they crossed. She stopped before the chalk-white entrance of a building intended for the working classes; many people entered and exited this building, many children played in front of it in faded pajamas under bathrobes grown too small for their siblings.

"Here we are," she said. "Thank you."

"The pleasure has been all mine," declared Charles. "Goodbye."

As he was turning somewhat slowly, she caught his sleeve.

"You'd like something to drink," she imagined. "Would you care for something to eat?"

"Do I seem hungry?" Charles worried.

"I can make you dinner" (she pointed to the bag).

"It would cause trouble at home," he stated. "Surely you don't live alone."

"No," she refuted respectively, "yes."

The two rooms of her apartment communicated with each other, there being no hallway. In one of them, a green shower curtain hid the corner opposite the kitchenette. The other one was furnished with a bed for one-and-a-half persons with a tobacco-colored bedspread and an armchair upholstered in garnet nylon, facing a television whose wire aerial formed a frame with the photo of a small boy inside it. A reproduction of Vlaminck and another of Modigliani broke the continuum of the wallpaper, with three photos of Rudolf Nureyev mounted on black railroad board and tacked above the bed in ascending order.

"It won't be anything fancy," said the woman, "I'll just make what I was going to for myself. I think there's some wine left. Wouldn't you like to watch TV while you wait? Wouldn't you like to have a drink?"

"I'd love to," said Charles, "I'd love to."

He sat in the armchair and followed the local news programs, then the mass entertainments, while she cooked things in the corner. He got up, offered his help when she set the extendable table, substituting a tablecloth for the felt ironing pad. She disappeared for a moment behind the green curtain, returned softened by a bit of makeup foundation, light-colored streaks on her lips and eyelids; she had loosened her hair without unknotting it. Charles saw her rearrange around the stove objects that (he was touched to notice) didn't require rearrangement. She no longer looked at him; she kept a certain humility in her smile.

They had eaten, then quickly gone to bed; Charles left early the next morning, promising to come back and see Monique. He did in fact return four times, bringing a can, a very ripe pineapple picked up at market's closing, or some flowers borrowed from the bunches at the general hospital. These haunts had become habits, formed in less than ten days, as was the inspection of the northern entrance to Le Havre, toward Bléville, where the garbage dumps occasionally yielded interesting souvenirs. Once while he was burrowing in this zone, to one side of Highway 147, a Ford Transit driving too close to the shoulder nearly ran him over. Charles hastily jumped into the ditch, and softly swore after the blue station wagon as it headed off toward the center of town, still keeping to its exaggerated right.

It was just that Paul had not yet gotten used to the vehicle's dimensions, nor quite mastered its controls. The poorly lubricated clutch was abnormally stiff, like trying to push in a fat nail with one's foot. He drove slowly, frequently changing program and volume on the Japanese tape player sitting next to him on the passenger seat. A little farther away, his overnight bag held some spare clothes and a novel by Mike Roscoe. Five metal trunks vibrating in the rear of the station wagon contained, wrapped in greasy cloth, the assortment recommended by Tomaso: to wit, eight rifles (six Herstals and two Armalites); an equal number of handguns named Viper, Python, and Cobra; and several hundred assorted shells, among which the 7.62-mm Soviet "short" predominated.

In homogeneous Le Havre, the buildings overlapped like long, dirty sugar cubes. Everything seemed to have sprung simultaneously from the ground circa 1955, fully furnished. It was clearly marked how to reach the port, but the *Boustrophedon* was not docked as planned in Théophile-Ducrocq Basin, Pier 2. Paul reviewed the other ships, a *Demosthenes*, a ragged *Star*, an attentively scrubbed *Suzy Delair*. From the deck of an indecipherable

Russian freighter, two blond-and-white sailors puffed meticulously on their English cigarettes while following Paul with their eyes. In a windowed office of the port authority, a man in shirtsleeves informed him of the four-to-six-days' delay that the Cypriot vessel would no doubt incur. He indicated the dock on which its freight was already waiting; Paul discreetly ascertained that customs would not take an interest in it until loading. The man in shirtsleeves delivered a voucher.

Thanks to the voucher, Paul could have access to the docks; he first set about finding a place to unload his trunks without attracting too much attention. He distributed them among other, rather similar trunks containing capacitors, machines labeled capacitors. This was only to be a provisional shelter while awaiting the boat's arrival. He would have to see later with the captain about the best way to shield the trunks from customs inspection; Pons had assured him that Illinois had no equal in this domain. Paul returned to the Ford, behind whose wheel he spent almost an hour searching for the center of town; but perhaps there wasn't one, or maybe there were several small ones. Back near the port, he reserved Room 24 of the very high-ceilinged Diamond Hotel, from where he immediately phoned Bob.

As Bob was not at home, Paul left the hotel number on his answering machine, just FYI. He went out again to return the Ford to the Le Havre branch of Hertz, swapping it for a black 104 coupe. At dusk, following the sea away from the port, he discovered a little stretch of broken glass and pebbles coated with petroleum, on which he could walk alone awhile by the water. Old shards, worn down by the movement of the ocean, shone like rounded caramels, like emeralds; Paul gathered them up and looked at them, put them in his mouth, in his pocket, sucked the salt from his fingers. At around eight o'clock he dined on beer and eggs in a brasserie, then returned to his hotel; Bob was still not at home. Paul soon slipped between the stiff, scratchy, chalky sheets, which were almost thicker than the quilt. A map of the city unfolded on his lap, Mike Roscoe within reach, he smoked several Senior Services while watching the extraordinarily distant ceiling, as if he were seeing a square of sky from the bottom of a well, starred with paint flakes, and under which, like a dropped anchor, hung the dry grapnel of a chandelier at the end of a chain measure. He fell asleep earlier than usual, the map of Le Havre spread over him like an extra blanket.

He heard it raining before he opened his eyes; recognized it at once as one of those long-lasting rains; finished off Mike Roscoe before getting up. After breakfast, running between the drops toward a newsstand near the hotel, he procured other books whose cheap paper immediately soaked up the water from the sky. Back in his room, the telephone rang: Bob. Paul explained the freighter's delay, his stay in town for four to six days at least.

"You'd be better off waiting in Paris," advised Bob. "Come on back. You'll go nuts."

"No," said Paul, "I'll stay. I don't do anything in Paris anyway, I don't feel comfortable there. That girl from the movies, you know." (I know, said Bob.) "I blew it, I'm sure I blew it. I might as well stay here. I'll call you later."

So he started reading, seldom left his room. Having convinced the reception desk to send up warm meals at the appropriate times, he could sleep at whim. Day or night, the rain did not make the same sound on the other side of the drawn curtains.

20

"THAT MAKES three days we haven't seen him," Toon noted, rummaging. "I wonder what the heck's he up to? Look out!" he cried.

Coming from La Ferté-sous-Jouarre, the brick-red 4 × 4 raced toward Château-Thierry. Toon had welded himself to his seat when they just missed a trailer-truck passing in the opposite direction. Constantly turning the dial on his short-wave, information from which might cause him to modify his itinerary, Van Os peered at the rearview mirror as much as through the windshield of the speeding vehicle.

"We should have taken the highway, don't you think?" Toon lamented, loosening the grip on his seat.

He went back to rummaging in the large glove compartment, pulled out a metal box whose lid was barred with a masking-tape cross.

"That's right," said Van Os, "and at the exit you run into the motorcycle cops. No, the highway is for suckers, I've told you a hundred times."

"Yeah," Toon said, preparing the bandage. Folding down the visor, he studied himself in the vanity mirror then, with a grimace, applied the Band-Aid to his skinned left brow. He studied himself anew, making several faces.

"You'd do better to count."

Toon grabbed the canvas bag sitting on the back seat, hefted it over the back of his own, and plunged his nose into it as if to inhale.

"It's a lot," he described. "This could take a while."

"All right," said Van Os, "we'll see at the house. What would you say, at a glance?"

"Two three hundred thou, but I wouldn't swear to it."

"All right," said Van Os.

They said nothing more until Château-Thierry, birthplace of a twisted road that bordered the Bois de Barbillon. Van Os lowered the radio, reduced his speed.

"He was an asshole, that cashier," Toon resumed while massaging his left shoulder. "He really gave me a good one."

"You gave him a good one too," Van Os reminded him.

"Of course, he got off easy," the young man observed, pulling a small pistol from his armpit. "Lucky for him I only had this small pistol. You really make do with what you've got."

"Since we can't find anything better," said Van Os. "And put that thing away."

Toon put that thing away and rummaged at the bottom of the bag under the sedimented franc notes, looking for a green rubber mask bristling with trembling pseudopods, which he then slapped over his face while emitting a buzzing noise.

"Take that off, you idiot," hissed Van Os. Giggling, Toon removed the mask, that was a gas, huh?

Their hide-out for the days to come was a small, very isolated, very subsidiary abandoned station on the edge of the woods, scarcely larger than a garret and flanked by a sheet-metal garage where they stashed the car. They entered the dark house, closing the door behind them, taking care not to open the shutters; Toon groped a bit before finding the panel box. Then he emptied the bag onto a large, very heavy, very cumbersome oak table, garnished with numerous mouldings and numerous drawers with bronze handles, which took up almost half the single room that constituted the ground floor. Spread over a wide expanse, the volume of bills was disappointing. Van Os, wearing a grumpy rictus, began stalking around the room while Toon started counting.

"It's freezing in here," noted Van Os, "and what's more, it stinks of mildew. Isn't there any heating?"

"Just the fireplace. We could make a fire if you like. There's wood in the garage."

"That's right," said Van Os, "and what about the smoke? Someone sees the smoke and you've got the cops in five minutes flat. It really is freezing in here," he repeated, rubbing his hands together. "Plankaert should have thought ahead. A little electric thing, I don't know, a little oil heater. You know the kind I mean?"

Toon arranged the wads of bills in three parallel rows. Van Os approached the booty, which he sized up, stopping the rubbing of his hands—not even a hundred and fifty thousand francs, you'll see. A minuscule television sat on the ground, which he turned on without raising the volume: the picture was rather fuzzy, streaked, ill-contrasted; cathodic phantoms of both sexes opened hazy fish mouths in a muddy aquarium.

"I was hoping for better," said Van Os. "And what about Bergman? Don't you see he's left us holding the baby? What do you *think* he's done?"

"We've already discussed it," said Toon. "And besides I'm counting here. I can't do everything at the same time, can I?"

"Of course not," snickered Van Os, glancing at his watch. "How about the other one, Bob, who's always trailing along?"

"He hasn't moved, he's staying put."

"And the girl?"

"I know who the girl is now, I know where she lives. It might come in handy, in case."

Van Os turned up the volume as the credits for a local news show paraded by: a brand-new report was devoted to a canvas bag from a bank in La Ferté-sous-Jouarre. The two men followed it with keen interest. First an ample camera motion presented a frame in which the forces of order bustled about, and out of which sped an ambulance containing the teller. "That asshole teller," recalled Toon. Then a witness, close-up, thought he might have to go at describing the assailants: two heavy-set blond men, one heavier-set than the other and afflicted with a southwestern accent, or something. "That guy's an asshole too," grated Toon. As the broadcast ended on aerial shots of Cergy-Pontoise, Toon finished his accounting. "One hundred thirty-eight," he said, "you were right. Which makes three times forty-six." On the table were three equal volumes of liquid assets; Toon pushed two of them toward the annoyed Van Os, then went to the television.

"Leave it, don't touch. In case we're also on at eight."

"Right," said Toon, "and besides there are some good comedy shows on now."

"Never mind the comedy shows, you imbecile!" Van Os suddenly cried. "Count again to make sure instead. And tomorrow you're going to handle this Bergman business a little better, you understand? Start with that girl first. Try to get something out of her. Tomorrow. I told you to count again."

That girl, however, was in her old room, on the third floor of her mother's house in Chantilly. She was cutting pictures out of fashion magazines, things that might give her ideas.

Jeff, at lunch, had announced his departure in dull tones, with confidential eyes. As Justine was amused by these conspiratorial mimics, he feigned to have feigned them, exaggerating them until she smiled less. Someone, he said, was coming to pick him up late in the afternoon. He had gotten up immediately after dessert to go pack his bags in his room. Nicole had followed to give him a hand. Justine in turn had gone to her room. They'd been packing that suitcase for three hours now. She cut her photos into smaller and smaller pieces.

Two short knocks sounded on the large door, downstairs. Justine heard Boris's hesitant soles clack on the tiles of the foyer, then the door shut after an indistinct exchange. Shortly afterward, Boris came up to announce in a reproving voice the unexpected arrival of a young individual who was asking for the Duke.

"You should be telling *him*," said Justine.

"I tried," said the indentured servant. "There was no answer. I didn't dare insist."

Bob stood stiff, square in the middle of a black tile in the foyer, his eyes raised toward Justine, who had just appeared in the upper reaches of the stairway. Ravishing, she slowly descended the steps toward him, for him alone. Then she led him into the green salon; Bob was frightfully intimidated. He contemplated his surroundings from the unstable edge of a rocking chair, not wanting to appear as if he were staring at her. On the walls, the works of art spoke eloquently of their authors' torments in the 1950s, careful to give a monied clientele some idea of what was going on in modernism these days—a well-dressed bastard of impressionism and abstraction—all the while reassuring it by a just barely recognizable representation of noble realities, such as equinoctial storms seen from the Grand Hotel in Cabourg, the Pont des Arts at tea-time, the Baie des Anges at Cinzano-time. Under glass between the two windows were arranged several fans, sulfides and snuffboxes; precious animalcules watched over by apocryphal ancestors.

Justine offered Bob a drink. Stuttering thanks, Bob was on the verge of finding something else to say when Pons joined them in the salon. His eyes shone with youth and fever; he seemed light, tired but refreshed, as a certain distraction made manifest.

"I am excessively happy to see you, Bob," he assured, restoring with a jocular finger the alignment of the mouldings with the Pont des Arts. "So you two have met. You've seen this stunning creature."

Decidedly at ease, he approached Justine, not without a certain menacing forwardness; she moved away by as much, smiling with exquisite indulgence; embarrassed, Bob examined the contents of his glass. "Off we go," said the Duke. "I'm set, so we're all set." They moved to the foyer. Nicole appeared all recoiffed, followed by Boris who brought down the ducal baggage, carrying it like a sack of refuse with the tips of his fingers, gripping the ramp with his other fingers. They went out; Bob opened the trunk so the Duke could deposit therein the object of Boris's repulsion. Circling around the vehicle, Baby Love checked the tire pressure by peeing. Then the Duke, having taken advantage of the fallen night to knead Nicole furiously one last time, climbed into the vehicle under the relieved gaze of the domestic workhand.

Mother and daughter saw him ride away, disappear. Inside the car, Duke Pons was already combing the radio for some music befitting his light mood, commenting excessively on any melody he came across, eventually settling for some harpsichord pieces by Scarlatti, rather irritating for the nerves. "Okay," he said, "so how do we go about it, finally?"

Bob explained: out of caution, given the harassment by the Belgian gang in particular, they had agreed to work separately. Paul would handle conveying the weapons up to Port Said, where the *Boustrophedon* was scheduled to call. Bob and Pons would join him there by plane in a few days. "In the meantime," said

Bob, "you can stay with me. We'll make do." The Duke liked this plan: Chantilly was getting a bit heavy, he admitted; Nicole was nice but, you know. The little one was sweet, but there was that Russian, not friendly at all; the Duke had felt his hostility from the outset.

So it could be worse—would there perhaps be a little pick-me-up to celebrate with? Bob pointed to the glove compartment: stiff with grease, a single glove sheltered a whole family of tattered road maps, a crumpled community of traffic tickets in green uniform, a couple of rags, a pair of dark glasses, an old tribe of Mobil bonus coupons, an idle gang of loose bits-and-pieces with no future, and a flask dressed in leather and filled with Jameson whiskey. "You're an angel," said the Duke, unscrewing the chrome cap. He drank, then caught his breath; wedged the flat bottle between his knees; emitted a snicker, then another, and then still another, taking his time. There was no sound other than that of the motor, punctuated by those snickers for private use, spiced by the harpsichord that buzzed like the insects suspended outside in the black air, caught by phototropism in the conical beams of the headlights, splattered on the windshield in transparent starbursts.

2 1

———————

THE RAIN stopped on Sunday morning, then the clouds dissipated, eviscerated by a fresh sun that brightened everything beneath it. Paul walked along the piers; the flanks of the docked vessels threw up high walls on both sides, as if he were following the tail of a parade. He finally noticed, at the end of the wharf, the algal prow of the *Boustrophedon*. The spinach on the hull peeled in sheets and the dirty banner hung, flaccid, on the ship's stern. Perched on the smokestack, the color of old lemon with black stripes, a transitory seagull stood.

There was no one to be seen on the deck bristling with derricks, except, at the rear, for a sailor seen from behind, held by a series of blocks against the bulkhead of the sterncastle, who was busy whitewashing its two upper levels. He suspended the movement of his brush, half turning toward Paul who had stopped below him.

"You the insurance man?"

He was thickset; his bare scalp was ringed with short blond fuzz; his austere, pitiless glance made you think of certain Foreign Legion chaplains.

"No," said Paul, "it's about a shipment."

"Port office," said the sailor. "Got to see them for that."

"I've seen them," said Paul. "Now I'm looking for the captain."

"Ain't here."

"But I have to see him," Paul insisted. "It's already been arranged."

"But since he ain't here," concluded the sailor, turning back to his work.

He resumed brushing a crosspiece. Paul verified, sighing, that no one else appeared to be on board. A pause: no doubt judging that the whole business had gotten off on the wrong foot, the seagull detached itself from the smokestack to go describe a wide arc over the port waters, opaque as mucus. Paul followed it with his glance, then returned to the painter:

"Isn't there anyone else? I really have to see somebody. Isn't there a second-in-command, something like that?"

The other didn't answer. The seagull finished its tour of the harbor on the jib of a blue crane that was loading bauxite onto a Baltic boat heading for Lake Ladoga, among the cries and bellowings of sirens and petrels. "Hey," Paul reminded him, "I'm talking to you." Without turning around, the painter sighed then called out a name, brutally. Paul did not really catch the name, which had been barked somewhat like a brief curse sanctioning some slip of the brush. Immediately the bearer of this name appeared at the freighter's opposite extremity. Paul discovered him as if he had already been there for a while, in imitation of the derricks; a discreet navy-blue subject who didn't seem to be answering a call, who leafed for all eternity through some yellow papers in the shade of his visor. He followed the guardrail in Paul's direction, neither hurrying nor seeming to have noticed him.

"I'm looking for the captain," Paul called out. "Is that you?"

The blue subject raised his eyes from his papers, as if to reflect on his reading, on that question, gradually focusing on the man who had asked it.

"Pons sent me," said Paul. "Mister Pons. He's a friend of the captain's. I'm a friend of Mister Pons's. Mean anything to you?"

"I can't know them all," said the blue man, who seemed to be freezing. "And what's it about?"

"A shipment," said Paul, using gestures to help him, "and then me. I'm going with the shipment."

"You know, we don't take passengers," the man shivered. "You know that, don't you?"

"It's already been arranged," repeated Paul. "It's all set."

The other shook his yellow papers. "If it's been arranged, it must be written down. If you say so, maybe it's been written down." (He consulted them.) "Not here. I'll have to check up above. Come, come with me, we'll go see above."

Paul crossed the gangway, and the other touched his cap: First Mate Garlonne, merchant navy. Bergman, explorer. Paul followed him between the cabins, then up the narrow iron companionway leading to the pilot house. "Naturally," said the mate, "they don't always tell me everything, I'm only the first mate, but still, even so—did you say Bernstein?"

"Bergman," said Paul.

"Let's see what we see," said Garlonne. He disappeared inside the pilot house. "Ah, right," his voice sounded offstage, "Bergman." He reappeared: "It's written down, you're right. Come in. So rare for us to take passengers, you know. Even those who ask we try to discourage, not very comfortable and besides the boredom, you know, the boredom at sea. You can imagine."

"I can imagine," said Paul.

"As for passengers, we can't legally take on more than twelve in any case. After twelve we become a passenger vessel, which changes everything, you can imagine that too. Where did you say your merchandise was?"

Paul repeated the number of the pier assigned to the ship's freight; his merchandise was already stored there with the rest.

"But it's just that . . . it's a bit special," he said, "it's a special case."

"I'll check with the captain," said the first mate. "Special cases are his domain." Another thing: it would be better to pay up front. Generally used by its owners to ship rubber, and secondarily palm oil and tin, toward the Occident, the *Boustrophedon* was always in need of a load for its return orientation, to avoid the lost revenues of coming back empty. But stiff was the competition, chancy the market; they had seen iron-clad arrangements fall through, contracts not be honored—better to obtain a commitment at the outset. "Cash would be preferred," Garlonne notified Paul, as the latter was reaching for his checkbook.

"Right," said Paul. "I'll go to the bank, be back this afternoon. Will the captain be here then?"

"We rarely see him before casting off. We're loading tomorrow morning in any case, as soon as Lopez has finished painting. We were late coming in, can't stay around. Just a short layover, you see? The guys are swearing like—you know."

He seemed animated by Paul's novelty, the happy excuse for a conversation that was not so easy to hold with Lopez. He showed Paul the pilot house, introduced the navigational aids: the precision of the autopilot, the range of the sonar. He moved with short steps from one machine to the next, in the made-to-measure uniform that he wore with the neatness of a steward. Then they descended the decks of the sterncastle, followed the guardrail toward the prow. Someone had completely removed the wooden hatch planks, and the holds, emptied of their rubber, gaped toward the open sky. Only a half-dozen heavy Chinese bicycles were to be found there, in a cluster, lacquered in black with gold threads like old typewriters or sewing machines; their addressee never having come to claim them, Garlonne explained, they found their vocation in ports of call.

Paul followed the first mate up to the forecastle where his cabin was located, along with the sailors' quarters, symmetrical to the captain's quarters located at the base of the sterncastle. Garlonne invited Paul in; the latter didn't want to impose, but nonetheless found himself with a glass of Banyuls in hand, while the other made him look at photographs of his daughter. Boarder in a Protestant institution in the Gard, she was all he had left. Mrs. Garlonne, bereft of the patience required of sailors' wives, had abandoned them eight years earlier for the owner of a large farming concern, thereby demonstrating in no uncertain terms that she had chosen her camp.

"Which hotel are you staying at?" asked this fellow desertee, this phantom brother. "So we can reach you, in case."

Slightly spinning from the fortified wine, from the freighter's rocking as it hiccuped at the end of its moorings, Paul found himself back on the dock, which was still deserted with the exception of a small, dark silhouette sitting way at the end. The banging of heavy objects, moved with great effort, rose from deep within the vessels' bellies. On the decks, calm interjections, braided into noises of metal, of sacks dragged and cables stretched, sounded too clearly in the iodine of the air. At the end of the dock, the man sitting on a crate was not much less imprecise from up close than he was as a silhouette: a vacant look, an unpolished morphology under his dark hobo's clothing. Paul paid him little mind. His short sojourn on board made him feel as if he had already left, almost as if he'd been kidnapped.

When he returned that afternoon with the money, the wandering man was sitting in the same place, on a slightly different crate, contemplating the loading operations from afar. No reason for them to identify each other. Lopez was now repainting the sterncastle's upper level. Using the wet coat retrovisually, he did not turn around when Paul came aboard under the aerial ballet of the derricks. Three crewmen, following the first mate's directives, received containers that they set down in the same order.

"We won't finish before late tonight," said Garlonne, not counting. "And even then."

At the very center of the hold, soon covered by other trunks, Paul spotted those he had escorted. They seemed neither more nor less inconspicuous than the rest, which worried him. "It's all taken care of," said the first mate. "The captain saw to it with Bloch." He let the matter go at that, too absorbed in his labors. Of the three men busy passing each other containers below them, two glanced at Paul once or twice: an African who seemed to have hip problems, and a young and handsome indifferent brunet. The third, named Sapir, acted as bos'n, an intermediary between Garlonne and the two others. He possessed a large, shovel-shaped head, topped with a bush of steel wool, and touched his nose in idle moments. This one threw no glances Paul's way.

On the sea Sapir held the position of engineer, and the African, who answered to the name of Darousset, held that of ablebodied seaman. The indifferent brunet was just a simple all-purpose sailor named Gomez, native of the same village as Lopez, not far from Cartagena. The captain had recently recruited Gomez on the recommendation of Lopez, who for a long time had joined his talents as a painter to those of helmsman on board the *Boustrophedon*. The indifference that floated in Gomez was no doubt akin to that of Lopez, albeit noticeably more Japanese in character, Gomez being able to smile whereas his compatriot could not. Sapir did not smile either, nor did Darousset, too concerned with his hip; that crew emitted no particular welcoming fervor. As for the captain, Paul had it confirmed that it was his custom to rejoin the ship at the last possible moment, still scheduled for early the next morning. Nonetheless Garlonne insisted that Paul remain at the hotel until then, ready for any eventuality.

Idle, Paul thus found himself stretched out on his bed, in his room at the Diamond Hotel. Someone in an adjacent room was typing—sometimes legato, a tetanus of castanettes, sometimes discontinuously staccato, reproducing involuntarily the scansions of slogans, brief refrains, catch-tunes, rhythmical reference points ancestrally acquired, almost as deeply embedded as things innate. From another contiguous room, a radio's primitive rock 'n' roll also made its way through the walls, whose paper retained the treble, filtering bass drums that were occasionally synchronous with the typing. The open window still brought the high and low frequencies of gulls and sirens, the fallen night purifying the sounds, accentuating their contours, their phosphorescence. In the shadows, Paul dialed Justine's number.

"She's not here," said Laure, "can she call you back? Oh, dear. Would you like to leave a message? All right. I'll just tell her you called. All right, I won't tell her." (She hung up.) "You were right, it was him. Have you got the car keys? Let's go."

2 2

An hour later, accompanied by bit players of both sexes, Laure and Justine were squeezed around a small table among other small tables in an opaque parallelipiped, smoke blue pocked with cigarette-ash red. A bar stood on one side, facing a minuscule stage on which a quintet performed. The conglomerated instruments threw back the lights, adding their own metallic, plastic, lacquered reflections, which sparked little golden flashes on the false teeth of the audience. At the bar three solitary men stood facing their beers, caught from behind by the music, along with Toon and Plankaert, the latter not so small as the former, each one beneath his hat.

"So," asked Toon, "you feeling better?"

By an illusion similar to the one that makes two identical segments, pinnated in opposite directions, appear of unequal length, their difference in height was aggravated by these hats: Plankaert's actually lengthened him, like an extra floor; whereas Toon seemed crushed under his, whose brim he pulled down. Plankaert had a rather conventional, placid look. His subsidiary hat aside, he was dressed, let's say, like the founding father of a mom-and-pop driving school; he had the patient look of a driving-school instructor. He seemed interested in the music.

"Much better," he answered without looking at Toon. "Although I hope I didn't catch another cold the other day, when I went to find you the house."

The musicians embroidered on a melody from Cape Verde. Out of time with the music, Plankaert crushed under the toe of his shoe the filtered ends littering the tiles. Greeting with his eyebrow a particularly well-placed syncopation, he gave the rapid soloists his full attention, as if at the wheel of a race car on a narrow mountain pass full of twists, rich in ravines.

"You like this, huh?" Toon said in a resigned voice.

"It's an era," said Plankaert, "it's an esthetic. Do you think they're going to stay to the end?"

Justine and Laure stayed until after the quintet had toured Cape Verde, then celebrated "Laura" at an unusually feverish tempo. Fidgety Toon showed impatience, hopped from one foot to the other, complained about his legs. "Let's have another round," suggested Plankaert, "it'll help pass the time." The bartender deposited two beers before them. Plankaert paid immediately out of professional habit.

"You're sure she's with Bergman," he worried. "If she's not with him, it's no use our being here."

"I didn't say she's *with* Bergman," Toon reminded him, "I said that Bergman's chasing after her. If we chase after her too, we'll end up crossing paths, anyway you get what I mean. That's what I said. Seems like they're finishing up, no?"

They finished up; the artists were called back for an encore, which they concluded by executing "Work," then they really had finished up. A hubbub rumpled the room. Justine and Laure passed each other their handbags as they stood; two male bit players were immediately standing to pull back their chairs. One of them, a more intelligent bit player, recited his inaudible lines to Justine, who smiled. "You'll see, she's going to leave with that one," said Plankaert.

"No," said Toon, "you'll see, she won't."

"This car really handles well," Plankaert later said behind the wheel of the 4 × 4, which he drove prudently, maintaining 100 yards of empty space behind Justine's.

"How come you get to drive it?" asked Toon. "He never lets *me*."

Plankaert chose not to answer. A pause.

One behind the other, the two vehicles headed down Rue du Faubourg-Saint-Denis toward the tunnel that leads to Châtelet; from there, to Bastille. Toon emitted a noise like an old door:

"Look, the girls are going home, it was all for nothing. Neither Bergman nor the— At least you liked the music. What do we do now? How about Bergman's pal, there, that guy Bob? How about we go see him?"

Plankaert had no objections to going to see the pal Bob, even though it was long past midnight—on the contrary, it would put the pal Bob in a more receptive frame of mind. And Bob in fact experienced a certain discomfort when he found Toon at his door at this hour, draped in his overcoat, displaying a choice expression.

"Good evening," said Toon. "We want to see Bergman. We're looking for him."

"But he isn't here," said Bob. "Hey, Plankaert, it's been a long time."

"I've been kind of tired," said Plankaert. "You haven't seen Bergman, have you?"

"He's not here," Bob repeated.

"No matter," Toon decided. "We'll come in for a moment."

Plankaert remained near the door, which Bob did not immediately shut. Odiously casual, Toon was already inspecting the studio, leafing through papers, tipping over a bottle, shoving aside the hangers in the closet. He didn't even glance at Duke Pons in his armchair, who watched him with indecision, caught all slumped in front of a television movie in which a miscast Burt Reynolds played a down-and-out lawyer.

"So," went Toon as if to himself. "Where could Bergman be if he's not here?"

"Go check *his* place," said Bob. "How should I know? You're getting to be a real pain in the ass, you know that? I don't know if you realize."

"What kind of a hockey puck do you take me for?" said Toon, "He's not home. Tell me where he is."

"I really think you're . . . " Bob hesitated. "I can't find the right word."

"It'll come back to you," said Toon. "Keep in mind that I've got my pistol."

Happy to be left out of the conversation, totally absorbed in his movie, Pons endeavored not to see the Belgians at all, as if they didn't exist, thereby hoping not to exist in their eyes either. "You're lying," he heard Toon exclaim. "I've got to punish such lies." Pons tried to merge completely into Burt Reynolds, who had been forced by life's ironies to defend the very blonde responsible for his decline, and who was now being tried for the murder of his, Burt Reynolds's, best friend. Toon penetrated the periphery of his visual field, stopped in front of the television as if to watch the movie; he contemplated the image for several instants from above, in a lopsided high-angle. Then he very brutally kicked the side of the apparatus, which jumped under the shock. The Duke jumped as well. Almost immediately it began to snow on Burt Reynolds, then Burt himself became snow, his delicate plea aggravating into a violent hiss while a fat white wire began to smoke from within the television's entrails. Toon turned to Bob with a nonchalantly apologetic smile—odious. Bob seemed weary. "Thug," the Duke snorted impulsively.

"It's not much," admitted Toon, "but it's the thought that counts."

Plankaert slowly leaned over to unplug the television. "No sense starting a fire over this," he calmly observed.

"Thug," Pons hissed again. "Little punk." As if he had just noticed him, Toon turned sharply toward the Duke, striking him in the same motion with the back of his hand. Pons fell over backward on his seat, holding his nose. Bob started to make a move, but Plankaert held his arm.

"We'll be back," Toon announced, "and it'll be worse if we don't find Bergman. It'll be worse next time around."

They disappeared. A line of hemoglobin oozed from Pons's nose and he looked frantic. First Bob settled him back into the armchair, ballasted by a glass around which he made the Duke close his fingers, his other hand closed snail-like over his proboscis. Then the hotel night clerk took a long time to answer; his voice was also laden with utter weariness over everything.

"We don't ring the rooms at this hour," he anxiously explained. "We can't, it's no longer possible."

"It's extremely urgent," Bob pleaded. "It's very very very important. Room twenty-four."

"Twenty-four isn't here in any case. Number twenty-four checked out."

"That's impossible," said Bob. "Check again, you'll see he's there."

"What do you think," asked the night clerk, "I'm making this up as I go along? I'm not making this up. I'm doing my job here. I know my job."

"Yeah," said Bob, "okay."

"I do it just like I'm supposed to. He checked out, I tell you. They came by to pick him up around midnight. Guys from the port."

And in fact the *Boustrophedon* was on the high seas at present. Paul was on board; no one spoke to him. Without going into the reasons that had precipitated their departure, Garlonne had too quickly led him to, then left him alone in, his cabin, which turned out to be dark. Paul explored the bulkheads with his fingertips, blindly, seeking—and banging against everything in the process—the light switch in the most improbable nooks and crannies; but once he found it, there was no more light than before. Paul groped his way back to his bunk and sat down, his bag, his only faithful companion, lying against his feet at the heart of the freighter's dark skeleton, among the crude odors of salt, diesel, and fresh paint. They must have known about the problem, since sailor Gomez soon appeared, flashlight in hand, spare lightbulb in his pocket.

Having explored his cabin, Paul went out on deck. Classic soundtrack for casting off. The sailors' shadows brushed past him; they let go the moorings as soon as Illinois came on board. The captain immediately shut himself in his quarters—Paul had time to glimpse only a stocky shadow disappearing through a yellow triangle that immediately snapped shut, like a trap. Garlonne directed the maneuvers, muted valves and heavy pistons soon pushed the freighter toward the harbor exit. Civilized, considerate, the port waters kept themselves in check up to the two lighthouses, which stood like a pair of obelisks looking out onto the vast sea. From that point on they permitted themselves allusions to their power; from that point on things began to stir. Under the effect of the movement, the first jostlings like nervous shivers running along the vessel's skeleton, the bells came unscrewed on the Chinese handlebars, which soon formed a herd, jingling chaotically.

Paul remained on deck all night, knowing he would not sleep. First it took him a long time to light his Senior Services, and then they didn't taste right. There was little activity in the corner where he'd taken refuge, under the network of companionways at the sterncastle, gossamer corbelings gleaming with all their fresh whiteness in the shadows. The sailors continued not to look at him when they passed by to go from one work site to another; Garlonne himself was no longer voluble, and the captain was still pulling an Ahab. Perhaps they simply didn't see Paul in the darkness, in the roll of the waves, in the cold absence of reference points. Much later a diffuse light situated the East, dissolving some early stars. Next the sun emerged, revealing Paul all alone on the deck of the *Boustrophedon*, fear in his heart, a drunken fear at the heart of a great fatigue. He leaned on the forecastle guardrail, studying the water ripped by the bows, astonished at the interminable, inexhaustible interest this ripping aroused in him—almost a reflex interest, infinitely self-renewed, related to the interests brought on by the sight of fire, the sight of storms, and the sight of pedestrians passing by.

23

PAUL FINALLY made up his mind to go back to his cabin. But as the porthole sported no curtains or shutters, the light was too strong and he couldn't sleep more than a couple of hours. He went back down on deck before noon to find Garlonne rather idle. The first mate exposed his viewpoint on wind velocity, water conditions, cloud formations, and his daughter's schooling. The others seemed unoccupied too; they ran the freighter as if without believing in it, as if it moved all by itself. Their actions seemed almost incidental—you coiled a line, you secured a crate, you sharpened the end of a stick, you gave Lopez a hand. You always found something to busy yourself with. You still didn't see Captain Illinois.

In the end, they hadn't waited, before casting off, for Lopez to finish repainting the sterncastle. He continued his job on the open seas. Truth to tell, he dispatched the last level a bit, just giving it a few touch-ups, daubing on patches of Rustoleum where the rust showed through, with a little paint on top. The upper level was thus spotted a heterogeneous white, all in superimposed repaintings, like the camouflage of a polar tank designed for an intercontinental snowball conflict. At the end of his swing,

Lopez, working his harness, moved like a Cartesian devil over the flanks of the sterncastle. He took great pains with the maintenance of the portholes, especially the one to the cabin where Paul had just finished lunching alone and was now seated before the remains of a tray brought by young Gomez. Exaggeratedly absorbed in its task, the inclement countenance was framed in the disk above Paul, who swallowed an awkward piece of cheese. He picked up a book for appearance' sake; his fingers greased the pages, his eyes skimmed along the lines. Lopez's harsh voice sounded from time to time, addressing Gomez who was passively leaning on the railing down below. Paul did not understand Spanish, still less anything about Cartagenan idioms, but, mistakenly relying on a general notion of southern languages, he managed to convince himself that his own case was being touched upon.

A little later, hanging around the forecastle, he had to efface himself from the path of Sapir, who was carrying several links of anchor chain in his allegory-laden arms. The man with the shovel-shaped head passed without seeming to notice him, like an informed Bedouin in a mirage zone, as if Paul, effaced, had no existence. Paul would have felt very alone if Darousset, at tea time, hadn't taken a moment to chat with him.

Darousset, a Sudanese bantam weight, was a native of the point at which the two maternal branches—the Ethiopian Blue from Lake Tana, the Kenyan White from Victoria—melted into a single, immense Nile. Eight years earlier, the first boat in his life had led him up the river to Port Said, recommended to one cousin by another cousin. Alas, in this sprawling city there was no longer any cousin at all, nor any money with which to go home; Darousset, stranded, had boarded a second boat, a run-of-the-mill tanker, and since then from one ship to the next he had never left the sea. He benefited from the stopovers within reason, distrustful of ports and large cities ever since his rotten memories of

Port Said, wanting to know of the world only its oceans and his native village at the fork of the Nile. One day, his nest egg sufficiently matured, he would return to his village and do nothing more than produce numerous children, right up to the end. Paul encouraged the able seaman in this life plan.

Lopez finished painting at the end of the afternoon, dismantled his scaffold, and relieved the first mate at the helm, leaving his handiwork to dry. But in the following days all this white would remain sticky; hands would adhere to ramps; it would never really dry. There was a knock on the cabin door and Garlonne appeared.

"It's me," he reminded Paul. "How would you like to dine with the captain? Just the three of us. We'll chat, it'll give us a chance to chat."

Pure figure of speech, for Illinois from the outset seemed mute. He had sat at the table before their arrival. He ate slowly, with slow movements that took their time—turning the bully beef in his plate to ensure his knife the best angle of attack, shoveling distinct portions of vegetables and rice, spinning his glass on itself, handling his napkin matador-style. Hunched over his victuals in an obtuse pointed arch, he decomposed his gestures in slow motion, measured them as if for a demonstration. As Paul entered the officers' salon, Illinois raised his eyes toward him from the depths of his beard, which he wiped, unfolding his napkin in a demi-veronica.

"Naturally it's the usual fare," the first mate apologized, "but there *is* cake. Frozen, of course. It's amazing what they can do with frozen food these days. We live on it, it's very handy. It represents real progress for us. On land, of course, you're not all that familiar with it."

"Oh, but we are," Paul assured him. "Frozen foods are constantly gaining ground."

"Ah," said Garlonne. "I didn't think it had gone that far."

So they spoke of frozen food for a moment, then of batteries, by association. The captain followed the interlocutors with his eyes, as if he had to read their lips. After the cake, Garlonne excused himself without wanting any coffee. Paul remained alone with Illinois, who readjusted his cup in his saucer, deducted a little tan froth with the tip of his small spoon, pushed the sugar bowl toward him.

"Long crossing," he said finally. "Boring trip for you, no? We're a small ship, not too well equipped. The minimum."

"I'll read," said Paul. "I brought some reading."

"Reading," the pensive captain repeated, "the decline of reading. They used to read in the Navy, once upon a time. I myself. We read less, on board, who knows why."

On land it was kind of the same, Paul pointed out, just like frozen food, and so they talked about it. The captain was endowed with speech after all; he expressed himself the way he ate: methodically and slowly. His voice hummed like a machine, a well-regulated motor that slightly planed down pronouns, articles, certain adjectives. "Your trunks, by the way, all your trunks." He pointed a knowing index toward the hold.

"Yes," said Paul.

"Everything is down there, way at the bottom. Well hidden."

"And customs?" went Paul. "No problems?"

"Right under their noses," said Illinois with a smiling movement of his thumb toward a point of the world where they imagined the outraged customs authorities hopping with rancor.

"How about the crew, do they know about the trunks?"

"No one knows, only us two. Elementary caution, minimum risk. Even Garlonne doesn't know what's inside. I told him they were boilers, parts for boilers. I told him you're in boilers."

The very next day, Paul discovered boredom at sea just as the first mate, then the captain, had described it. The tour of the ship was short work, the ocean perpetually unvarying. At its surface two sperm whales came up for air, a sight he examined in its slightest detail; then it once again became featureless. The sky alone offered a little variety. Even when it formed a perfect blue unity, pure backdrop, empty stage, you could sense that the clouds were waiting in the wings beyond the horizon, rehearsing a thousand ways of not bungling their entrance: by eczematous flecks, entwined threads, tenacious slabs, or flows; by streaks or diffusion; coming undone in fibrils, as if on contact with the air; compressing into organ-shaped threats from which rain would spurt. They could appear light, in profile, sparkling; or else gravid and swollen, lugubrious; or else fickle, indecisive, fuzzy—half-open or ripped apart. If they appeared principally in packs, certain anchorites or freelancers also drifted to other altitudes without mixing in, ignoring each other, all puffed up with montgolfier pride. Sometimes, without warning, one of them committed suicide in creamy dissolution, dispersed into the ether, leaving in its wake some pellucid nebulosity, the floating overcoat of a guardian angel.

All that second day, then, Paul studied the sky—so much so that by evening, at dinner, he was squeezing his head and rubbing his eyes. Debating with the captain a fine point of personnel management, Garlonne was slow to react. Paul had to exaggerate his symptoms in order for the first mate to rise toward the ship's pharmacy—a locked, painted metal box, hanging from the bulk-head, that contained the therapeutic minimum: lots of aspirin, several antibiotics with a wide range of uses, and rolls of crepe bandages. Nothing for the afflictions that one would imagine to come with the job: sea- or homesickness. Paul downed three aspirin tablets, letting Garlonne resume his complaints: Lopez didn't like him, Lopez was far too surly, even if his work was beyond reproach.

"It makes for a bad atmosphere on board," the first mate deplored. "I can barely talk to him."

"That's your business, Garlonne," said the captain. "Harmony on board isn't my department. That falls under *your* responsibilities."

Garlonne opened the second panel of his dissatisfaction: conflicting in his view with the office of first mate, his secondary function as the crewmen's representative weighed on him. The hammer and the anvil, you know?, it was no kind of life always to be caught between them; couldn't we find someone else? As Illinois shrugged his shoulders without answering, Garlonne began to pout before announcing, without looking at anyone, that he preferred to retire for the night. After his departure, the captain offered to lend Paul his spare cap to shield him from the sun: too large, it floated in unstable balance on Paul's ears. Illinois showed him how to tighten the hat by folding the inner leather ribbon. Paul thanked him and immediately went to try out the headpiece on deck: a little fresh air at night helps you sleep.

He made the rounds of the ship. The lights were off in the first mate's quarters, but they still shone for the crewmen. Paul, glancing through the panes of the crew's quarters, noticed Garlonne with them. He monologued without stop, persuasively it seemed; Paul couldn't hear what he was saying. Near him, young Gomez and Darousset listened attentively. Sapir himself appeared absorbed, sitting a little farther away on the edge of a bunk. He continued to touch his nose, to sniff his fingers, which he occasionally stuffed into one nostril or the other; he caressed their jutting hairs, pulled on them as if on a rope. He seemed motivated by the need to establish a permanent relation, a kind of aerial bridge between his prehensile and olfactory centers. The surly Lopez, on watch at the wheel, was absent. The first mate was perhaps describing his daughter for the three others, in terms that flattered their enforced celibacy; and the documents that he slid toward them, on the table covered with Scandinavian magazines and playing cards, might have been selected photos of said daughter, chosen from among the most appropriate to their reveries.

"Say," Paul said to him the next morning, "I saw you last night with the others. I didn't dare come in."

"Ah," went Garlonne, raising his eyebrow. "Yes, well, in the evenings I teach them reading a bit. You should have," he added without conviction, "you must join us next time."

On the evening of the fourth day, they met with a violent squall. All the clouds observed by Paul—the rival tribes of haughty cumulus, endogamous altostratus, and proud cirrus which, the day before yesterday, had still kept at a respectful distance, jealous of their nebulous identity—all of them now banded together under the threatening power of a single, fat, absolute nimbus, in an opaque precipitate that closed ranks to examine the freighter more closely, from all angles, reducing the horizon to the diameter of a hula hoop. It didn't look good.

At the height of its thickness, the nimbus burst, whipped the boat with an immediately fierce rain, propelled a buckshot of fat, heavy drops to gnaw at it, pierce it, destroy it, while a violent wind toppled hearts and minds, scooped out waves with breathtaking facades. Horrified, the *Boustrophedon* began to lurch every which way, with no discernible pitch or toss, trying instead to twist in on itself the way a maniac cat vainly chases its hindquarters, at times. The hull produced violent, raging, pained creakings that covered all voices. Against the gunwale, on deck, enormous blocks of liquid exploded in showers more enormous still, populated with fish in unstable balance, who were themselves beginning to worry. In the hold, the Chinese bells howled ceaselessly, hanging onto the handlebars with all the strength of their nuts and bolts. Soon the monstrous shudders no longer even succeeded each other, but attacked all at once as if to kill the very idea of succession, to abolish the time massed in its apocalypse. Scarcely had the freighter tried to bend under one blow than another blow was already bending it in the opposite direction, at the far limit of dislocation. Nothing seemed solid or right anymore, including ideas in heads.

The captain, uneasily followed by his first mate, had joined Lopez in the pilot house. First they tried to maintain a smooth course, attempting to negotiate blow for blow, to come to terms with the seaquake. Then the controls became useless; they could no longer hold onto them, nor even glance at a dial. The men began to bounce off the bulkheads, with no more free will than a pinball wrapped in yellow oilskin. Garlonne managed to grab the wheel, and his body for a moment swept the air as if he were hanging onto the tail of a crazed horse; then he flew off and went to collapse among the marine charts that were heaving through space in long accordions. After that he stopped even trying to get up, slid like a mop cloth across the deck at the whim of a blind order.

Shut in his cabin, Paul also kept falling in every direction. Soon he couldn't even orient himself in space: the reference points normally constituted by up and down, left or south, were abrogated by the storm as time had been. Convulsively he managed to hug his bunk, gripped by a chronic hiccup and emptying everything onto it, vomiting his very organs as if in a vast regurgitation of the self—his spasm at times was not even finished before he found himself projected across the residence, his bolus describing behind him long curved sprays like handfuls of grain. Beaten black and blue, Paul finally lost consciousness; briefly he saw his consciousness sink into a deep, thick, darkly viscous liquid, in which only a few vegetative functions bothered grumpily to remain afloat.

What met his eyes, when numerous hours later he reopened them, was at first glance an abstract thing, and his brain had some trouble processing this information. Then it all fell into place: envisioned in sideways low-angle, it was but debris and shreds of objects, bottoms of objects, traces of the banging of objects against other objects, all of them more or less flecked with more or less digested food. The bunk had come detached from the bulkhead, and the smashed frame, scattered across the middle of the cabin, had let its mattress escape, the latter having run aground during the tumult on the unconscious Paul. The mattress weighed on his chest like a dead shark. The rest of his body was crumpled under the disarticulated leaf of the bedside table, his head half-caught in a blue bag come from elsewhere.

At present there was no movement anywhere, as if to compensate for the damage. Through the stencil of the porthole, a tube of smooth light formed an impeccable disk on the soiled bulkhead. No sound either, except for the hypocritical wavelets clucking with all their tongues against the hull, calmly, as if nothing had happened—it was just a joke, lighten up, it's over now, no hard feelings—at times letting some stronger wave rise up, an affectionate chuck from the blue-green element, gentle reminder of what it could do. With infinite precaution, Paul began to stir, dragging his body full of hematomas toward the demolished bunk, mounting it almost as easily as he would a horse.

His headache, bearing no relation to the one from two days before, was cancelled out by all his other pains, everywhere. Paul was no more than a single muscle, one enormous ache. His very consciousness hurt: the future was scarcely brighter than the present, nor, retroactively, was the totality of the past. He remained prone. He wished he were sleepy. He tossed over negative ideas during the hours that followed, equally criss-crossed by contingent thirst, nausea, hunger, and heat—dead hours in which, once again, all duration was abolished. It fell to seaman Darousset to reestablish the continuity of things: far off, hovering from the altitudes of the sterncastle, his voice called out to whoever wanted to hear it that Port Said had been sighted.

The city pushed a hot clamor out to sea, past the machinery of the port. As soon as they had come alongside, the men extracted from the holds the bouquet of bicycles entangled by the storm, using a hoist. Scarcely recovered from the ordeal, exemplary was their energy in separating then repairing the cycles, before scattering into the city, the gratification of several basic drives in mind. On their vehicles, the sailors passed almost unnoticed. The closer the Orient, the more natural cycling was, before blooming in Asia where this common means of transportation allowed one to melt at low cost into the social body. Paul preferred not to take his chances in town, but remained on board in the company of the officers. They dozed off under their caps, breathing the dampness of the estuary in the hollow of lounge chairs unfolded on deck. Garlonne lavished refreshments on them.

"I don't go," he said, serving Paul, "I don't go ashore very often. But my little girl would like that, you know."

He was thinking of treating his only daughter to a cruise when she finished school: with this in mind, what could be more appropriate than the *Boustrophedon*, what could be more economical and safe? This way he himself would always be present to explain things to her and teach her about life. Informed of this project, the captain procrastinated, hanging his answer on a dilatory thread.

"Have you given it any thought, by the way?" the first mate inquired.

Illinois mumbled a difficulty: only men on board, right?, it was a real risk—but let's see, Garlonne, we'll think about it, we'll see. Morning's end calmly slipped by, in contrast to the swarming cries and gestures of the longshoremen on land. Their feverishness lowered at around noon, then the idea of a siesta made its way into everyone's reasoning, soon led astray by dreams of power and love.

Sudden cries shattered the general torpor: on the docks, Duke Pons waved his arm, hopping in place; behind him, Bob still seemed weary. Immediately the Duke spoke too loudly.

"It was a real hassle trying to find you," he stamped his feet at the bottom of the gangplank. "So much noise, so many people. Three hours just to get information. Anyway, here we are."

24

THEY WERE glad to see each other again. The captain
congratulated the Duke, the tales of the storm impressed
Bob. Before so much sudden animation Garlonne rubbed emotive hands together, steeped in a matchmaker's sentiment; he
scurried off to find more deck chairs and cold drinks.

"Well," said Pons, "we haven't seen much of the town. We just
got here. Maybe we'll have time to catch a few sights, what do
you say? The pyramids, for example, are they far?"

But they would be leaving that very evening, and already the
sun was beginning to wane: the men returned one after the other,
worn out but happy, each one on his bike. From afar they saw
Darousset pedalling at top speed; erect as a dancer he mounted
the gangplank without braking, as if it were a diving board at the
end of which, after a short hyperbole, his machine collapsed with
a crash. Garlonne ran to help the acrobatic Sudanese, whose
exercise everyone saluted: young Gomez uncovered all his teeth,
Sapir himself brightened up a little; only Lopez showed a her-
metic face. "He's sulking," sighed the first mate. "He's always
sulking."

The two cabins adjacent to Paul's were given to Bob and Pons, who had already been put to the test in the airplane by several pockets of turbulence. For his part, Paul had not fully recovered from the parallel phenomena of the humid night before, and so everyone went to bed early. Then life on board resumed as in the preceding days, soon tiresome when the sea behaved itself; but with three of them, they could at least resort to games. They met up again in the officers' salon for dinner, after which the captain did not refuse to be the fourth for a few hands of stud poker.

Keeping to its twelve-knot cruising speed, the *Boustrophedon* slipped into the Red Sea, after which it headed for Colombo, next stop. Nothing remarkable, nothing notable happened: every evening, on the ship's log, the officers countersigned the nothingness. Even so, brief altercations persisted between Garlonne and helmsman Lopez. One of these broke out on the quarter deck, just above Bob's cabin where they were killing time with dice—five mismatched dice found in a trunk along with a mat, provided long ago by the Byrrh company, whose green felt, shriveled to yellow, peeled like a lawn in drought. One of these dice, surely loaded, too often came up five, but they could make do, overcome the obstacle by a system of coefficients whose workings they perfected all the more minutely in that it was raining that day—you couldn't even go out on deck. Apart from the storm, it was the only time it rained. Cosmopolitan small change stood in for chips.

Through the half-open porthole, the sound of voices reached them just as the Duke was about to attempt double-fours to match three-of-a-kind. He suspended his motion: they looked at each other. Outside, Garlonne spoke in a voice that was more emphatic but less audible than usual. They heard him breathing between propositions, to which the Spaniard retorted bitter diphthongs beyond meaning. They couldn't understand a word, except when Lopez yelled three times at the first mate to go fuck himself, with progressive mutations of the *u*. Then the two men moved away, no doubt separately, and silence reconquered the ship. The Duke threw two dice: after their brief choreography, instead of the desired fours, an ace appeared in the company of the ubiquitous five.

"Five," he said, "so I go again. It's five, I can go again."

"No," said Paul, "we didn't say that. It just gives you a handicap for the next turn, you know very well that's what we said."

"That's right," recalled the Duke, "but after eight handicaps you're allowed to go again. So I had seven. Remember, we said *that* too."

"Right, we said it, but then we said no."

"Why not," the Duke became indignant.

"Because it makes things too complicated," Paul said plaintively, "things were getting too complicated."

"*You* are disloyal," concluded Pons.

What was to remain engraved in their memories as the major event of the *Boustrophedon*'s odyssey happened on the evening of the ninth day at sea, shortly after the stop at Colombo. They were advancing pleasantly into the Bay of Bengal; the weather reports were at their most favorable. Pons, on deck, had momentarily enjoyed the sweetness of the air before going to join Illinois. Paul and Bob arrived shortly afterward, as the Duke was doubling his aperitif. The captain smiled gently; they were awaiting only the first mate to begin dining. As his delay was becoming prolonged, they took their seats at the table, Pons next to Paul. The Duke immediately refilled his empty glass, then turned to his nephew:

"You think I go at it too hard, don't you? You think I overdo it, go ahead and say so."

"I don't know," said Paul. "Do you always drink so much?"

"All the colonials do, my boy. All the colonials do."

Then the door opened to reveal Garlonne, who did not immediately take his seat as was his custom. He remained immobile on the threshold; they looked at him. After six seconds, they knit their brows.

"How about closing the door, Garlonne," said Illinois. "And come sit down, the food's getting cold."

Standing at a kind of attention, the first mate did not respond to the invitation. A solemnity tried to emanate from his person, as if for the raising of the flag. He opened his mouth to speak, but the saliva was lacking in his coalescent mucous membranes; his Adam's apple bobbed up and down like a furious yo-yo. He seemed extraordinarily moved.

"I'm not alone," he managed to emit. "The others are here."

His voice conveyed something mashed, as if reduced to its residue, filtered by a vocoder. He took one step forward, like a robot; Sapir indeed appeared behind him, followed by Gomez and Darousset, who seemed a bit frightened. Garlonne cleared his barren throat:

"That is, they asked me, as their spokesman—they're not happy, you know?"

He halted, pulling a sheet of paper from his pocket. The captain waved an evasive hand.

"Go on, Garlonne. Say what you have to say, old man."

"In any case, it's no longer bearable," the first mate soliloquized, twisting the paper in his hands. "I *said* it wasn't right, as second-in-command, for me to speak for the crew. I always said it. But anyway, since they asked."

They all watched Garlonne unfold his trembling sheet of paper, except for young Gomez and Darousset, who didn't appear very concerned; they cast curious glances into the officers' salon, having entered it only once, to sign on. The moment the first mate began reading the list of grievances—after having hemmed and hawed some more—the captain looked surprised; he slid a hand under his cap and pensively scratched his scalp. Paul shook his head when Bob, interrogatively, turned toward him—a discreet lateral shake, softened synonym in non-verbal language of the twirling index finger around the temporal fossa. Indeed, if the demands reworked classical themes—salary, hours, food, social security—it was scarcely necessary to be in on the deal in order to discern its excessive turn, exorbitant on certain points, venturing beyond reasonable limits to toe the line of the delusional system. They were attentive; the Duke set his glass down. He picked it up automatically, set it back down without having drunk.

His recital finished, Garlonne attempted to refold the paper while pronouncing several words on his own behalf: of course he, as spokesman, allied himself with these requirements (he stuttered on this last word). For his part, he would present but one, which was precisely to be relieved of his status as spokesman, for reasons many times enumerated but which he felt it necessary to repeat. He spoke more easily at present, although his voice wobbled a bit on the tonic accents—curiously, he pronounced several very common words badly, as if, not understanding them, he could only mimic them phonetically. The first mate seemed imbued with a discreet exaltation, most unusual for him; it was the color and skeleton of his peroration. A brief silence elapsed at the end of his speech; the captain waved his hand anew, no less evasively.

"It's excessive, Garlonne, it's very excessive. I agree with you, I'm on your side. Whatever you want. But it's not my department, you have to take it up with the company."

Seeing that his uncle was getting ready to intervene, Paul lay a gently deterrent hand on his forearm. "It's a shame," said Garlonne, bowing his head. "They won't take it kindly." Behind him, marvelously relaxed, Gomez and Darousset seemed not to take it at all; a finger in his nose, Sapir contemplated his espadrilles. Garlonne repocketed the sheet of paper.

"Just one small overture," he insisted, "as a gesture. You give in on one point, a tiny little point. Sometimes hearts are appeased with a tiny little point."

"Don't be ridiculous," went the captain without undue harshness. "Tell the men to get back to work and come sit down. The food's gotten all cold."

Without raising his head, the first mate began fumbling in his pocket again, from which he finally pulled a minuscule, fourth-rate gadget, something like a Browning Baby for ladies. Discreetly verifying that he was holding it the right way, he pointed it toward Illinois, then in a circular motion toward the three dismayed passengers. But his little object gave him no credibility; he looked as if he were offering it for sale. Having swallowed his saliva: "Let's go," he emitted, not without effort. Instantly blunt instruments flowered in the hands of his smiling escort. The passengers started, but Illinois simply moved his shoulders and adjusted his visor, turning back to his plate.

"I'm afraid I am forced . . ." said Garlonne in a forced voice. "I'm taking command, you see."

Without answering, Illinois planted his fork in the pâté, impaling a half-cornichon at the same time.

"The crew is with me," the first mate elaborated, "you have no choice. They're the ones who want it, you know. There is no other way."

"You're losing your mind, Garlonne," chewed the captain. "You really disappoint me. Where's Lopez, by the way?"

"He's with us," cried the first mate, increasingly nervous. "Lopez is with us."

"These days," the captain said into his napkin, "I mean, you simply don't realize. You don't know anything about anything anymore. This is mutiny, no ifs, ands, or buts. It's unrealistic. It's completely unrealistic."

"I'm in charge," the other affirmed shrilly, "I'm taking charge here."

"All right," said Illinois. "What are you going to do?"

"You stay here," Garlonne suggested. "Don't move from here until we let you off the ship. No one must stop us," he explained, "you mustn't try to stop us. Nothing must stop us from doing anything."

He had approached the table, all the while speaking in a constantly rising register; he waved the ladies' accessory in the proximity of Bob, who suddenly unfolded toward him, shouldering him off balance. Almost at the same time, Paul grabbed Garlonne's wrist. The captain stood, followed with a slight delay by Pons: Sapir and the smiling seamen were already rushing toward them. Brief commotion, then they distributed the roles two by two, one on one. Young Gomez tackled the Duke; Bob dragged down the man with the shovel head. As he rose again in confusion, he met the wild eye of Garlonne, the black eye of his little weapon aimed at Paul. "I'm going to shoot," whimpered the first mate for the benefit of Illinois, who puffed heavily, contained by the Sudanese's double nelson. Garlonne cried out and then the detonation sounded, a sharp noise in the black space of people, who froze for an instant. As no one was hurt, they started up again, had another go at each other, in couples, while trying to move toward the door, as waltzing lovers turn imperceptibly toward the dark terrace to remove their embrace from the prying eyes of the outside world.

25

THE FISTICUFFS continued on deck. Garlonne having resumed shooting, captain and passengers ebbed as best they could toward the ladder of the sterncastle, where they scrambled up the metal spiral to the pilot house. They rushed into it, locking the hatch behind them; they heaved a sigh.

"Lopez," went Illinois, "what are you doing here?"

His voice sounded curiously severe. The helmsman didn't answer. He remained at his post, standing before the compass. Outside the mutineers were banging on the iron door.

"You're not with them."

Lopez still didn't answer; he continued to function at his post. Whether he acted this way out of legalism or out of simple dislike for the first mate, who knows. "Steady as she goes," commanded the captain, heading for the radio. "We're going to call for help." He took his place before the transmitter. They soon stopped trying to break down the steel hatch; they were no longer banging. They must have gone back below.

It seemed that the transmitter was out of order, no longer even working as a receiver. "It's broken," said the helmsman. "The Negro was on duty before me, it was surely him."

"Weigh your words, Lopez, if you don't mind," went Illinois in a preoccupied tone that heightened one notch when, three decks below, the sound of the engines suddenly ceased.

Sapir had halted the machines, whose vibrations were ordinarily so regular that you didn't even hear them anymore, that they erased themselves. Now that you really didn't hear them anymore, their absence was deafening. It is often the same with a missing tooth (let's explore this), the volume of empty space can be surprising; it's enormous, without relation to the space one attributed to that humble tooth, which one immediately misses, which one suddenly discovers post mortem, which one blames oneself for not having brushed in the time of its splendor, and which ends up occupying much more space than when it was there, even if one keeps it in a little box (enough). The captain glanced toward the foredeck, in the direction of the anchor; the insurgents not being of a mind to drop it, the *Boustrophedon* began to drift on the dark water, toward the frothy heart of the Indian Ocean. "A fine mess we're in," said Pons.

Although they were of no further use, Lopez stayed at his post before the navigational instruments, spread below a long rectangle of glass that looked out toward the bow. Near him, the captain stared at the empty deck, the sea around it, the fallen night; light appeared in the crew's quarters. Piled onto the deck of the pilot house, the three passengers slept little.

They were all standing before the rectangular port at first light of dawn, under a televisual grey-blue glow, poorly defined, ill at ease in these cinemascopic dimensions. It had already become hot by the time noise began rising from the deck: the rebels had slept late, perhaps hesitant to leave their quarters. Knowing they were being watched, they showed an insincere casualness, an awkward triumph; Garlonne came out last, adjusting his uniform. They hung around on deck all morning long without being able to conceal their enforced idleness, nor the slight confusion into which this plunged them. Although forcing themselves not to look at the hostages who were lined up behind the pilot house window, eventually they gave in, irrepressibly loosed brief glances toward the sterncastle. They looked at the sea, they looked at their hands; Garlonne suggested some paltry tasks, too soon accomplished given their enormous good will.

Upstairs they consulted with each other: it was a stalemate. One side holding the engines whose controls were held by the other side, each camp found itself neutralized, rich with half of the same banknote. "We'll have to wait," said Illinois, "we'll wait." Conferring in the first mate's cabin, Garlonne and Sapir arrived at similar orders and conclusions. As the heat was rising in the immotile vessel, each side panted from time to time; each side wiped its forehead and cursed. Between the antagonistic forces there was but a single exchange, fairly brief, when Lopez shouted something Spanish to Gomez, no doubt exhorting him to join the side of law and order. The sailor answered without turning around, with a word of very few letters that had Darousset in stitches. Aided by Sapir, the Nilotic seaman dropped fishing lines from various parts of the ship.

They must have been biting, for after an hour a heavy cloud of frying enveloped the freighter, spread over the surface of the water, gave rise and cruel definition to the appetite, then the hunger, of the besieged; on the other hand, catching a whiff of the horrible, unnatural odor, several flying fish dove precipitously back into their habitat. Soon even the Duke didn't want to look at the deck, where the brazen mutineers picnicked, raising glasses to their health; to forget his cramps, he chose to sleep.

Still, the sailors' excesses seemed to weaken them; young Gomez went more and more slowly to renew the bottle supply. Garlonne retired to his cabin, entrusting his little weapon to the man with the shovel head. The latter seemed less vigilant, and the two others were beginning to doze off. "This might be the moment," Bob suggested, "don't you think?" Lopez rested on him his scarcely amenable glance.

"We'll wait a little longer," said Illinois.

A long half-hour later, the dazed crewmen lolled in the requisitioned deck chairs, letting themselves fry in turn under the tropical rays. Drifting in silence, littered with sated dreamers, the vessel became a snoring Dutchman, the raft of a gorged Medusa. At a sign from Illinois, Bob unlocked the door.

Following Lopez, who went ahead to scout, a solid iron bar in hand, the three men gently stepped over the sleeping Pons—it seemed they did not deem his help indispensable. Then on tiptoes they descended the flights of non-skid spiral; excessively moist, their hands still stuck a bit to the white rail. They regrouped against the guardrail of the quarter-deck, under the limp flag. A simple plan was formulated: at Illinois's signal, coming simultaneously from port and starboard, Lopez and the captain would surround Sapir and disarm him, while Paul and Bob would neutralize the two others; three sleepers can't hold out against four starving men. Let's go.

Immediately it was too late to pull back, immediately they were caught in the trap: at the captain's signal, before Lopez could react, the three mutineers jumped to their feet in hostile poses; immediately they attacked. Sapir eliminated Lopez by grabbing his iron bar from the other end, diverting above him the helmsman's forward momentum; the latter described a Gaussian curve head first before immobilizing at the foot of an air shaft. Without transition, the man with the shovel head pulled Illinois by his wrist, jammed his shoulder in a wrench-lock, compressed his larynx with his left arm, and the captain began to suffocate. Before his eyes young Gomez and the Sudanese seaman, in better shape than Bob and Paul, were exchanging increasingly advantageous blows with the latter; one's laugh deflagrated in bursts, the other's smile sparkled. They fought more scientifically, efficient as stuntmen. Bob landed barely one blow to the bantam weight's three; Paul was no longer trying to do anything but parry those of the handsome, indifferent brunet. As Garlonne bolted from the doorway of his cabin, Sapir tossed him the Browning Baby, freeing for an instant Illinois's trachea. Garlonne missed the object, which fell on his foot; he grimaced picking it up, then brandished it toward the combat zone, wishing aloud for all this to cease. As no one seemed to take his wishes seriously at first, he started shooting again; everyone hit the deck.

The impacts and sharp cries had jolted Pons awake. From behind the window of the pilot house, he anxiously considered the mutineers' victory. These latter, quickly back on their feet, jubilantly kept their enemies on the ground. No one seemed to want to worry about the Duke; perhaps they had forgotten him in the heat of the action—if not, there would be something humiliating about this. Pons saw the first mate triumphantly point his little firearm at Illinois. He did not hear him softly singing that *he* was in charge of the boat now, that he would take charge of his life as well, that he'd travel the world with his daughter, that *this* was true happiness, that it was finally here. Garlonne's recitative amused the younger men who were tying up the enemy, saluting the main points of his delirium with shouts, tightening the knots. "I *know* that's right," cried Darousset, "I *know* that's right." Sapir bound Lopez silently, staring him in the eye.

So Garlonne was humming, full of himself, his chest puffed up with an unknown happiness. Details seemed to stand out unusually clearly, with himself the clearest detail of all. He would have liked to rise into the air, leave his body, take a bath. An energy with no outlet teemed within him, a thirst for further action made him breathless, weighed on his throat. For want of better he waved the Baby, his finger trembled on the trigger: a projectile headed off, ending its parabola in a little splash. The first mate looked at the others, then at the weapon with great contentment; then a reflection of sunlight struck his eye, from above, on the window behind which Pons was afraid. Garlonne aimed, fired on the reflection without making out the Duke who threw himself to the ground under a shower of safety glass. Then there was only one bullet left in the chamber, and he didn't know what to do with it. There was a knot in the wood of the deck, at his feet; the knot flew like a cork. Garlonne was happy, his weapon empty, his conscience empty as well, every little thing was clear and everything had been won despite that sound of planks.

A new noise sounded below deck, toward the middle of the ship: a violent noise of long planks. Then immediately, from a hatchway, appeared an Armalite rifle held by a hefty arm followed by a large shoulder, a large thorax, and so on, in a stereophonic noise of broken crates, as if all this were emerging from several crates at once. "Charles!" cried Pons through the shattered window. But Charles did not hear him; he kept his rifle on the mutineers with one hand, while with the other he shielded his eyes blinded by ten days of night, spreading one finger after the next to try to make someone out in all this light.

26

HERE'S Miss Odile Otero, who will turn thirty-nine on the twenty-sixth; who has kept her mother's apartment; who hasn't changed the wallpaper. On weekdays she types invoices at Kosmos Auto, and she occasionally spends her holidays with cousins in Pontault-Combault. Every Wednesday, between Lotto and yoga, she withdraws eight or nine hundred francs from Branch Office N, near her home.

A repetitive destiny, a long white face are Odile Otero's, beneath a mop of very thick yellow-grey hair; her general bearing denotes discontentment. In the pocket of her coat lies a pamphlet published in Monaco, entitled *The Secret Doorway to Success* and wrapped in brown paper. Odile is ashamed of this particular volume, but she is also ashamed of her coat. She has felt bad ever since childhood, ever since school where they used to call her Double Zero. They didn't bother her quite so much at Pigier secretarial school, 'and at Kosmos they don't notice her at all, peaceful as a corpse at last. Having attempted suicide three or four times, she has also slept with nine men since the age of twenty-three, several times in a row with some of them, and yet she would do the same thing all over again.

On Wednesday, Odile Otero opened the door to Branch Office

N, endorsed her check payable to the order of "myself," and presented her account number. Exaggeratedly virtuoso, the teller counted the banknotes a little too rapidly for her taste, although she didn't dare recount them at his window for fear of offending him, nor in the street for fear of being mugged. She was therefore doing it discreetly, her back to the teller while walking toward the exit—although this furtive count didn't satisfy her either—when two Martians entered the branch office with resolute steps.

Greenish Martians: serrated chins, fusiform noses, excrescent antennae, no ears, plenty of pseudopods that shook with each movement. They needed neither speak nor show their equipment more plainly; everything was perfectly clear from the outset. Behind them a third personage, taller, dressed in lighter-colored clothes, wore a heron's head at the end of a naturally long neck: as it was sheltered by the outsized beak, all that Odile Otero could see of his face were false teeth between grey lips. It seemed to her that this heron exerted a certain authority over the green men.

A young, average-sized Martian, the one carrying the athletics bag, headed for the teller's window, while his compatriot watched the streets from the glass door. At a curt signal from the heron, everyone fervently hit the ground. The green young man placed the athletics bag before the bullet-proof cage, opened it, pulled from it a sawed-off shotgun whose natural orifice he introduced into the window, without a word—no doubt counting on the teller, trained well in advance for such a scenario, not to require any further explanations. The employee immediately went to work, counting even faster than usual, dropping his count altogether when the sawed-off shotgun started to wave. Not far from Odile Otero, a spread-eagled old lady began crying silently, under the collapsed tent of her garments. As she seemed ready to put more energy into her sobs, the heron braked her momentum with a nervous nudge of the heel.

Once the treasure had been transferred, the teller pushed the sports bag back toward the Martian. The latter glanced briefly inside, then placed his shotgun on the mattress of bills at the bottom of the bag, which he zipped up. At that very moment, his counterpart was still scrutinizing the public pathways and, with his irritated beak, their boss threatened to peck the old lady to death. Noticing that the bearer of the athletics bag was unarmed, an unthinking young bank exec, perhaps weary of his station in life, tried to jump him: immediately the heron fired. Everyone on the floor thought this was the end, but the projectile missed the banker, preferring instead to go lodge itself in the right arm of Odile Otero, who cried out loud, and the fallen banker also cried out very loud when the elder extraterrestrial rushed over to rest a foot on his face.

"Stay on the ground," yelled the heron as panic began to ripple the floor. "Face down, goddammit."

The gangsters then ebbed synchronously toward the exit. Plankaert got out first, removing his mask in the same motion. He ran toward a Peugeot double-parked before the branch office, turned the key amid the slamming of doors. Two metro stops away, in a parking lot under a building, they abandoned the Peugeot for a green Alfasud, registered in the Rhone, that took them across Paris due southeast. In the Alfa, Van Os chided Toon for his carelessness.

"Do you even see what you're doing? You put the thing back in the bag and you *closed* the bag. Do you even realize?"

"So all right," said Toon. "We got out okay."

"We got out okay, that's a good one. We're lucky enough to borrow something that works, and *you* put it in the bag. Do you see what could have happened? When are you going to stop being such an idiot? Maybe never. Maybe you've got a worm in your brain, did you ever think of that?"

Toon abstained from answering, sunken into a back seat that

absorbed him almost entirely. Plankaert, at the wheel, refrained from taking sides. Their boss, moreover, calmed down soon enough. "Well," he said, "I guess we didn't do too badly." He began playing with his mask, introducing the tip of the beak into one of his nostrils, distractedly, then into the other one.

"What do you think, for the girl?" asked Plankaert.

"Her arm, I think," said Van Os. "Maybe her shoulder," he grimaced, "or her elbow. Joints are the worst."

It was only her arm, but Odile Otero was still in a fair amount of pain. Luckily everyone immediately rushed to her aid, most notably the suicidal young bank exec; his attentions irrigated Odile's arm with morphine, slathered honey on her dry fate. No doubt she and this young exec would henceforth watch over each other forever, give each other back a taste for life; it's the beginning of another, rather moving story, but for the moment the Alfasud braked in the middle of Kremlin-Bicêtre before a large sporting-goods store. Toon stepped out of the car.

"Do I really have to go right now?"

"You certainly do," said Van Os. "And try to do a little better with Tomaso this time. See you tomorrow."

Via ever-varied routes, Van Os and Plankaert then returned to their railway shelter near Château-Thierry. Autodidacts trained on the job, so to speak, they counted the money much more slowly than the teller. A routine evening: Plankaert rearranged the bills into three uneven piles, took the one in the middle, then turned on the portable TV; Van Os was already dealing with dinner, slicing palm hearts into tokens.

The next day Van Os awoke at around seven, then left the house and opened the door to the garage where the 4 × 4 and the Alfa waited side by side, rosy in the cold exhaust fumes. Maneuvering the all-purpose vehicle, he crossed over the remains of railroad gravel to reach the local highway, which he followed to

the nearby forest; disdaining his own safety precautions, he had
no goal other than to take a spin. Anyway it was during the week,
and the woods would be empty that early in the morning: no
hunters, no gymnasts, no families devouring insect sandwiches
on a blanket, no pairs of lovers parked frantically behind foggy
windows. Van Os let himself wander a moment along the paths,
following the side roads; then he felt like some exercise. Engaging
the four-wheel drive, turning up the radio, he veered abruptly
into the hilly underbrush. To the limp syncopations of a calypso
he drilled a passage between the trees, jumping the fallen ones,
hurtling up or down inclines of nearly fifty degrees, skating on the
moss and the spongy mud. It was exciting. Low branches
whipped the sheet metal, dead branches scraped it, thorn bushes
bit it; Van Os felt all this in his very body, even the stings of the
crushed nettles.

He stopped short at the foot of a hornbeam, as a news bulletin
gave an account of the attack on Branch Office N the evening
before: Van Os listened for the comments with the stage fright of a
seamstress. The man on the radio soberly described the event—
traditional, well-executed operation, without notable technical innovations; neoclassic technique, in short. Van Os started up again,
more slowly; his pace was more distracted, his driving less sporty.
Skirting a rut, he nearly fell in. He was no longer in such a good
mood; he meandered less. He soon found himself out of the woods.

The edge of the woods was bordered with arable undulations;
in the distance men circulated on tractors. Van Os retraced his
path under cover, knowing farmers' memories to be long and
precise, and not wishing to complicate matters with witnesses to
his presence in the area. Rejoining the network of forest roads, he
lost his way twice before finding it. From the outside, he verified,
the little train station seemed completely deserted. A small 125
motorbike, still warm, blocked the garage; he had to move it to

park the 4 × 4. He closed the door to the garage, opened the one to the house. Plankaert was still asleep upstairs, but Toon, standing in the middle of the room, was watching television from above, the sound off. He had not removed his helmet, nor his coat, nor one of his gloves.

"Tomaso is jerking us around," he immediately announced.

"You could at least say hello."

"Sorry, did you sleep well? I've never seen these morning shows, must be tough for the guys who host them. I sure couldn't, that early. He's really been jerking us around."

"Explain," said Van Os.

"I found out through Briffaut. We should have seen him earlier, Briffaut, he's worth knowing."

"Indeed," said Van Os.

"Tomaso took a delivery about two weeks ago, a big deal, combat stuff and everything. Then all of a sudden it disappeared, nobody knows where to. What they *do* know, what Briffaut knows, is that Bergman came by a lot before that, and not at all afterward. They were jerking us around. We're not in the circuit anymore."

His glance elsewhere, Van Os protractedly scratched in his pocket. Toon had turned back to the silent screen. They heard Plankaert above them getting out of bed, his bare feet making the floor creak, then the clinking of a belt with a little coughing, an involuntary moan, the cry of the faucet, steps on the staircase. He appeared, knotting his tie under his swollen chin; his damp hair, combed rearward, shone like licorice threads. "I heard," he said as Toon was about to speak, "I got it."

"We will have to do something," said Van Os, pulling his hand from his pocket to examine it. "One must react quickly in such cases, otherwise the damage is done. After that they lose respect, they don't talk to you anymore, and finally you're in the toilet. It's bad for one's position. We are going to make an example, first of all, we're going to check the oil."

Aided by Plankaert, he inspected all the vehicles' humors: the gas, the brake fluid, the water, along with the air in the tires, the visibility of the windows, the correct angle and reflection of the rearview mirrors.

"I'm going with the kid," he said. "Take the Alfa. You'll try to see about Bergman again. We'll meet by the Stock Exchange at lunch time."

"Right," said Plankaert.

"Would you like me to drive?" asked Toon.

Van Os did not answer. Van Os said nothing all the way to Paris. Toon stared at the landscape without managing to get interested: beyond the grey-green roadsides, scarcely varied cultivations spread featurelessly. The occasional houses seemed empty, their dogs were attached to nothing; these dogs didn't even know what they were guarding. As a preface to the suburbs, several early sheds seemed to contain nothing either. Then it filled up; more and more things appeared, with more people to carry them.

"You think he's open?"

"What," Toon started.

"Tomaso," said Van Os. "You think he's open this early?"

Yes, Tomaso was already killing the chilly morning in his overheated shop. Narrow rivulets of perspiration ran down the lines of his hand. Regularly the discount man pulled up the tails of his grey smock to wipe his palms on the thighs, shiny with use, of his trousers. He also wiped his watch crystal with a corner of his smock, then wiped the displayed objects with a blue rag.

The little bells tinkled when Toon appeared; he immediately headed toward the back room without a glance for Tomaso, who heard him lock the rear exit. Van Os appeared in turn; behind him Toon now locked the main entrance. Van Os circulated a bit among the appliances, inspecting them wearily, with that critical detachment that already spells trouble even with a normal customer. Tomaso coughed. Van Os raised his eyes toward him. "Mister Van Os," said Tomaso, "will you be needing anything?"

"I will always be needing something," answered Van Os.

"Naturally," said Tomaso.

"I don't know. I wonder if it really *is* natural, sometimes, this kind of perpetual appetency."

"It's human," Tomaso rushed to concur, "that's how we are."

"Perhaps something important was missing in my childhood, I don't know. I don't remember, maybe love."

"Come now," Tomaso squeaked, "how could that be."

"It's a question that still plagues me in my adult years," Van Os continued. "Please believe that it hurts me. For example, you don't like me, I know. It hurts me. You also laugh at me behind my back. That I cannot abide."

"What? Never!" Tomaso tensed. "Never in my life."

"I have nothing more to say," concluded Van Os.

The discount man immediately feels his body being gripped, pushed, turned around, thrown, then pinned to the floor by Toon's pointy knee, against a freezer inaccessible to the external gaze of the clientele. He has just lost his beret. A large piece of metal begins to warm very slowly against the back of his neck. "If they kill me," he tells himself, "I'll have taken all those thermal cures for nothing." Could this be his final thought? Is it conceivable for the last idea of a lifetime to be quite so trivial? No. This answer reassures him, for an instant.

Three hours later, Toon having gone to wash his hands, Van Os studied the menu. Near the Stock Exchange, lunch hour filled the restaurants with brokers who called to each other in their coded language. A swarm of quotes and percentages darkened the air.

"Veal paupiettes for me," said Plankaert. "There's nobody at Bergman's friend's. Everything's locked up tight. I went in to check it out. The gas has been cut, electricity, everything. Seems like they'll be gone for a while. What now? What are you having?"

"I don't know. I don't know," said Van Os.

It troubled him to have to study the menu at the same time as the situation. They cancelled each other out.

"It might be better to let it drop," recommended Plankaert.

"No," said Van Os. "I want to hurt Bergman. I've been humiliated, do you understand, I feel excluded. I cannot stand that. I've made up my mind. What *is* that imbecile doing?"

The latter returned, blowing on his hands.

"You're going to try to find that girl," Van Os told him. "I've decided to kidnap her. Call us here as soon as you've got something, ask for me by the usual name. We'll stay here and wait for your call."

"But," said Toon, "I thought we were going to have lunch."

"We'll eat first," Van Os established, "and you can eat after. Or go get yourself a sandwich at the bar, quick. Go on."

"But I'm hungry," said Toon, "I'm really hungry."

"Don't rile me," said Van Os. "Veal paupiettes for me, too."

Said paupiettes ingested, the crowd in the restaurant bubbled less brightly, the hubbub became decaffeinated. Rounded off by the Côtes-du-Rhône, the interest rates snapped more sluggishly in the smoke of lite cigarettes. Van Os, a tiny bit dulled, did not hear the voice of the man at the cash register that rose without apparent power, although perceptible at a long distance, the way actors know how to do: they were paging Mister Schmidt, Mister Schmidt, Mister Schmidt to the telephone.

"It's for you," said Plankaert.

Van Os wiped his fingers, sticky with muenster; his lips, to which a unit of cumin clung. He groaned while standing up.

Toon was calling from a phone booth near Square Trousseau, at the corner of Rue du Faubourg-Saint-Antoine and Rue Charles-Baudelaire.

"She's home, it wasn't so hard. I don't know about the other girl, but *her* I saw, she's there, do you hear me? Are you happy?"

"We're coming," said Van Os. "Stay where you are."

"How far have you gotten?"

"We're coming. We're just having coffee, we'll be right there."

"Good," breathed Toon, "I have time to get a little something. There's a little cafe just next to here, red seats, today's special lentils and ham. I'll wait for you there."

"No," said Van Os, "I said stay where you are."

"But you promised. You promised."

Everything was not taken care of that afternoon, which was only a dress rehearsal of the action to come. Everything would really be taken care of a few days later, when they would leave Paris via Porte d'Orléans, in the Alfasud, whose trunk would be better outfitted for transporting Justine. Plankaert would drive (where to, by the way?), with Van Os next to him reading the map (we're changing hideaways; I've found something better); Toon would pout in the back seat. Every so often, and with great momentum, Toon would propel his jaws toward a sandwich stuffed with lettuce leaves, blades of Swiss cheese, and slices of ham that stuck out of the oblong bread like onionskin paper from an ill-kept file. The green car would eventually leave the highway at Nemours to cut across the open countryside, under an enormous sky with American overtones. The completely flat landscape would immediately reveal the horizon; they would notice from afar the rare constructions that beckoned on its thread, on its line. It would be like reading a calm text scanned with punctual farms, underlined lakes, suspended towns, exclamatory water towers.

27

A s CHARLES had nothing to wear, the captain, who was of similar build, offered him his spare uniform—but although it suited him, Charles did not feel comfortable in it. They ended up finding him something among Sapir's belongings. He moved into the first mate's cabin.

Once neutralized, Garlonne and the three others had been fettered in a corner of the hold, which they blocked shut using crates full of tiles. As the first mate kept moaning about his daughter, what would become of her now, Illinois hinted that he'd keep an eye on her report cards. In their bonds, young Gomez and Darousset remained in even moods; Sapir suffered mainly from not being able to touch his nose.

The rebellion quelled, the radio repaired, the engines started up again, and Charles having been introduced by Pons, the captain cabled his report to the shipowner who, from Limassol, immediately notified his offices in Bombay. They were once more heading for Singapore, at low speed, Paul and Bob compensating as best they could for the sudden reduction in crew members.

A star member of the Indian police force finally appeared, accompanied by four proud men with very white teeth under very black mustaches, dressed in green short-sleeved shirts and coiffed in matching berets, with four other men in less impeccable dress, with less self-assured looks—replacement sailors that they swapped for the mutineers before heading off again full speed ahead.

Even if his body had rejected the graft of such an appendage, trying on his uniform had brought Charles closer to the captain. Most of the time he stood next to him in the pilot house. The Duke, gabbing incessantly, reminded each one of the memories they had in common, narrated these memories to each other one while exaggerating them. Below, Lopez paced up and down the freighter, checking the work stations without departing from his rugged severity. Although promoted to acting first mate, he had not really celebrated the defeat of Garlonne's men with the others.

This part of the voyage, more animated, was brief. Around the table they talked endlessly of everything: the mutiny, Malaysia, the past that they replayed over cards. In the cool air, Paul and Bob circled around the deck on bicycles. It happened that Bob referred in front of Paul to the young woman met in Chantilly; it happened that Paul spoke to Bob of the one from the cinema that he'd had so much trouble seeing again. It never occurred to them that these portraits might bear a certain resemblance to each other, and the fact is that they bore none at all.

Leaving the Nicobar Islands portside, the *Boustrophedon* entered the Strait of Malacca. On either side, in clear weather, one could make out Indonesian and Malaysian lands, pink and green on the planisphere posted in the officers' mess. In Singapore, Pons having tried to convince Charles of the advantages of new clothes, Illinois provided them with the address of one of those speedy tailors in whose shops, under these skies, all kinds of multi-piece suits flower in fast motion. Then they shipped out, passing the tip of the peninsula, heading north while remaining near the coast where the traffic was relatively calm. A little farther toward the rising sun, on the other hand, near the Celebes Sea, the atmosphere was such that navigation became untenable. This area beyond Borneo, the most dangerous in the world, was overcrowded with pirates perpetually on the attack: devastating plunderers who killed men, raped women, dismembered infants, kidnapped virgins, set fire to ships, then headed for the horizon howling with laughter.

So they preferred to hug the shore, drifting toward the usual port located near the mouth of the Rompin River, less than sixty miles from the plantation. The captain and the Duke knew a few people at the port authority as well as in customs; it would be as easy as in Le Havre to unload undeclared merchandise, along with Charles and his expired passport. Initiating the new suit into what henceforth would be its life, the wandering man settled into a crate while the freighter came to rest among the floating houses and the deckless boats that trawl for horse mackerel, tropical tuna, and barracuda. The captain recommended the Hotel Regal in the center of town, near a small snake market—average hotel, small well-kept garden in front, manager not very curious about people's identities; a fan abetted by a tap provided air and water to all the rooms.

Normally, the captain would simply go take delivery of the rubber. But things at the plantation might have changed; they would await his return to decide how best to invade it. Furthermore, Pons having immediately notified the Aw brothers of his arrival, no doubt the latter would send someone out to report. While waiting, they went into town: from one place to the next people talked, bet, ate noodles, drank Tiger beer; such was Malaysian life. Steel tops hummed in bunches without touching, their spinners hunkered over them with feet wide apart, in their element, like bocci players in the West. On the roofs of squat dwellings, children's silhouettes held the leashes of kites too simple, too light to cast the slightest shadow. Other children threw overripe pineapples at each other, which exploded in a thousand sticky pieces. Still other children escorted Bob and Paul, *what is your name what is your name*, offering to extract from them some fraction of a Malaysian dollar. Very soon it was very hot, but a sudden light rain fell at times, which dirtied little and dried instantly.

The Aws' emissary appeared the following evening, as they were dining on octopus with rice under the technicolor of a neon light; clouds of glimmering midges haloed this neon like escaped gas. The emissary had at his disposal a Land Rover rented from a godfather; he called himself Djalaluddin Din, and he announced that the situation had changed. Jouvin, informed by Kok Keok Choo of the peasants' discontent and worried about Pons's absence, had thought up the idea of arming the seven foremen, who at present formed a veritable militia. Working conditions had stiffened, the constant surveillance was undermining morale. Private life was less so. A committee had formed, which met constantly about the timeliness of a strike. Pons's features bent downward; his very nose seemed to fall. So they would actually have to use these weapons, which would no longer be mere arguments, scenic accessories; now they would be called upon actually to touch the metal. This idea gave the Duke a chill. Aw the younger planned to move the day after next, the emissary specified.

"We'll see," said Pons.

Brought back a little later by the plantation truck along with the cargo, Illinois confirmed Djalaluddin Din's statements, while giving them further nuance: as far as he could tell, the Chinese were equipped with only three or four hunting rifles; otherwise it was just your basic chop-chop, or even simple club. Despite their martial science, the balance of power in no way favored them. Duke Pons hesitated, then decreed, well, okay, that they'd leave the next morning. As a precaution, the *Boustrophedon* would prolong its stopover until they had notified the captain of the happy outcome of things. Lopez would take advantage of this break to repaint the forecastle. Early the next morning, despite the general reticence, the Duke settled in behind the wheel of the Land Rover.

After leaving the city, they briefly followed the Rompin against its mangrove-lined current, then took a bad dirt road hovered over by the massive forest, bordered by plots of land, crumbling into high yellow dust. Certain plots were flanked by equally yellow, sometimes reddish, dwellings, often grouped in the perimeter of a well. Peasants in doorways furrowed a glance at the passage of the tall vehicle full of dirty white men, besotted by the heavy air, the screams of the gearshift, and the dance between potholes, their eyes full of yellow sand. Far from the dwellings, tiny deserted temples lined the road, crammed with foodstuffs and fresh flowers for the exclusive use of vipers high on incense. Finally Pons shouted that they were almost there.

Three miles before the plantation, Djalaluddin Din pointed out a narrow side road that they followed more slowly up to camp. The camp: mats in the middle of a clearing, eight men sitting on them around three stones from which rose a chalky line of smoke, a pallid plumb line that wound around the lower branches as if around the fingers of a smoker, became entangled, and then dissipated in the upper archways.

Aw the younger was there with all the others. Still the only one to know everybody, Duke Pons made the introductions, pronouncing names that were not always entirely understood. They pulled the trunks from the car and removed the utensils with collapsible stocks, which they handed out; there were two too many. The Malaysians still demonstrated scant enthusiasm for this arsenal; as Bob tried to explain its particularities via gestures, they turned skeptical eyes away, spoke quietly among themselves. Aw Aw had taken Din and Pons to one side. He explained the situation in measured tones.

The timid locals continued to exchange brief sentences with smiles, soft laughs, examining Charles and the others on the sly. One of them finally took the plunge, *what is your name;* Paul answered too quickly the first time, then articulated better. The Malaysians laughed, repeating the names with comments, deforming them with sharper laughs; this new material seemed to lend itself to native puns.

Aw Aw, seconded by Din, ended up convincing Pons to go into battle as soon as possible, exploiting what the captain had described: the Chinese's scanty equipment would mean certain victory. And even if—around the hard core constituted by himself and his brother, Din, and their close companions—the resolve of the locals formed a slightly overripe pulp, they could at least count on their passive support. Nonetheless, rather than attacking frontally, even with the certainty of winning, it would be better to operate by surprise, subdue the foremen without undue bloodshed. Aw suggested they act one hour before daybreak, when the imminence of dawn means that everywhere, every time, sentinels let down their guard.

The green light around them darkened softly, from olive via absinthe to bottle, then malachite. The noise changed character with the darkness. Nearby they heard quadruped footraces, which were buried during the day by huge, heated conferences that opposed five hundred species of birds, several among them migratory; deploying their inverted V on the tip of a conifer, they were sometimes called to testify as special delegates, sometimes booed as foreign agents, depending on the avian ideology of the moment. At nightfall these flying creatures took a bit of a breather, prepared for sleep, plumped the down cushions under their wings before burying their pointy heads in them. Soon only isolated, hesitant exclamations filtered down, repetitive and disillusioned, the belated soliloquies of birds in their cups; they embroidered a texture of melancholy riffs against which the vesperal merbok, a brilliant virtuoso with an established repertoire, occasionally deigned to improvise.

The men shared the soup, then remained seated, leaning on elbows by groups of affinities. They were fairly bored, not daring really to sleep. Still to one side, Aw, Pons, and Din fine-tuned their strategy, honing their tactics while passing around a thermos decorated with red flowers.

Charles pulled two dice from his already rumpled pocket, made them jump in his hand. He threw them on his corner of mat, read the score, threw them again. The Malaysians, from rather far off, began to observe him; their attention quickly sharpened, then they approached more and more noticeably. Using sign language, Charles was soon able to introduce them to the beauties of craps. Paul having kept the set of dice found on the *Boustrophedon*, they added the cubes together, which they then distributed, instituting three craps workshops; Bob, reserving for his own use the die that liked fives, failed to mention this fact. The locals played ardently, reinventing rules and discovering throws, devising strategies according to exotic premises, original postulates; they were delighted with this novelty that they explored in depth, until finally all their dollars, all their shyness had disappeared, while they waited to go out and fight. They remembered the cans of Tiger left in their bags; aluminum against aluminum they toasted. Bob fraternized while counting his winnings. Gambling night under the banyans.

2 8

Y OU ARE tired from the sleepless night. An hour before daybreak, you are so anxious for it to come that you imagine signs of its presence. You see it, there, just behind those trees; you expect the sun to rise any minute now. Then it comes less than ever. You begin to worry, you lose patience. This distress aggravates your fatigue; you might also lose your nerve when you find yourself at the edge of the pond with its occasional croakings, near a barracks full of sleeping men.

You are a Chinaman named Lu. You have this two-shot rifle in your arms. You have nothing to do other than keep your eyes open in the dark while listening to the batrachians snore. Not even the song of a bird, the most inveterate night owls having collapsed on their nests long before; no biological clock rings this early. And yet, from not far away come muffled steps: beasts sometimes cross the plantation, their gait rapid, light—and that's just fine. You wouldn't like it to be the clumsy, massive rumble of the hippogryph dragon, who eats rot and sweats poison; who, overall, is easily twice the size and weight of the average Chinaman. Best to banish this idea; the noise vanishes as well. You begin to feel relieved.

One minute later you smile when you recognize the merbok, in one of its most classical verbal attacks. If the virtuoso is already singing its theme song, you think, the others will certainly follow suit and take up the challenge, in a rasping voice at first, all hoarse before the first worm of the day. Dawn will seem to come more quickly; it's encouraging. Your confidence returns. But the bird immediately falls silent. Maybe it was singing in its sleep, the way humans speak in it, in snatches, oohing at some star turn in its operatic dream. Disappointment tarnishes your confidence; then, no sooner has Djalaluddin Din finished mimicking the merbok than something heavy falls on your shoulder and your knees buckle, then on your head and you fall. You roll into the pond and the leeches rush at you, latch onto your dermis with all the might of their three jaws.

After Din retrieved Lu's weapon, Aw Aw forced open the camp gate. Alerted by the prearranged signal, Aw Sam was waiting nearby with the other members of the strike committee. His younger brother handed him the wet rifle, showed him his own more modern, heavier one with a knowing look, a finger on his lips. The unionists regrouped in silence, then headed toward the foremen's barracks, where the look out offered not the slightest hint of resistance: very soon everything was almost over. The Chinese, awakened without violence, made no trouble after Kok Keok Choo had bowed to the Aw brothers' arguments, which were advantageous in all respects. The Europeans, who up until then had been content simply to watch the operation (handled in a scant fifteen minutes), were disturbed by its ease. They felt utterly useless, embarrassed at their own presence, out of place in the middle of the work site; they had been told to shove over. Pons offered to take care of the Jouvins himself.

Raymond Jouvin slept so soundly that they took the time to rip out the telephone cords before tying him up with them, on his bed, as he was. For Luce there was nothing to be done: she lay at the height of imbibition in the villa's indoor garden, among the palm leaves of the castor-oil plants. Her bottle had not rolled far on the flagstones of the patio, emptying itself of part of its contents; leaning on the edge of a stone, a couple of geckos lapped up the puddle, in no hurry. So it was all over almost too quickly. They would have liked to see the sun rise on their victory. They had to wait before making out its contours.

If, by an alliance between their leaders, the foremen and the trade unionists had officially joined camps, the rank-and-file was still somewhat divided. The two factions began to grumble, then pared down to two representatives, who confronted each other vocally, then manually, with bare knuckles. Aw Sam wanted to intervene, but Aw Aw, like the Duke, was of a mind to let the combat continue as a boxing match, a sports exhibition that would be a first celebration of the victory. And indeed, the two groups began cheering loudly as soon as the pugilists had thrown themselves on each other. They saluted the noble holds and low blows with equal fervor, chanted one name or the other depending on their camp; a few irresponsible souls, partisans of total war, alternately chanted both names.

The fistfight petered out with the sunrise. Everyone's eyes smarted a little. On the threshold of the Jouvin villa, Aw the younger and Duke Pons turned toward each other. Their smiles expressed bonds forged in combat, as well as the probable budding of their rivalry in seized power. They were tired, especially the older Pons; they had a brief board meeting. The Duke showed reticence before the Aws' proposal of an immediate week off for everyone, to start with. Proposing instead that from this day forth the anniversary would be officially commemorated, even celebrated with a large cock fight, he obtained that everyone would return to work the day after tomorrow. Once the holiday had been established, they divvied up the rooms. Din led Paul and Bob to the best one, that of the fallen couple. He and his men would make do with the living room, and Charles would share Pons's bungalow.

"Preferential treatment," said Paul, exploring the bedroom. "Why are they giving us the best room? We didn't help. We didn't even join in."

"Forget it," said Bob. "Help me pull off this mattress. I'll take the box spring if you like."

Outside, neither the Duke nor Charles felt sleepy. They toured the buildings, then advanced into the fields, between the rails of shrubs; Pons named things as they appeared in this new day. Charles walked in their midst, a little haltingly, as if he'd just been let out of the asylum. Then, once back at the bungalow, they weren't just going to go to sleep like that, not without a last beer. And by the way, Pons wanted to show Charles his plans, the plans for that gnomon he'd mentioned the other day on the boat. Charles leafed through the working drawings while the Duke uncapped the conclusive Tigers, still complaining about the age-old problem of building materials, his stumbling block.

"Why don't you just make it out of rubber?" yawned Charles.

"Shit," said Pons. "I hadn't thought of that."

"Maybe allow for a solid frame, even so."

Charles went to sleep without taking off his suit or exploring this idea, which the Duke examined alone, in bed, imagining the object, visualizing it more and more clearly. No, no frame. Duke Pons was conceiving of a new model of elastic gnomon, whose every variable he would control, whose flexible shadow he already saw floating, softened by the veiled sunlight, like his own flag on the reconquered territory, the figure of his reestablished power. If, as to this latter point, the Aw lobby displayed too many pretentions, the Duke would make use of the Chinese via proven methods. The situation had been won. Soon the gnomon would rise. Pons defined all its parameters, lingering on its every detail. As he imagined painting it he fell asleep, his eyes closing softly on the pillow of things accomplished.

Four hours later, the plantation was completely surrounded by the police, assisted by a detachment of ground forces. There were three or four times fifty men, most of them armed with Ingram explosives. They had come in trucks and jeeps, led by light armored vehicles equipped with MILAN anti-tank missiles, followed by a small Leopard tank and two Saladin armored cars, overshadowed by a Lynx helicopter built for ground attacks. It was too much. It was way too much.

29

ACCUSTOMED to rude awakenings, Charles immediately identified the grumbling of the real helicopter while the others were still dreaming: some of shutting up that pipe organ, others of annihilating that mosquito—maybe with that chainsaw? Leaping to his feet, Charles spied through the bungalow window several clusters of idle peasants raising their noses toward the ruffled sky. In the distance, a dotted line of soldiers materialized on the outline of the plantation, at too small a scale for one to delineate their faces, even with a very fine brush.

Firmly shaken on his bunk, guided toward the window before he'd even finished opening his eyes, Pons considered this without understanding. His thoughts assembled with difficulty, in fits and starts, like the pieces of a puzzle. An instinctive terror lubricated his system; everything fell into place all at once to bring forth a deduction. "It's fucked," he murmured. "We're screwed."

There was only one possible recourse: he in turn grabbed Charles by the arm, pulled him toward the door; they surged dazed into high noon. Dragging the uncomprehending Charles behind him, Pons began to run toward the uniformed men barring the entrance to the plantation. The helicopter just above them stirred the heavy air with its canopy, in a din of indefinitely shredded phone book; all arms and legs, they crossed its small round shadow.

The officer in charge of the operation did not even put his hand to his holster at the approach of these two white men of mature age, slovenly, out of breath. The thin one with red eyes cried for help in correct Malay. Rapidly introducing himself (Duke, Duke Pons), he panted a resume of the facts whose disjointed character might have been the result of his panic. It was only the broad truth, with few elaborations, relieved for its own good of pertinent details: fanatics had just invaded the plantation, holding the bosses hostage, bullying the supervisors, and terrorizing the employees. Things seemed critical, the Duke diagnosed; these men were coldly determined. The soldiers could nonetheless take advantage of the momentary lull in their vigilance, to which he and his colleague owed their escape. With urgent, ill-synchronized movements, he indicated the foremen's dormitory behind a committee of mangroves, offering to guide them: the moment seemed ripe to quell the subversion, even if they still had to contend with a few pockets of resistance.

The officer reflected briefly, then raised his hand while turning toward his men, who followed his quickstep in unison. They posted several guards at the entrance, toward whom Duke Pons ran to make their acquaintance. Still followed by Charles he returned to flit about the head of the column, haranguing the officer with breathless suggestions, buzzing among the troops under the snoring of the fat iron fly, which doubly annoyed everybody.

On the strength of his information, the forces of order invaded the barracks of the Chinese. A certain disorder ensued, a confusion fertile in denials, protests, rancors. Everyone grabbed everybody else, seizing the occasion to settle old, unrelated scores. The officer couldn't make heads or tails of it, asked for someone in charge, demanded they find him someone in charge. Kok Keok Choo finally came forward, reestablishing the truth of the matter and designating the Jouvin villa as the true nervous center of the disturbance. A moment passed before the officer realized that this version of events differed considerably from the one given by Pons, to whom he turned, full of questions—but of course the Duke was no longer there.

Of course he was running through the forest, his friend Charles right behind him. It had been a little more difficult to detach themselves from the squadron than it had to then leave the plantation, those fine guards having recognized them as allies. And now they ran, heading back up the path taken several hours before. In much less time than for the first semi-circle of the round-trip, they returned to the bivouac where earlier they had joined Aw Aw and his comrades. Deserted, this place had all the elegance of a picnic site on Monday morning, in some wooded area of the European outer suburbs—although the Malaysian forest, more powerfully biodegradable, accorded wax paper a much feebler status, a lesser life expectancy than in Fontainebleau. The Land Rover was still there, all misted over with green. The Duke approached it, trembling, then stopped short, dug frantically in his pockets. "Oh shit," he uttered in a dead voice. "The keys."

But Charles and his Swiss army knife knew how to dismantle a dashboard, read an electric circuit, connect the right wires, and soon they were speeding toward the coast. They reached the banks of the Rompin just as, in the recaptured Jouvin villa, the officer was methodically conducting his inquiry; deciphering a counterpoint of witnesses, he interpreted the share of responsibilities. They didn't brake a single time before arriving in the city, then they crossed the city toward the port. Having crossed the port, they pounded down the dock, at the end of which they leaped onto the gangplank of the *Boustrophedon*, which immediately cast off. From the beginning its engines chugged full ahead toward the wide open spaces. While the officer, having finally grasped Pons's role in all this, alerted the central authorities; while hasty anchors were raised and three cutters, packed with coast guardsmen, raced off in pursuit of the freighter, the latter left Malaysian waters to penetrate the neutral, profoundly hospitable high seas, out of reach of any repressive force since no territorial sovereignty had jurisdiction over them: this point has been commented on at length since the *Lotus* affair of 1927.

"It was bound to happen," Pons allowed four days later, gazing out at the ocean.

Daily, the ex-Duke analyzed the Malaysian situation, tirelessly projecting the same film for himself, each time discovering a few more awkward splices, admitting his mistakes. Charles looked at the sky, which a DC-9 split diametrically, trailing its white line straight across the dome, disguising it as a scored pill.

"You didn't get to see much of the country, after all that."

"Still," said Charles, "I was able to get an idea."

Inside the DC-9, they had lowered the window shades so that the passengers could watch the movie with Burt Reynolds. Everyone was indeed watching, except for Bob who, having seen it already, had not completely lowered his. Paul was sleeping in an aisle seat. Sitting next to Bob, a nearsighted man in brown was leafing through a brochure about hair implants. Interrupting his reading to clean his glasses, he attempted to exchange a few words: business, pleasure? "Little of both," said Bob. "And you?"

In the final account, there had been nothing to hold against them. No one could prove that it had been they who had fraudulently transported the weapons, which had immediately been confiscated, ticketed, and exhibited for investigative purposes in a room in the basement of the court building; this room adjoined a smaller office, lit night and day, where they had nonetheless been asked, protractedly, several times over, a whole series of questions. In their favor, the various testimonies concurred that Paul and Bob had proven scarcely inclined toward action, toward inciting to action; they were plausible pawns in a situation they swore they didn't understand. The fact that they knew the principal instigator, presently at large, was too minor a charge to press. After three days of redundant interrogation, it had been decided to release them. Firmly they had been seated on the first flight home, in economy class.

"Technology transfer," answered the nearsighted man, donning his spectacles. On the pale screen, Burt smiled broadly. Bob stretched, dug in his pockets, discovered at the base of the pectoral a frayed Egyptian souvenir, almost entirely emptied of its tobacco. He raised the shade a little more: nothing but the eternal azure, scarcely distinct from the crumpled water which a lone black dot marked way at the bottom, a blackhead on blue goose bumps.

On board the dot, Pons was finishing his self-criticism. He fell silent. He seemed annoyed. Charles was looking no longer at the sky, but at the water, nostalgically: how good it felt to be on the water, how much better you moved. He was perhaps surprised not to have been reincarnated as a pike, a tuna, even a simple carp as had surely been planned. No doubt some technical slip at the moment of his orientation, a wrong move at the last minute, had diverted him from his initial fate, wrenched him from his rightful environment: he would have made a good carp, a rather good fat psychasthenic carp wandering alone between two fresh waters, rehashing his fears of ending up stuffed, his regrets at not having been born a piranha.

"The fact is," said Pons, "that I have nothing left. I don't own a thing."

Charles turned. Jeff had not yet broached this subject.

"What you see," he resumed, "is what you get, and nothing more."

They headed toward Europe. Pons, impatient until the stop at Aden, darkened in the Mediterranean. After the waters approaching Le Havre had changed color nine times, Charles headed off in the rain to see Monique, leaving the captain and the Duke to their farewells. Would they ever see each other again?

"You're leaving just like that"—as Illinois understood the situation—"you don't have anywhere to go."

"I know a few crash pads in Paris," Pons presumed. "Obviously it won't be easy, there's my age, this weather. Can you believe this weather? I don't know if I can get used to it again."

The captain pulled at his chin, moved a divider on a chart, coughed in the way one hesitates to propose marriage, to slip a ring on such a long-standing liaison.

"You could stay," he blurted. "I could find you something. On board there's always work to do. The company won't make a fuss."

One day, Pons would admit that he had hesitated. But no, I couldn't get used to that either. Better to die where I come from. The captain lowered his eyes.

"On the other hand the train, Charles and me, we could use . . . I'd pay you back . . . "

Illinois took a wad from the ship's safe. "That's an awful lot," protested Pons, "it's too much."

"Come, come," said Illinois, who then rifled among the books above his bunk, pulling out a small volume, a small souvenir, Nordenskjold's *Journal* of his travels in the polar regions, 1880, here, take it. To read on the train.

At the station Pons met Charles, who now sat facing him next to the compartment window. The fallen Duke leafed through the Nordic opus without conviction, lingering over anecdotes concerning the effects of extreme cold. Charles gazed out the window. Pons showed him the captain's money, handed him half, and gazed out the window in turn. They spoke once of the train's speed. At Gare Saint-Lazare, on a scrap of paper, Charles inscribed the address of his mailbox in the suburbs. They were standing in the middle of the concourse; people rushed by them in all directions. What are you going to do?

"I'm still not sure," answered Pons, staring at his foot as it pushed a cigarette butt.

"You could come with me, you'll see you could do it. I'd show you how."

Pons reflected too long before answering, then raised his eyes toward Charles but he was no longer there, Charles was no longer there. Pons remained alone in the company of four hundred francs and change, out of which the ticket for Chantilly would take a bite. With neither job nor family, neither home nor anything, he had no prospects other than Chantilly. And even then.

Iffy recourse: Nicole might not spontaneously offer to underwrite Pons's needs, the unmentionable goal of this expedition. He'd have to know how to convince her; he felt confused just thinking about it. In case of failure there would still be the Charles solution—but his convictions, his ducal conception of the world rebelled against this. For Nicole to accept Jeff as a permanent guest, he especially had to say nothing, induce nothing, play at the back of the court so that the idea would seem to suggest itself; she must take the initiative and he must refuse, at first. It was rather delicate. The Duke had been quite fond of such maneuvers in the days of the plantation, when he danced among the Chinese, the Jouvins, and the unionist sensibilities; but he no longer had the energy for them, and besides they had not borne such fabulous fruit.

Aged, hunched amid the comings and goings, he left the station via Cour de Rome. Before taking the train again, from a different station, the preparation of a little speech for Nicole might be in order. He composed this speech, of which he eliminated the second half, then the first under the drizzle. He was alone; he was hungry; he watched the buses maneuvering.

Night and the rain fell coldly on Chantilly when he rang at the door of the villa, giving just the brief buzz of an apprentice salesman, a debutant Jehovah's witness. Boris opened without a glance, indicated the entrance to the green salon without a word, disappeared. Pons walked uneasily into the salon, to discover Nicole prostrate in a wing chair in the dark. She stood as soon as he appeared, collapsed in tears in his overlong arms; Pons was very embarrassed. "She's all gone she's all," sobbed Nicole, "gone."

"It's nothing," said Pons uncomprehendingly. "It's nothing," he repeated softly. "*I'm* here," he indicated.

As Nicole sobbed all the harder, he changed tactics: calm down, tell me what happened—it was surely nothing but they wouldn't be able to eat right away. He made Nicole sit down, sat next to her, tell me what happened, calm down, I say. An hour later he knew everything about Justine's disappearance, in other words very few, but extremely lachrymose and repetitive, facts. The consulted police threw up their hands.

"She went off with some guy, most likely," guessed Jeff. "A few days, a little trip, you know what it's like, they never tell you. They don't think ahead."

Nicole began crying again, for the rest of the day. Early the next morning her tears had already salted her cold tea. Pons left the house, without knowing what to do with himself. He had been able to take back his room, that wasn't the problem at all; he paced over the cold gravel. Magpies flew above him, exchanging hoarse points of view, crossing the air taut like segments of a line, anamorphoses of penguins. He heard other birds, without seeing all of them; he climbed into the Austin.

At Chantilly station, Pons wrote a postcard (we have to see each other at once, call at meal times, Jeff; on the verso, the castle), which he tossed into an incredulous mailbox, with the address that Charles had given him. From an equally bemused booth he tried to phone Paul. Then he let it ring a long time at Bob's while watching the people beyond the cabin windows: rattled by a sudden gust of wind, the sky with great effort held in a terrible need to rain; people, dressed accordingly, busied themselves below him. He hung up. He joined the people.

30

A T BOB'S, the telephone had not even rung, as it happened to be out of order. Its wires were ripped out, and the instrument itself was broken, like the majority of objects around it. In Bob's absence, during one of Van Os's vengeful tantrums, the latter's men had demolished the studio, smashed every accessory, even ripped up the phone books, then concluded their labors by burning several well-chosen plastic appliances in the sink. Their greasy smoke, coating everything in a thick gluey soot, compromised the future of the few items left intact.

Disembarking from a taxi hailed at Roissy, their watches still on Malaysian time, their sorry faces showing the difference in zone, Paul and Bob stood before the open door, in the hallway, as if on the threshold of a coal molecule: the space was uniformly black, bristling with black carcasses, littered with sharp black debris. They didn't dare enter. Bob hadn't reacted too badly.

"We can't stay here," he simply concluded. "Let's go to your place."

"Don't even think about it," said Paul, "it might be worse. Maybe they did worse."

"You think it's them?"

"It wouldn't be too good to bump into them. In my opinion.

We'd better not take the cars. Can't you think of somewhere else, meanwhile? Somewhere safe?"

"No idea," said Bob. "We could go see Bouc."

They went just to have a drink, without desiring a consultation. They sat down to chat in the pocked canvas armchairs, ran through the various subjects that came up, such as cold cuts, orchids, indigo, hope, until aperitifs, after which Bob went out to do some shopping. They dined on red meat, red wine, and oranges while watching the television news, then the beginning of what came after. Bouc Bel-Air got up to change the glasses.

"You'd like to stay the night as well," he finally assumed.

"Well, that is, it would be great," said Bob, "but we're not imposing. We don't want to impose."

Bouc returned with a decanter of marc and three jelly-jars, pulled from a closet two cots of the same model as his own; Bob and Paul drank to his health. Soon they'd already been there a week. You always felt a bit cold at the geomancer's; the collapsible shower dribbled barely lukewarm, and the heater was a little resistance thing that scarcely threw off its meager puff of burnt dust. Thumbtacked to the door, a gymnastics chart, which they stared at just about every morning, depicted the twelve basic twists and bends.

At the beginning it was all smiles, but you know how, often, in a limited space, these situations quickly turn sour. At the beginning everybody's happy, the host less lonely and his guests sheltered. But time passes, taking the novelty out of things and ruffling feelings; soon it grates, then it weighs. Bouc Bel-Air stopped being the first to laugh, withheld his replies and averted his gaze; he demonstrated ambivalence about everything. During the day, Bob and Paul were generally to be found sitting in one of the rooms while he, in the other, received the distraught clients whose future was his beefsteak. The door separating the two rooms was thin, and it displeased Bouc that the two others should hear him, even listen to him patch together his prognostics whose character he knew to be limited. When he tried to improvise, to introduce variations, it was annoying to imagine their silent smiles. Even if they never alluded to it, he did not like them to witness the sometimes delicate reactions of the clientele.

So Bouc began to pull such things as: drink all the Kronenbourg and all the Tropicana, finish the reblochon; never buy anything; lose the soap, stop up the drain; leave the place as is, go out without notice, forget to drop off the key. More and more frequently stranded outside due to forgotten key, Paul and Bob waited, usually in department stores.

"Do you really think the Belgians are looking for us?" Bob asked at the foot of the escalator. "You think they're still after us? Personally I think it's over."

They wandered around the ground floor, among the perfume stands; the firm and rigid saleswomen seemed of a different essence from their sisters in the middle of the bottles and sprays. Grasping the samples, Bob vaporized the back of his hand.

"We can't stay at Bouc's anymore," he continued, "it's unbearable, let's go to your place. Come on, we'll go to your place. It's nice at your place. It's big."

"No," said Paul, "but I have another idea. Maybe we can phone from here." (They could.) "Hello, could I speak to Jean-François?" (He could.) "So, there you are," he said in a husky voice. "I thought so."

"Only since yesterday," said Pons, "I just arrived. I tried calling you, this morning, your timing is perfect. We have to see each other right away."

"That's a good one," said Paul. "Don't you remember how you just let us drop, back there? We didn't even speak the language. Is that any way to treat someone?"

"But you see that you're here," gambled Pons, "you see you had nothing to fear. If they found *me*, I'd have a ton of problems. And Charles with his expired passport, did you think of that? You don't know where he is, by the way, do you?"

"Listen," Paul cut him off, "you have to put us up, me and Bob. We've got a big problem" (because of him, Bob whispered, make him understand our problem's because of him). "There must be room where you are. Bob said it's big."

"Ah," went Pons, "I don't believe that would be possible. Let me talk to Bob." (That's right, said Bob, let me talk to him.) "Bob, someone dear to me has disappeared, can you imagine, could you possibly help me find her? I'm asking you, because I get the impression that Paul—"

"You're not serious," Bob interrupted in turn. "You dream up these schemes without a plan. You don't have any common sense. I'm not buying it this time."

"Little Justine, you remember her?" (Yes, said Bob.) "You saw her in Chantilly, do you remember? She's the one who's missing, get it? You see how important it is." (Yes.) "Try to explain it to Paul."

"He doesn't know her," Bob seemed to recall in a troubled voice. "Maybe he won't understand."

"Try," repeated Pons before hanging up. "Call me back afterward."

"What's going on?" asked Paul.

"Let's go sit down."

On the table of contents displayed at the large store's entrance, Bob looked up the floor devoted to furniture. They chose two squat, eggshell-white armchairs in which they discussed, then decided: the bestowing of aid, as requested by Pons, would only be imaginable in exchange for safe haven. They called him back. "All right," he said, "I'll see what I can do."

As the despairing Nicole no longer left her room, it was difficult to explain the situation to her discreetly, without Boris listening in. "It will make our search easier, Nicole," shouted Pons
through the door. "We'll centralize our information that way. It's
better." She didn't answer; Pons considered that his case had been
pled. "It's okay," he said on the phone, "come over. We'll work it
out." Two hours later, casting a radiographic pupil on Paul and
Bob, Boris prepared two rooms for them in the attic, adjoining his
apartments.

The next day, it was no use having gone so early to Levallois: it
was a whole production just to find Rue Madame-de-Sanzillon,
and in the latter Charles's mailbox, and in the latter Pons's postcard under a sediment of offers for goods and services—nothing
for Vidal. Pons reread his card; they waited for hours in Nicole's
Austin, watching the street. Charles did not appear, nor did anyone else, save for a new gang of Lusitano-Mauritanian garbage
men in a noisy green truck. It was the end of the morning; the
crew put the finishing touches on its collection by ending with
arteries as eccentric and scattered as Madame-de-Sanzillon.
These streets were restful, for being stingy in refuse, they constituted the lap of honor of the sweepings, a farewell to use value, to
exchange value, before the dump and the incinerator.

They returned to Chantilly for lunch, downcast, trading vague
outlines of plans. Nothing encouraged them to move in one
direction or another; when you got down to it, they knew nothing
about Justine. They became discouraged. Boris had set the table
for four.

"But Nicole's dining in her room, Boris," objected Pons.
"There are only three of us, no?"

"I'm eating with you, sir."

"Forgive me, Boris. And call me Jeff."

In fact Boris ate little, deducting only the margins of foodstuffs, crust or rind, which he chewed thoroughly. He spoke to them; they listened to his voice carry a grave ardor, Bukharin and Chaliapin resurrected. Alone they would never find Justine, he foretold them, whereas with Charles it would be possible. He seemed to admire Charles a great deal. But alone, he continued, they would not be able to find Charles either. He also seemed to hold their own abilities in doubt. Perhaps he might be able to find Charles. He rose, stacking the dirty dishes, which he replaced, then he returned with the next course. "We'll eat the next course," he concluded, "and afterward I'll find Charles."

The afternoon was spent following him through metro stations, under bridges, across squares, and finally into the vaulted canal. They hopped the fences, skidded on the slime at the tunnel entrance, nearly fell into the venomous Styx that flowed at their feet. They were cold, not unafraid in the black dampness, on the narrow quay; they held onto each other's clothes behind Boris's feeble penlight. The latter walked much straighter than normal, and more and more quickly, as if he were reaching his goal. Indeed, a light grew in the distance: fire in a trash bin, four cannibals around it at the Chemin-Vert marker. Three stood at their approach.

Boris seemed very excited to see Vidal again. He was no longer the same man. He spoke with gusto, as if just back from Africa; memories echoed under the vault. Vidal wanted to know: was Boris feeling better? wasn't this new life in Chantilly too hard on him? had he seen Charles? "As a matter of fact," said Boris, "I'm looking for him."

"It won't be easy," said Vidal, "you know what he's like. Did you check Saint-Ambroise? There's always Levallois, he goes there sometimes. That's where we've got the mailbox."

"They've already been by there," said Boris, waving his thumb toward the others.

"Ah," Vidal said without looking at them. "There wasn't anything for me, by any chance?"

"No," answered Pons, intimidated, "I don't believe so."

"No matter. Would you like to have a seat?"

They sat, the regulars squarely on the ground, the others squatting on their cautious heels. As he settled in, Boris identified Henri the one-legged, the only person not to have risen.

"I won't get up," said Henri, "because of my stolen leg."

A plate with twelve screws, he explained, wasn't very hard to remove; it didn't take much time at all. In broad daylight at Jaurès station, while he was asleep, in front of everybody, it hadn't woken him up. He hadn't even seen them. "I've sort of ordered another one," said the unijambist, showing his crutches, "but it's a long wait, as you can imagine." And still these pains in his phantom limb, which the dampness surely wasn't helping.

"You haven't seen Charles, have you?" asked Boris.

"I know he sleeps in the seventeenth sometimes. I don't remember exactly where, though. It's pretty big, the seventeenth, it's a large arrondissement."

"Brochant?"

"Could be Brochant," said Henri. "You know it?"

"He took me there once," Boris recalled.

After midnight, then, the Austin headed for Brochant. Boris had a little trouble finding the street, then they were finally in front of Gina de Beer's. The windows were dark behind the closed shutters, behind the openwork fence delimiting the polygon of rose bushes.

"Lights are out," said Boris. "We shouldn't disturb them. We'll wait here."

"Here?" they said skeptically.

"Here," he specified. "This way we can't miss him."

When the day and its noises rose, the four men in the Austin were full of dew, sweat, mist, and joint-aches. Bob was the first to give up feigning sleep; he went out to buy the paper and some croissants, if there were any to be found in the neighborhood. On his return, Paul and Boris were talking cars in the front seat of the car; only Pons persisted in faking it. Bob distributed the croissants, opened the newspaper while yawning, cast a glance; his eyes latched onto the first lines they met, like a cat thrown at a curtain, then slid down them, mechanically skimming an article on Monaco. They had rolled down the windows; they bit into their dry pastries. Separated from Bob by the raised newspaper, Pons read the headlines on the back page.

Creak of a handle, squeak of hinges: their glances converged on the ground-floor shutters, which opened onto a nude Charles. Hands emerged from the Austin, waving around its midsection like fins. Charles blinked, focused, recognized the faces behind the hands, made a sign while shutting the window. In the time it took him to get ready, Bob was able to finish another article, on the State of Andorra.

3 1

A THIRD, devoted to Lichtenstein, completed this series on the midget principalities. Toon scowled at the arrangement of consonants and folded the paper, which he handed to Justine. Sitting on her bench, the young woman instinctively recoiled. Toon scowled some more.

"Hold it just like that," he said, "front page toward me. Don't move."

She found herself bound, by a light chain of solid white plastic, to this little bench bolted to the middle of the round, high-ceilinged room—moreover, you couldn't see the ceiling. The floor was bare cement. No furniture except for the mattress; no window; no provisions seemed to have been made for air circulation. On the floor two burners under a glass lid, fed by butane, released whiteness. Plankaert emerged from the depths of the cornerless shadow, approached while pawing a flat case; he avoided looking at Justine. Toon turned to him:

"Will that be enough light, you think?"

"Turn on the lamps in back," Plankaert said cheerlessly. "Anyway there's the flash."

He unfolded the instant camera and adjusted the focus. Justine trembled a little in small doses of fear and cold. "You don't seem to be doing too well," said Toon, regulating the knurls on the burners (she thought it was *she* that he . . .), "what's wrong?"

"What we're doing is so stupid," Plankaert groused. "It's out of proportion."

She didn't understand what they were doing, but she was less afraid of the man with the Polaroid—he was less nervously unpredictable than the other one, not so young, more conversant with manners. The mute, daily visits of a third man who always came alone did not at all help explain what they were doing there, what she was doing here, what they wanted from her; they simply marked the succession of days in this airtight world.

"Hold the paper right in front of you," Toon said again, turning toward the other. "That okay? Is she all right like that?"

"That's fine," said Plankaert. "Sit up a bit straighter, Miss."

Through the viewfinder he saw her straighten up; she could not see his eyes, then she saw nothing at all under the flash, followed by the little whine of the machine as it vomited the picture.

"Let's take another one," Toon suggested.

"That's enough," said Plankaert, "that's enough."

Mirthlessly he shook the photograph, waiting for the image to clarify. Justine rested the paper on her lap. "You can keep it," said Toon, "I'll bring you some magazines later on. Any in particular you'd like? Aren't you getting hungry?" She didn't answer. Plankaert leaned toward one of the lamps to examine the portrait, straightened up while grumbling something; she remembered that she didn't have her bag with her, nor the mirror inside it. Toon stretched up toward the Polaroid, over Plankaert's shoulder, then took it to study up close. She saw them walk away, return to the shadows from whence they were regularly reborn, carrying things to drink, eat, change into, wash with, read; and pills to sleep. Toon bumped against something, swore, then dissolved into the ground.

Tomb-like noise of a trapdoor, then the silence returned. She glanced through the newspaper. No mention of her kidnapping.

Toon methodically descended along the wall, gripping with all his vertigo the rungs that he squeezed excessively tight, moving only one of his limbs, then the next—as in the trees of Hainaut, when he was a little boy—and telling himself not to look down.

"Why are you making that face?" he insisted.

"Because it's an assholic idea," answered Plankaert fifteen rungs below. "That's why."

"*He* wanted it," Toon reminded him, testing with his feeble weight the resistance of the next bar. "It was *his* idea."

At the foot of the ladder, all wired, the idea's author brandished at Plankaert a sheet of paper covered with revisions, inserts, and cross-outs:

"I've finished. Read that."

More stage fright: embarrassed to have someone read his prose in his presence, Van Os literally paced in circles, this room also being round. But it was also much better lit; four windows underlined four views of a large hydraulic machine located in the center, whose purpose was not readily discernible to the layman—they guessed only that it was out of order, ossified under greasy rust. The portable television was perched unsteadily on this machine, among clothes, cans of food, a heater, a transistor radio, and a bag containing more clothes. Another bag, smaller, containing East German Zeiss binoculars and a Czech Vzor pistol, was placed on the floor near the cot. Plankaert and Toon sat on an unoccupied part of the machine, a tarpaulin folded under them. Plankaert read the text over; Van Os passed in front of them.

"By the way," went Toon, "what'll we do if we don't find Bergman? Do we let the girl go?"

"That's right," cried Van Os, braking exasperatedly. "So she can go tell everybody everything, is that what you want?"

"She'll tell in any case," prophesied Plankaert without raising his eyes. "Someday."

"You're against me," said Van Os, "that's what it is. You're plotting against me."

"No," said Plankaert, "I wish you well."

"Then we won't discuss it. We'll do it like they do in these situations—a recent photo of the person with a note that spells out what we want. That's the correct procedure."

"This is pretty violent stuff," Plankaert observed as he handed the sheet back to Van Os. "It's kind of threatening. Maybe a bit too much."

"It's an accurate expression of my thoughts. And besides, this way Bergman will do something. He'll have to show himself."

"Not certain," said Plankaert, "not even certain. And besides, what if the newspapers get into it? Up to now it's been quiet, but imagine if the paper prints the photo, it becomes a whole big deal. It's too much."

"I don't give a good goddamn," said Van Os, handing Toon the paper.

"One second," went Plankaert, intercepting. He reread it, suggested some changes that Van Os refused, then some grammatical corrections that he accepted, embarrassed. Plankaert took advantage of that embarrassment to pass content off for form as much as he could, but it was only details; Van Os stood firm on the essentials. They passed the message to Toon.

Armed with scissors and glue, the young man had been ordered to recompose it anonymously, using capitals requisitioned from old newspapers. First he balked at this task, which was hardly in line with his aspirations; then it was no less fun, all things considered, than the scrabbled word puzzles in the quiz magazines. He found certain words ready for use, others that he had to shorten, lengthen, reorganize; certain smaller words were discovered intact in the body of a large one, and sometimes several ones cohabited there. It was interesting. The others had resumed their talk, but Toon was no longer listening, perceiving only the music—Plankaert's persuasive, Van Os's yielding—of their interventions.

His work completed, while the conversation was dying under fatter and fatter bubbles of silence, Toon handed the paper to Plankaert who handed it to Van Os who crumpled it into a ball and shot it nervously toward the wall, then picked it up, unfolded it, and reread it with a sigh. Toon watched, uncomprehending.

"Very well," the boss said to Plankaert, "all right. You win. We'll drop my idea. But that means you have to find Bergman for me, you guarantee you'll find him."

"Of course," said Plankaert. "We're leaving now."

"So wait," went Toon, pointing to his crumpled collage, "so we're not using it?"

As no one answered, he ventured:

"Could I have it, could I maybe keep it? As a souvenir, is that okay?"

Van Os began yelling again at Toon, who recoiled fearfully toward the door while Plankaert burned the anonymous letter in a bowl. On the threshold, their boss spat Flemish curses at the outside world; Plankaert had to push him gently aside in order to get out. He crossed two hundred fifty yards of open country before reaching the byroad, where Toon had already taken refuge in the car. As he was about to join him, he heard Van Os stop yelling and slam the door of the water tower.

He turned around: it was a fifties' water tower, shaped like a fifties' vase; its curve was also reminiscent of certain hourglasses, certain pepper mills. A lot of use had been gotten out of it for thirty years before they had built another, more capable one, six miles away; then they had abandoned it after emptying it of its water. It now stood very alone in the heart of the interminably changing cereal flats. There were no visible constructions in the area save for a single ruined farm, very far away, which Van Os had studied with his binoculars. A semi-primitive lived in it, in the company of a decalcified horde fanaticized by the search for some proof of the bone's existence; no hierarchy was distinguishable between these beasts and their protégé.

Abandoned, the water tower was peeling. A column of short moss gnawed a triangle of its septentrion. Rising above the four cardinal windows, a flight of rungs behind a dotted line of portholes permitted access to the old first-floor reservoir—windowless, naturally. Plankaert got into the car and started up. Behind the middle porthole, Van Os watched his men leave before going to visit the girl in the reservoir, as he did every day. Toon turned to his colleague:

"What's with him, you think? Did you see how irritable he's gotten?"

"He's tired," said Plankaert. "We're all tired."

Toon liked that girl in the reservoir. Therefore, out of sympathy, he would not have abused her. But she was never satisfied. This dissatisfaction was not really visible on the Polaroid, no more than the trembling of the newspaper stretched before her. They might have destroyed his collage, but they hadn't thought of the photo which Toon had saved, which he would keep.

Division of labor: while Plankaert took care of the neighborhoods that Paul frequented, Toon stood watch at the foot of his tower on Quai André-Citroën. All day long it was in vain, and the next day as well, while Van Os looked after his captive alone. Fortunately, Plankaert spotted Paul the day after that, at around noon, near Chaussée-d'Antin.

Paul was stifling in Chantilly, where the vanished Justine haunted everyone's mind. The absence of a recent photo of her

did not help their search and, despite the army of migrant infor-
mants raised by Charles, no trace of the young woman could be
uncovered. So they waited, not knowing where to go next; they
spoke less. Using his shoes as a pretext, Paul had taken the afternoon to go breathe the exhaust of the big city, contained in the
perimeter of Gare Saint-Lazare, where he inspected the shops.

Professional, Plankaert followed the thread of shoe stores, as
dictated by his art, until Paul seemed to decide on a model that
might have been English, embellished with a shark's-tooth collar
on either side of the laces. The other watched him through the
store window, thinking, strange taste. As Paul sat to try the things
on, Plankaert went to find a telephone.

"Come on," he said. "I found him."

Toon was happy to be for once at the wheel of the 4 × 4, happy to
listen to the frequency modulation, happy to use the telephone.

"You're brilliant," he said, "but why don't you take care of it
yourself? I've got a good radio here, I don't really feel like moving."

"Don't be an idiot, there are too many people. And besides, he
might not just come along quietly. And besides, I'm tired. Come
on, we'll do it like with Gonzales, you remember how easy it
was."

Shortly afterward, at the aftershave counter in the Printemps,
Toon applied the Gonzales procedure, one method of kidnapping
among hundreds, whose principle involves anticipating the vic-
tim's behavior. Toon spoke loudly, loudly swelled his high voice,
demanded an imaginary lotion. The calm saleswoman tried to
appease him, to distract this nervous little customer. She pretended to look again, leading her long purple nails among the
vaporizers, the sticks, the fat promotional bottles full of artificial
fluid. "It existed," the nervous little man went up a notch, "it
can't no longer *be*. Where's the manager?"

He fidgeted his little heart out, hoping to be very noticed, and indeed shoppers were looking at him all over the store. "I can't believe it," thought Paul, hidden behind a pyramid of gels. He had recognized, from afar, the young man's high-pitched squeak coming from over by the perfumes, wafting over the fragrances; he had been startled. All the same he moved closer, hid, identified the silhouette in the overcoat; he followed the dialogue with the floor manager, then, the Gonzales effect working like a charm, followed Toon himself. Toon was very easy to follow in the huge department store. "It might not be too smart to follow him," thought Paul. But it was easier still outside the huge department store.

Toon crossed Boulevard Haussmann. Paul did not lose sight of him along rues de Rome and de Leningrad, at the end of which, on the border of Batignolles, rose the church of Saint-André-d'Antin. Toon entered the church; Paul followed a moment later. It smelled of stearin and cool granite, not at all of incense or disinfectant; no organ rumbled in the extraterrestrial silence. No one was there but a man collapsed in prayer against a pillar in the back and an old woman in a stone-grey suit, melted into the transept. Toon had disappeared. Soon the old woman rose from her knees and crossed herself; she left without glancing at Paul. It was even emptier. Then everything happened very fast.

Plankaert removed his hands from his face, detached himself from the pillar, approached Paul, who recoiled and immediately felt the contact of something hard between two of his vertebrae. No doubt related to this contact, Toon's breath reached him from very close behind his shoulder. Plankaert came nearer, pained but decided, the very picture of an undertaker. First he confiscated the plastic shopping bag, with the new shoes inside. This bag then contained Paul's head. Still attached to the latter, his bound body lay under a blanket in the back of the 4 × 4, which had started off. In the front, Toon examined the shark's-tooth collars: too big for him, and too small for Plankaert.

The car finally stopped and they dragged Paul out, his head still in the bag. After they'd cut the engine, there was a different silence from the silence in the church; now it was a silence full of sky rubbed by birds. They guided Paul over pliant, uneven ground. They stopped, then opened a door, behind which they heard music turned down low and strong, regular breathing shot through with wheezes. "He's sleeping," Toon went softly. "What should we do?"

"Turn that off," Plankaert whispered, "then we'll take him up." Three steps; the music died; then they pulled and pushed Paul. He felt himself moving vertically, tried to imagine his surroundings.

Toon and Plankaert hoisted him into the reservoir and deposited him on his side; he was still prevented from doing anything by his cowl and his bonds. Justine watched them work, the butane burners at her feet attending the altar of a pouty goddess. They threw her a regulation glance before closing the trap door. They went back down, tiptoeing past the still-slumbering Van Os.

"We'll wait," said Plankaert once they'd gone back outside. "We won't wake him up, it would get him annoyed, and he's already— I'd rather he rested, then saw Bergman after."

They strolled around the water tower, in no hurry. From time to time the wind thought about rising, dozed off again, then stretched seriously; it yawned in scattered, conflicting gusts, under which the colors of the crops changed hue. The cereals bowed their heavy heads in masses that were lighter on the obverse side; the long, limp, mobile stains formed a progressively twisted declension of the chlorophylian mood.

"It's pretty," said Toon.

"Yeah," said Plankaert. "Impressive." But then cries resounded from within the edifice—cries of fury or pain, perhaps both. The two men ran for the door.

The cries originated in the reservoir. Awakened with a start, Van Os sat wild-eyed on his seat.

"What's going on?" he said in a frantic voice. "Who turned off the radio?"

"Nothing," said Plankaert, "don't worry about it. This'll only take a minute."

Toon followed him in his assault on the rungs. They had a little difficulty opening the trapdoor at first, as Paul was lying on top of it—albeit temporarily, since he was moving without stop, rolling crazily in an attempt to escape Justine's grievances. Still holding the bag that she had pulled off him, the latter brandished in her other hand her high-heeled shoe, punctuating each future bruise with a war cry. Paul also cried out, in the middle register. "Whoa," said Toon, "we've got to separate them."

Plankaert tried to grab Justine, but it wasn't easy. "It's because of *him*," she was panting, "it's all because of that *asshole!*" He finally spun her toward him by force.

"That's enough," he went. "That's enough right there. You don't beat a guy who's tied up, I mean after all. It's not dignified. You're forcing me to shorten the chain."

They rolled Paul out of reach, then went back down, a little worried about their boss's mood. But they found Van Os peacefully seated on his cot, having turned on the radio that now broadcast some Herb Alpert. Before his eyes, hanging from two fingers, swung the two new shoes with shark's-tooth collars.

"What's this?" he asked. "Whose are these? They're nice."

32

CHARLES HAD alerted his network after Justine's disappearance; now Paul's was the occasion to circulate some new particulars. As Bob (who accompanied him on his rounds) had spoken to him of Van Os (whose shadow hovered over events), Charles indicated this trail to his colleagues. Boris also came as soon as his duties allowed, thereby taking up again with his former confraternity, reminding Charles of such-and-such an attic or basement.

Pons soon stopped going with them. He had trouble—after they had searched late into the evening—seeing why he should sleep on a bench in the metro just so he could be ready to get to work early the next morning. For this purpose, Charles had taken measures: if you wanted to get up early, all you had to do was bed down in any station of Line 8. Since it had been arranged that the friendly conductor of one of the first morning trains would give three short horn blasts as soon as he saw Charles, Number 8 acted as a long alarm clock, all the handier in that it covered numerous neighborhoods. If, on the contrary, you wanted to catch some sleep, you simply avoided settling in at Bonne Nouvelle or Liberté stations, for example. Boris did not mind sleeping in the metro, and Bob got used to it. Night after night they searched the system's entrails, even those least open to the public; even the phantom stations—Arsenal and Croix-Rouge, stricken from the map of the world, haunted by a fringe of cavernicolous wanderers whom they interviewed like the others, one by one.

In Chantilly, Nicole had emerged from her room. She began to reappear in the house strewn with spare beds; Pons kept her company as much as he could. They saw her during meals, which Boris maintained the habit of sharing with them. They started talking again. "So in the end," Nicole said to Charles, "you never married."

Charles bowed his head, departed alone that evening in the car—again toward the canal, under whose vault Henri awaited his prosthesis. Generally well informed, the unijambist was all alone beside the cold stew; Vidal and Jeanne-Marie were vacationing on the Ourcq canal. This time he came up with two names, which might yield other names. In two hours Charles crossed the city twice, followed his leads up to the aforementioned Briffaut; on the return highway he knew everything. The moon was much fatter and lower, much redder than normal when he parked the Austin, headlights off, in front of the house in Chantilly. He got out of the car; the gravel shone, rusted by the satellite. He approached the windows: the others had retired to the salon. "So in the end, no," answered Pons, "I couldn't go through with it. There was Jacqueline, but you remember Jacqueline, you know what she was like, and then there was that business with my sister. Besides, I'm terribly suggestible. And there you have it."

Charles scribbled two sentences in pencil on a scrap of cardboard. Then he opened the door to the villa, climbed without being heard to the upper floors, and placed the cardboard on Bob's bed. Back behind the wheel of the Austin he waited, looking at the ignition key, a firefly in the shadow of the dashboard. He heard the others go to bed. Bob appeared shortly afterward.

They skirted the west of Paris. Charles drove slowly, even on the highway that they abandoned at the Ury exit. Night over Nemours was black and liquid. Then Charles found his way surefootedly in a maze of secondary roads without lights, which undulated like the languid arms of an estuary, without bumps or dips to disturb their ride, with no existence other than to direct them. They made out no dwellings on either side, or weren't certain of their reality. Finally, daybreak having passed into dawn and low beams into sidelights, they saw, in the distance, to the right, the water tower, dark lighthouse against a grey swell. Grasses continued to roll as far as the eye could see, by ample brushstrokes, under the risen wind full of vigor and pollen.

Charles did not slow down, drove until the edifice was almost imperceptible behind them. Leaving the car by the side of the road, the two men then retraced their path, on foot in the damp blades under the white sky. First they followed the narrow road, then headed across the fields, running bent over, under cover of the tallest plants. They lay among the sunflowers two hundred yards from the water tower; above them, already pointed straight West, the courtesan flowers awaited the rising of the radiator. Charles cleared a small flat surface, but the dice rolled badly on the loose earth; in the shadows they had to read the scores in braille. They nonetheless tried a few tosses, then a light appeared in the ground floor of the tower.

A long moment later Plankaert came out, followed by Van Os, to take a leak; it was then five past eight. A little before nine Toon and Plankaert appeared, the latter swinging an empty fishnet bag ballasted by a housewife's change-purse. Toon watched the 4 × 4 maneuver and head off, then reentered the water tower. "Let's move up a little," Charles suggested.

After the heliotropes was a haywagon toward which they dragged themselves with the curved motions of deep-sea divers, making tiny critters jump and burrow up to the edge of the alfalfa patch, almost at the foot of the round building. Through a window they saw Toon pass by, hat on head, towel in hand. They inspected the other windows, crawling around the stronghold, as soaked with dew as if at the bottom of a real moat. They didn't spy Van Os, but saw Toon with a tea kettle, then a beer bottle, without transition. "He'll have to come out to piss, too," judged Charles. "That'll be when."

He would in fact get the better of the young man, who ended up coming out as predicted, unzipping in anticipation, immobilizing his turned back a little farther off. Charles struck once, not too hard: Toon jumped lively and turned, off balance, raising his shoulder and hip while describing yellow figure-eights in the air, handicapped by the maintenance of his member; then he collapsed under Charles's reexpedited fist. After that they neutralized his boss, whom Charles grabbed, spun, emptied of his air as if to fold him with the other tires; who crumpled to the ground, his apron undone. Then Charles indicated the rungs, saying: "Let's go up."

33

L'AVENIR almost borders the Loiret. Located in the south-west horn of the Seine-et-Marne region, it's the locality nearest the water tower. The 4 × 4 returned from it, stuffed with provisions, with all the daily press on the back seat. For some undefined reason, the second he saw the tower in the distance, Plankaert knew things had changed. He slowed: in front of the edifice, strapped to a chair like an old man, Van Os caught his breath while contemplating the landscape from the height of his compromised career. They had left him there near the entrance, the plywood emblem of a roadside restaurant; at his feet, Toon lay without additional surveillance. Whoever they were—Plankaert could not place the Austin—the newcomers must have been busy in the reservoir. Plankaert continued to slow down, contemplated his subjugated chief, weighed the balance of power, discreetly picked up speed, and exited to the landscape's left.

Charles wanted to bring the freed Justine immediately back to Chantilly. She seemed shocked, looked at nothing and nobody; a shadow, she got into the Austin; only Bob tried to speak to her. As he and Paul were a bit hesitant to get in beside her, Charles, in a hurry, cut the matter short, promised to send someone for them right away, and instantly took off. While waiting they would watch over Van Os and the sleeper, whose fate they had not yet decided.

From the first phone booth he came across, in a village named Bromeilles, Charles called Chantilly: immediately Pons commandeered another Austin, lent by a neighbor and identical to Nicole's, two options aside. He made good time but seriously lost his way after the Ury exit. They waited for him. The air grew warm, fat blue flies hummed nearby, little tractors leveled the horizon. When Pons finally appeared in the new vehicle, they got in, still not having decided anything about Van Os. "Well," said Bob, untying him, "we'll be leaving now." Still seated, the other jumped at the slamming of the doors:

"Couldn't you give us a lift back?"

"Fend for yourself, Van Os," said Paul with a gesture. "There are already three of us and it's a small car. Fend for yourself. Count yourself lucky."

"Let me come with you," begged Van Os. "I don't take up much room and I'm willing to admit my mistakes."

"No," said Paul. "No, okay?"

"Please, take just me. I'll come back" (he pointed to Toon) "to fetch him. Then I'll stop" (he stood up), "I'll stop a moment. At my brother's, in Bastogne" (whose probable direction he indicated), "just for a moment. Please take me with you. Please."

So they shoved over, sighing; they began to drive all squeezed in together. Before noon the sun did not yet smother things; on the contrary, it supported, disseminated the colors. Clothes hung with all their blue in front of farms, from lines; like a tongue sticking out of a window, an egg-yellow coverlet was extremely egg-yellow. Several cats, themselves extremely run over, spotted the road like little prayer rugs, rarely Siamese, never Persian. At the entrance to the highway, Van Os instinctively tensed.

They let him off in the fourteenth arrondissement, at the city limits. He got out; smoothing his clothes on the sidewalk he said thank you, thank you very much. Left alone, he approached the first window he saw, stationed himself before it to reflect on the order of things to do. Warn Plankaert. Get the Alfa back. Get Toon back. Call Bastogne. Or maybe not. Maybe better to write. He hesitated, felt impoverished, looked at the things behind the window, a mixer, a food processor: suddenly the prices of these things seemed very high.

Pons was in no particular hurry to get back to Chantilly. He parked the Austin under a mulberry tree near Saint-Paul, where they had lunch; then under an acacia in Belleville, where Pons wanted some more coffee. It was one of the first nice days, with that sincere warmth—not a single after-chill—that urges bodies toward café sidewalks, where these bodies can see each other better, move more freely under less cloth. He was in no particular hurry to get back.

"We could go see someone," Bob suggested. "Bouc, for example, we're not far. You want to come, Jeff? Do you want to meet some people?"

"Of course I want to meet people," said Pons. "Since I'm starting over. It's a must."

Suspicious at first, Bouc Bel-Air discovered in the ex-Duke a rare interlocutor: with shots of Ulug Beg and Jagannath Bhatt, citing the same passages of Wallace or Charbonneau-Lassay, the two men recognized each other as strollers on the same out-of-the-way sidewalks of human knowledge. Forgetting Paul and Bob, they soon spoke only between themselves; soon they were obscure, soon in disagreement over Samarkand and Baghdad, whose observatories opposed their views. "Cosmic error," spluttered Pons, who didn't notice Paul and Bob as they stood up and left without a sound. Outside the afternoon was still in full swing, as were the violent odors all down the Faubourg. They had nothing to do, were in no particular hurry to get back either; they walked. More or less southwest, toward the high-rises of the fifteenth arrondissement.

In a general southwesterly direction, in other words turning around, often deviating from this axis, moving in fits and starts, retracing their steps. You going to see her again? Looking, in turn, at new things gleaming behind shop windows, but also at old ones thrown in a heap in large green bins. Could they see her again? Skirting a high-risk zone where they might run into Elizabeth. You think it'd be possible? Remembering an object they had to buy, forgetting it for another one. They thought about Justine, each man for himself, mechanically reading the numbers of cars and names on doors, names on street signs, names on mailboxes; thirty years later they would still remember her. Their distraction, this wandering idleness, although they had no care at present other than to avoid dog disjecta, seemed no particular luxury to them. They had not even gotten midway the course of their walk toward the fifteenth when the afternoon waned; people went home to be reunited with their names. The sun was setting when Paul and Bob crossed the river (reflections) via Pont Neuf.

They stopped off in a bar near Square de la Charité, a long dark bar with a small stage in back, a real wooden bar fringed by high wooden stools. A singer was going on shift, adjusting the mike, checking her voice in a minor key, stopping at the chorus, negotiating chords with a pianist in a checkered jacket. The pianist seemed worried, as if forced to leave his fingerprints over the entire keyboard. Early evening, few customers. They sat at the bar.

Music lets you talk less, lets you stare at your glass, the parchment lampshade, the multicolored collection of liquors, rather than at your neighbor. So they said little, except that it was nice out, that it wasn't very crowded, that they'd really felt like walking. The singer hit a few high notes—she knew several ways to reach a high note, to lead the high note, which the pianist spattered with sprays of arpeggios. Paul began to drink a bit fast, to fidget on his stool, to slide off it.

"I'm going to call," he said. "I'm going to go call."

"Okay," said Bob.

"Just a quick call, then I'll come back. A quick telephone call."

"Yeah, okay," said Bob, "so go call."

He turned back to the bar, the lampshade, the comings and goings of the white-clad bartender. The pianist now dried out his playing with brief chords, little metric strides—in the houses, in the gardens, his partner warbled, nothing can be heard. Paul settled back on his stool.

"It's busy. The phone is busy."

"You'll call back."

"Yeah," said Paul, "I'll call back."

But a little later it's his turn to be alone, to look at himself alone in the mirror that doubles the lampshade. Now Bob has gone downstairs to phone; it seems that for him it's no longer busy. It would seem that he's not coming back. Paul shows the bartender his glass, the piano slows down, calms down—in the heart of the tropical night, the singer insists, all is silence.

But it's getting toward the end since, seven hours away, the Malaysian day is starting to break; black night is actually yellow. The men are asleep on their bunks. An argus pheasant stands near the pond, beneath the kapok of the silk-cotton tree; he is not in heat, so he will not sing. The rubber continues to grow as expected, but Bob still hasn't come back.

ABOUT THE AUTHOR

Jean Echenoz is the author of four other novels: *Le Méridien de Greenwich*, *Cherokee* (which won the Prix Médicis in 1983), *Lac* (winner of the European Literature Prize), and *Nous trois*. *Cherokee* was published in English by David R. Godine in 1987, and a short novella, *L'Occupation des sols*, appeared under the title "Plan of Occupancy" in a recent issue of *Translation*. Mr. Echenoz lives in Paris.

ABOUT THE TRANSLATOR

Mark Polizzotti has translated works by Jean Echenoz, Maurice Roche, René Daumal, Paul Virilio, and the Surrealists. He is currently writing a biography of André Breton.

DOUBLE JEOPARDY

has been set in a film version of Electra by Huron
Valley Graphics, Ann Arbor, Michigan. Designed
by William Addison Dwiggins for the Mergen-
thaler Linotype Company and first made available
in 1935, Electra is impossible to classify as either
"modern" or "old-style." Not based on any historical model or reflecting any particular period or
style, it is notable for its clean and elegant lines, its
lack of contrast between the thick and thin ele-
ments that characterizes most modern faces, and its
freedom from all idiosyncrasies that catch the eye
and interfere with reading.

Designed by Stephen Dyer
Printed & bound by Haddon Craftsmen,
Scranton, Pennsylvania